IMMORTAL PASSION

Louis pulled upon the loop of her hair, bending her head back, arching her neck into a pale curve. Cassie gasped as his mouth fastened fiercely upon her throat. A charge of anxiousness and expectation shot through her system, awareness so acute it sizzled like fire along her limbs and beat like a wild thing within her breast. It was desire, it was madness, it was a lack of control so overwhelming her will ceased to be her own. There was only Louis and she clung to him for stability as her senses soared.

Her body reacted to the shock of his bite but her mind was far beyond the recognition of anything akin to physical pain. Reality raveled into a loosely woven mesh of strange sensations: floating, drowning, fire, and a vast empty chill. That last began to grow, surmounting the rest, that chill that was like dying. A whisper of fear wound through the heavy strands of pleasure and her thoughts groped outward in hopes of solace.

Louis, I'm afraid.

His voice sounded within her head, a stroke of reassurance flowing like the pulse of her blood from her to him.

Have no fear. You belong to me now. We are one, just as you wished, but not quite as you wanted. You are the slave of my needs, an extension of my will. You sought the darkness and now it resides within you. You wanted me and now you will pay the price of that desire for all eternity . . .

Also by Nancy Gideon

MIDNIGHT KISS
MIDNIGHT TEMPTATION

MIDNIGHT SURRENDER

NANCY GIDEON

PINNACLE BOOKS
KENSINGTON PUBLISHING CORP.

For Sandy,

*who shared my teenaged obsession
with the supernatural
(remember racing home to catch
"Dark Shadows"?)
and
who first encouraged me,
with my eighth grade scribblings,
to become a writer.
This one's for you!*

One

He was as one with the shadows, steeped in the same darkness, the same deep chill. He moved alone, silent and undetected where the soft glow of street lamps fell short in their conquest of the night. Winter was in the air and crystals of it hung in the rapid plumes of his breathing as he waited.

As he watched.

There was a sudden burst of sound overhead, a woman's laughter. He sucked in a quick breath of anticipation, beginning to ease from his hiding place. Then a man's voice mingled with her merriment and he darted back into the anonymity of blackness. He pressed back against the cold stones, closing his eyes, calming the shiver of his impatience.

Soon. Soon she will come.

The couple crossed over the bridge oblivious to him and continued on in their late evening stroll, unaware of the evil they brushed past.

A few more minutes went by, then he was rewarded.

She approached the bridge with a hurried step, probably tired and cold and eager to gain the warm comforts of her flat. Her haste made her careless as thoughts focused ahead on those waiting pleasures. Pleasures she would never know again. The tap of her boots made a hollow reverberation as she passed over him. He eased from the shadows just far enough to get a glimpse of her. She was bundled up in her cheap coat, her blond hair all but hidden under a silly hat. Her arms were laden with paper-bound parcels, articles of clothing she meant to alter that evening so they would be ready for her customers the next day. She didn't sense her danger.

The cold gleam of lamp light glittered in his stare as he turned slightly to follow her progress down the grassy incline that led to the walk below. To where he waited. She stumbled, uttering a soft, unladylike curse as her packages shifted and threatened to tumble. She juggled them for a precarious moment then continued down the gradual slope with a more confident step once they were under control. She was looking ahead as danger, swift and certain, moved up from behind.

He struck without warning, muffling her startled cry with the clamp of his hand, silencing it forever with a quick slash across her throat. The packages she held tumbled to the ground and lay scattered, forgotten.

Her blonde head wobbled loosely as he unwound the handknit scarf she wore. A more vivid hue dominated its subtle pattern. He held it up against his cheek, breathing in the fragrance held by its yarns: the floral hint of her perfume, the heavy scent of her blood. His glazed eyes slid closed as if in some dreamy rapture. There was a soft thump at his feet as her body crumpled, purpose served and now discarded without care.

"For you," he whispered in a tender reverie.

Cassie Alexander sat back in her chair, giving her head a slow revolution upon a stiff neck. It was late, much later than she'd realized. The papers spread across her father's desk would have to wait until morning. There was no way to straighten a five-year tangle overnight.

Brighton Alexander had been a top-notch newsman, but in business he'd been a disaster.

Her fingertips stroked along the glossy mahogany surface of the desk and she smiled fondly. She wasn't sure whether to bless or curse her father for the legacy he'd left her. At the moment, it felt like a millstone of incredible tonnage. But tomorrow, when she pushed open the frosted glass doors of the *Lexicon,* and was heralded by the scent of newsprint and energy, she knew she wouldn't feel that way. This was her dream, all she'd ever wanted.

One didn't abandon a pampered child just because it was teething.

But one didn't get much sleep during that time of upheaval, either.

"Good night, baby," she murmured wryly as she turned down her desktop lamp. The outside offices were already dark, everyone else having gone home to their families at the dinner hour. Cassie had no one to go home to. The *Lexicon* was the only family she had left.

She collected her long velvet coat and, with a ream of proof pages under her arm, she started through the empty office. She was reaching for the knob of the outside door when a distorted shadow loomed large and threatening on the other side of the glass. She stumbled back with a cry of alarm, her papers flying every which way like an early blizzard.

The door nudged open.

"Miss Alexander?"

Cassie clasped a hand to her laboring bosom. It was just Tim, one of their postal delivery boys. "Oh, Tim, you gave me quite a startle! What are you doing out this late?"

"I'm sorry, ma'am." He blushed hot, finding himself the cause of her distress, and bent to help her gather her work into an untidy pile. Once it was all collected and they stood, she gave him a questioning look.

"Well?" He was staring at her through the rapt eyes of an awkward adolescent, full of manly urges and boyish timidity. She fought against the desire to give him a firm shake back to reality. "What is it?" she prompted again with a fraying patience.

"Ma'am?"

"Did you want to see me for something?"

"Oh! Yes, of course. I was to deliver this package to you." Pulling his gaze from the curve of her lips and blushing furiously, he extended a crudely wrapped brown paper bundle with her name and the office address scrawled across the top. She took it curiously.

"And it couldn't wait until morning?"

"I was slipped an extra note to see that you got it tonight."

"Hmmm." She gave it a rattle. There was a soft shifting.

"Maybe something from an admirer," the boy suggested with a deeper flush of color.

Cassie made a noncommittal sound. More like another packet of debts she couldn't afford to pay. "Well, thank you for your diligence, Tim. Go on home now. You shouldn't be out on the streets at this hour."

"Beggin' your pardon, Miss Alexander, but neither should you. Can I have your carriage brought round for you?"

"I didn't use it this morning. I'll just catch the late streetcar. It drops me off almost at my door."

The lad lingered a moment, looking uncomfortable then all at once bold. "Maybe I should see you home. It is awful late and you being a lady out alone . . ."

She held to her smile. "How old are you, Tim?"

"Almost fifteen, ma'am." He puffed out his slight chest and stood taller.

"Your parents should be proud. They've raised themselves quite a gentleman. Go home. I'll see you in the morning."

His shoulders fell in disappointment. "Yes, ma'am. Good night, ma'am. Don't forget to lock up tight behind you."

She did smile then. "I won't." Really! Almost fifteen and all patronizing male already. She waited until the sound of his heavy boots sounded on the stairs leading down to the first floor before she turned to lock up the office. Then she brushed her fingers over the gilded plate on the door proclaiming in bold letters, *THE LEXICON*, C. Alexander, Owner and Editor. Owner and editor and still peach-fuzz-faced errand boys felt she needed their protection.

The moment she stepped out onto the front walk and the night wind snatched away her breath, Cassie regretted the need for public transit over the comfort of her personal carriage. Hunching her shoulders against the chill, she started the two-block walk, having to run the last half of it when the illuminated car pulled in ahead of her. It wouldn't do to miss it on such a night.

Gasping slightly, she climbed aboard and paid the fare to an indifferent conductor. As she found a seat close to the front, she scanned the car with a quick glance. An old woman snoring loudly. A dapper gentleman reading from the evening edition. Two large fellows way in back with feet stretched out and arms folded over massive chests. A lively group. She wondered what they were going home to, but her mind was too tired to play its usual game of making up histories to go with their faces. Her father always told her she had too active an imagination to be contained by just the obvious. That's what made her a good writer and reporter. She settled onto her seat and laid her papers and the package beside her. She gave the parcel another curious look. It was light. Too light to contain text from some want-to-be author. Maybe it *was* from an admirer. Smiling at that unlikelihood, she leaned back and watched the New York City scenery drift by.

She was almost twenty-five, too long out of the social light to be considered anything but a self-proclaimed spinster. She'd been more interested in getting an education than in grabbing up a husband and now, at her ripe old age, a man might look twice but he would also think twice about courting someone too obviously difficult to have made a match while yet in her prime. The idea didn't distress her. She, like her father before her, considered herself wed to the world of journalism. He'd once said the front cover was his mistress, and now it would be her master as well. And it would prove much

more responsive and satisfying than men of
this Victorian age.

Few men or women would share her views.
They considered her odd, some even said
dangerous, with the way she insisted upon
keeping her own home and holding a promi-
nent position in a male-dominated field. She
cared little for their opinion. She knew hers
was not the popular choice but then, hers
never had been. For a score of years, she'd
squared off against tradition and had refused to bend before its stuffy demands.
Where was it written that a woman had less
intelligence than a man? Where was the
proof that a female could not reasonably
control her own destiny? She'd posed these
questions to her father and he'd been impressed by her vinegar, as he'd called it.
Had his wife shown some of that same vinegar, she wouldn't have collapsed under the
strain of everyday living and ended her days
in an opiate daze in an upstate sanatorium.
No one was ever going to fault her for that
same debilitating weakness, Cassie had determined at a very young age. She was going
to be strong and in control. No one would
ever mistake her for feeble-minded and lock
her away from the world.

She knew and understood the world she
lived in, though she disagreed with many of
its philosophies. She saw harsh realities in the
pages of the *Lexicon* every day and never
shirked from them. If it was news, its exis-

tence could not be denied. If it existed, it would not go away if one pretended not to recognize it. She preferred to be the aggressor at the end of this ever-changing century and when the next era dawned, she would be ready for it. And the *Lexicon* would be her sounding board, taking a forward-looking stand amid a backward-looking populace.

Hers was a necessarily lonely position, both in the professional and personal sector. Those who worked for her bent before her decisions because she paid them to. Those who were not on her payroll shunned her society as if mere ideas could contaminate. She hoped they could. The people of New York could afford to suffer through an epidemic of new ideas. How could industry rush so vigorously ahead when mankind lagged behind in ignorance?

She missed having her father to argue these points with over evening brandy and cigarette smoke. She'd joined him in both vices, feeling wonderfully independent and decidedly wicked. He'd been gone for almost two months and she hadn't touched a drop or had a taste of tobacco since. Decadence was no fun unless it could be shared. Her father had been fun. He'd been a brilliant writer with the sharpest instincts she'd ever seen. He'd had a caustic wit and a cynical world view that allowed her freedoms no other female could claim. He saw her as an equal and when he died, he'd paid her the ultimate compliment. He'd willed her the *Lexicon* and paved the way for her eternal independence.

He'd also left her nearly penniless.

But oh, how she'd loved him. And now missed him.

And she was so deep in her reverie, she almost missed her stop.

"Oh, wait! This is where I get off," she cried to the conductor. She heard him mutter unflattering epithets as the car shuddered to a halt. She gave him a sweet smile in passing. "You're so kind. Have a pleasant evening."

"Same t'you, ma'am," he growled, not meaning it.

When the lights of the tram disappeared, Cassie found herself swallowed up in a chill midnight fog. Its rising billows cloaked all in a silvery haze and she shivered in spite of herself. It was only three blocks to her huge rambling house. Long, silent, empty blocks. She'd never been timid with her own company. Even so, she set out at a brisk pace.

She'd gone the first block when a feeling of unease crept over her. It wasn't a definable sensation. More of a tingle of intuition. She was very female in that sense. Keeping to her rapid pace, she tuned her ears for any untoward sound.

And there it was: the soft echo of her own steps, redoubled.

She refused to glance behind her. She

would not be intimidated. With a casual move, she put a hand to her elaborate hat as if to straighten it and removed a long pin. Clutching it in her hand the way she would a dagger, she dared any cutpurse thinking to make a quick score to tangle with Cassie Alexander. He'd find her no easy mark.

But she was wrong on two counts. Her money wasn't the focus. And it was two sets of footsteps, not one.

She'd just rounded the second block. She could see her house, big and dark, looming just up ahead. She considered running, weighing the distance against her own fleetness of foot. She considered a moment too long, for suddenly she was flanked on either side by large, threatening forms.

The two men from the streetcar.

One grabbed her wrist. Without hesitation, she jabbed her hat pin into his meaty hand. He let her go with a wail. She managed one quick forward stride when the other nabbed her about the waist, whirling her around and thrusting her hard up against the narrow iron fence rails of a neighboring home. Still clutching her armload to her chest, she drew a big breath, preparing to scream, but a fierce blow caught her on the jaw, skewing the sound along with her senses.

She didn't remember falling but suddenly the ground was cold beneath her palms and cutting into her knees. She tried to scramble forward, to break free of them. All she had to do was bolt down the nearest front walk to the safety of the family within. All she had to do was unleash one cry for help.

But the back of her coat was seized and she was flung head first into the wrought iron bars.

The twilight world grew darker as fog rose in her mind. She uttered what she'd hoped would be a loud plea for aid. It sounded like a whimper. She groped about rather blindly for the hat pin she'd dropped— for anything she could use against her assailants— but she was too disoriented, too dazed by the brutal blows to effect any kind of struggle.

"Stab me, will you," came a low growl from out of the cresting blackness. A rough hand cuffed her arm, dragging her up to unsteady feet. She got a glimpse of hard features, cruelly drawn in their vicious intent.

"Take my money," she panted, throwing her handbag out into the misty street, half hoping they would go after it. They didn't.

"It ain't your money we want, missy."

She tried to slap the one closer to her but her hand was intercepted and crushed until she moaned in pain. These men were going to hurt her . . . or worse. And there was nothing she could do to prevent it from happening practically on her own doorstep.

Then, amazingly, her attacker was gone, yanked back into the fog by an incredible force. She staggered, clutching at the fence for balance. A terrible wail came from out of the mist, then silence.

The other man lost all interest in her. He'd pulled a knife, a long thin-bladed weapon that he bandied before him with murderous intent as he whirled to face the gray-cloaked street. He took a cautious step off the curb, the mist sucking at him, veiling him partially. He gave a sudden shout and drove his knife forward with all his might at some target Cassie couldn't see. Then he, too, was lost in the swirl of evening haze.

Cassie leaned back against the rails, breath rasping from her, panic and pain shaking her knees together. She'd dropped her papers and her slick-soled shoes slipped on the spill of them on the walk beneath her. Sobbing softly, she started to pull herself along the fence, afraid to take her eyes from the spot where her assailants had disappeared.

She screamed hoarsely as one of them lurched into view.

He was stumbling, reeling, his hands up at his neck. Blood gleamed black in the faint reach of the closest street lamp. He made a gurgling sound and reached out for her with one wet hand. She couldn't move. His hand caught on her sleeve, tugging as he began to fall. Frantically, she jerked back to free herself as he slid down silently into the low curtain of mist.

Movement brought her frightened gaze up from the cloud that had swallowed him. She

shrank against the unyielding bars, small
sounds of terror escaping her with each labored breath.

A lone figure approached from out of the
icy clouds. A face, familiar yet unlike any
she'd seen before. Pale as the wisps of mist.
With eyes like fiery coals.

"Do not be afraid."

Yet when he spoke that soothing sentiment, two monstrous teeth were exposed:
sharp, animal-like fangs all tinged with crimson. Cassie tried to scream, but the noise suf-
focated in her horror-constricted throat.

"I will not harm you."

He reached out a slender hand, the gesture an offer of aid, not threat. It cupped
beneath her elbow just as the strength in her
legs gave way and he held her up without
any effort. She was aware of her own fear,
of how it fluttered about a heart gone mad,
but she was helpless to act upon it even as
he placed his other hand gently against the
tangled disarray of her blond hair. His touch
was cold, so cold it made her tremble.

Then the shock of the situation overcame
her. Consciousness gave way before a numbing swoon. And just as she sank into its embrace, she felt his hand pass across her eyes
and heard the low croon of his voice.

"Remember nothing."

Two

"I couldn't just leave her. I had no choice."

"No. No, of course you couldn't. You did the right thing by bringing her here."

The pair of voices played about the edge of her consciousness, teasing Cassie with their familiarity. A low resonant drawl that was subtly European. Thin female tones that still held a British clip. She should know them. Bewilderment crowded her brow as she struggled back to awareness. Her head was thundering with a persistent storm of misery while thought remained calm and perplexingly serene, processing information with a sluggishness not unlike the numbing balm she'd experienced after a glass or two too many.

Where was she?

Movement brought a luxurious yielding to the mattress beneath her. Comfort swaddled her body even as vagueness cushioned her brain. Her very absence of alarm confused her but the sense of safety was strong, as consoling as a mother's embrace.

Her eyes blinked open. Images swam for

an instant; an elegant half tester overhead—
not her own— paneled walls, soft gaslight,
two faces, neither clear enough to identify.

"W-what . . . ?" The sound whispered
from her, as uncertain as her other senses.
When she reached up toward the muddle of
her head, her unsteady hand was enveloped
in a gentle grasp. Small fingers, thin and
parchment frail, yet instantly soothing, patted
her own.

"It's all right, dear. Let it come back to
you slowly. You've had quite an ordeal."

Using that light touch, that soft voice for
focal points, Cassie dragged herself up from
the placid waters of confusion. Her wavery
gaze cleared, filling with the concerned features of her elderly neighbor, Arabella Radcliffe.

"H-how . . . ?"

"Just relax, my dear. Don't force the memory to return."

Cassie rebelled against that kind advice.
The void of her thoughts frightened her. It
was like waking to find one's self in a
strange place after a bout of sleepwalking.
The questions were immediate and intense:
What had happened? What had she done?

What had been done to her?

"H-how did I get here?" Here was obviously the Radcliffes' home, this one of the
sumptuously styled bedrooms of their West
End brownstone, but it didn't explain what

she was doing there stretched out fully
clothed.

"Two ruffians were bent on robbing you.
Thank goodness Louis happened along. I
hate to think what might have occurred had
he not been out walking and heard your
cries for help."

Cassie's gaze shifted from the old woman's
benign smile to the darkly brooding expression of the man who lingered back in the
shadows just beyond the clear reach of gaslight. A pang of excited longing leapt within
her and was quickly entangled by an unexpected shiver of . . . of fear.

It was as unmistakable as it was mystifying,
that eerie tingle of alarm. She didn't understand it. Louis Radcliffe was no frightful menace. Quite the opposite. In fact, despite all
her independent ways and assertions about
needing no male figure in her life, in Arabella's handsome grandson she saw her every
ideal. Four months ago, she would never have
dreamed she'd go weak-kneed over any man.

How wrong she'd been upon meeting her
new neighbors.

The Radcliffes had taken up residence in
the mammoth brownstone quietly, without
much ado, settling in almost overnight: the
gracefully gray Arabella, who was eighty if
she was a day, and her simply gorgeous
grandson, Louis. Theirs was a household
nearly as atypical as her own, with a single
housekeeper who came in by day and a

seemingly ageless and mute Oriental man who took the wheelchair-bound Arabella out for daily excursions to the park. They did no entertaining and, despite the nods of society's initial overtures which were quickly discouraged, they seemed to prefer to be left alone.

In his last days, Cassie's father had been intrigued by the reclusive Radcliffes. Something wasn't right about the two of them; old woman and young man, living alone in the rambling house. His newsman's nose was twitching to the scent of possible mischief but Cassie admonished him, saying he was looking for a story where none existed. Arabella was a genteel old lady whom she found gracious and surprisingly contemporary in her views on life. Cassie genuinely enjoyed their visits together in the waning hours of the day.

And then, there was the extra enticement of catching a glimpse of the elusive Louis.

Her father was right in one sense: there was something decidedly different about Louis Radcliffe. It was more than his compelling looks, for Cassie had no fondness for pretty-featured men who seemed more attached to their own reflection than the world around them. She would have to admit a certain helpless feminine response to her fatally attractive neighbor, a fluttering of heart and faintness of breath that she thoroughly deplored as a silly weakness. But his was more than a surface appeal. Her fascination with him went soul deep. In the treasured times he'd joined the two ladies in their twilight tea, Cassie had been entranced by his old-world manner of politeness and was nonplussed by his sincere interest in her often outspoken opinions. Nothing she said discomposed him in an era when men were appalled by the assertiveness of a female mind. Perhaps he was simply used to strong-willed women. Arabella was never one to be shy when voicing her thoughts.

And Arabella was the other reason Cassie was so enamored of the handsome Louis. It was the way he treated the older woman, with respect and attentive kindness. Cassie had never seen the members of his set consider the elderly with such a degree of sensitive compassion. It quite overcame her jaded views. Those slight, thoughtful gestures hinted at a heart filled with tender passion, and considering that quality wrapped up in such an exquisite package, left Cassie in an awkward state of palpitations.

She wasn't sure what to do about her feelings for the quixotic Louis. The unresolved nature of them left her in a frenzy of giddy desire and restless frustration. While he was unfailingly courteous to her, he held himself aloof from any not-so-subtle signs of her interest in him. She'd almost talked herself into dismissing him as a girlish fancy.

And then her father died.

She'd been devastated, but Arabella and Louis Radcliffe had become her lifeline to sanity. They'd invited her to spend her evenings with them, just talking or not talking as she gave in to frequent bouts of weeping. Their understanding of grief touched a spark of gratitude within her that could never be repaid. Her fondness for Arabella and her desire for Louis grew apace since those first lonely days and nights.

And now Louis had been her rescuer, saving not just her fragile emotional state but her very life.

Where had that tremor of fear come from?

Arabella looked between Cassie's strained countenance and the object of her attention. "Can you remember nothing of what happened?"

There was an element in her tone that distracted Cassie from her thoughts. Did the older woman sound agitated? Perhaps it was just worry over the trauma she'd suffered. Cassie managed a weak smile to calm her while her own emotions trembled with mounting panic.

"It's all so vague. I remember taking the streetcar home. I was carrying packages." Her gaze darted about to rest upon the bundles she'd borne stacked atop a dresser, all accounted for but worse for wear. It looked as though they'd been trod upon. She was beginning to feel equally misused. Her brow furrowed as she forced her mind beyond the haze-draped remembrances.

"There were two men on the car with me. They followed me. They grabbed me and . . . and . . ."

"What?" Arabella's prompt was surprisingly sharp. It startled Cassie from her frail hold on the moment.

"I can't quite recall. I almost have it, then it slips away from me."

Arabella smiled back with a sweet reassurance. "The shock of it, I'm sure." Then her warm gray eyes honed with an edge of steel as she watched the younger woman's response. Cassie wasn't mistaken this time. Had Louis done something dangerous . . . or illegal in his rescue of her? If that was what Arabella feared, that Cassie would become an instrument of some recrimination for his brave act, she would put her mind at ease at once.

"Whatever becomes of those two, I'm sure it will be better than they deserve."

"Oh, I don't know about that, Miss Alexander. Consequences can sometimes be amazingly cruel."

With that cryptic statement, Louis Radcliffe stepped into the light and up beside the elderly woman seated at her bedside. He moved like no man she'd ever seen before, with a grace that was fluid, with the power of a tidal wave behind it. Neither the superb cut of his clothes nor the refined cast of his features could overcome the eddy of raw strength he exuded . . . disturbing, dangerous, and to Cassie, unbearably inviting. She was reminded all at once of the glossy big cats she'd seen pacing behind bars at the zoo. He was like them, a primal animal surviving on the basest of instincts: sleek, cautious, calculated in every move. A man capable of acting with swift, brutal measures if the ends were justified. The shiver returned to ravage her.

Then Cassie smiled to herself. She was, of course, allowing her creative fancy to overwhelm the facts. Louis Radcliffe was gorgeous but the rest was a product of an overtaxed mind and a too-barren heart. She wanted to see some deadly avenging hero so in this confusing hour of need, he became one. It was a nice dream, if only for the moment. And when the moment was over, he would be once again just a man.

But what a man.

He was made with delicate lines over unshakable strength. His facial bone structure was all abrupt angles and intriguing hollows, squared by a determined jaw and the brooding slash of dark brows. That harsh effect was softened by the rich rumple of short-cropped dark auburn hair, by a mouth that was all wide sensual swells and by eyes that glowed with green and gold sparks of mystery. Perhaps there were men better looking but none half so magnetic in terms of pure appeal.

His long-fingered hand came to rest on Arabella's thin shoulder and her blue-veined one rose automatically to cover it. The gesture was one of intimacy and devotion and Cassie was all at once taken by the emptiness of her own life. She turned her head to one side to blink back the sting of tears.

"I should be getting home."

Catching the tremor of hesitancy in her voice, Arabella was immediately protesting. "It's too soon. You need rest."

Cassie had started to sit up, aware of her embarrassing position upon the bedcovers and the steady glow of Louis's gaze. The pounding in her head intensified but she tried to ignore it. Tried and failed. The room began to swirl in great sickening loops. Even the frail strength of Arabella's hand was enough to press her back down upon the coverlet.

"You can spend the night here," the elderly woman said with unquestionable authority. "If you feel stronger in the morning, then you may leave. If not, you should be in company in case you need medical attention."

"But I'm— "

"You're not fine," she overruled grandly. "You would not suggest such nonsense if you could see yourself."

Cassie's hand rose self-consciously to her

face. There, along her jaw, she could feel an impressive contusion. Sure she must look a fright, she ceased all active struggle but her reluctance was still plain in the pucker of her brow.

"Do not argue with me, child. I was a doctor's daughter. I know the danger of head injuries. Morning will be soon enough for you to get up and on with things. Until then, you must make yourself at home and we will care for you."

The tears that threatened earlier returned at the older woman's kindness, but Arabella brushed words of gratitude aside.

"Now, you need to rest. I'll find you something more comfortable to put on for the night. Do you think you can manage your own disrobing?"

Cassie flushed hot at the personal nature of the topic, too well aware of Louis in the room with them. "Yes, of course," she murmured brusquely, wondering over her blushes. She had thought herself too sophisticated for such feminine flusters.

Arabella wheeled herself with surprising agility toward the door, leaving the two of them alone. In sudden discomfort, Cassie began to worry the lacy stock of her rumpled gown with awkward fingers. With its bulky back drapery and form-molding corset, her attire was hardly conducive for rest. Nor was the way Louis watched her. She was unbelievably clumsy in her struggle against the ever-tightening knot of fabric.

"Let me," he offered abruptly, and she was too startled to object. While she reclined in a paralysis of mortified longing, he bent and pushed aside the fumble of her hands to work the delicate bow loose. As his graceful fingers began down the row of tiny buttons that ran the length of her throat, he couldn't have mistaken the agitation in her hurried swallowing. So he spoke softly to distract her from her modest horror.

"Those two men, did you recognize them?"

"I— no. No, I didn't." She held her breath as he leaned nearer, concentrating on the fussy pearl buttons and the tight loops that held her linen stock snugly in place against the column of her neck.

"Do you know of anyone who would have reason to want to harm you?" The remote calm of his tone was in direct contrast to the giddy surge of her emotions.

She paused to consider his question. "It was a simple robbery," she finally answered. "Nothing personal, I'm sure." But she wasn't sure, was she? A whisper of memory said it was very personal. She remembered throwing her bag into the street and the growly voice saying it wasn't her money they were after.

What then?

"Those men," she began in a failing voice. "Did they run when you came upon us?"

His fingers stilled and he glanced up at her for a moment. In the muted lamplight, his eyes gleamed with a molten fire. A reflection, no doubt, but it quite unnerved her. And so did the low, smooth caress of his words.

"I would not worry about them, Miss Alexander. They will not be troubling you again."

And suddenly she lacked the courage to ask what exactly he meant by that. She saw all sorts of terrible imaginings in the sharp planes of his face and in that unnatural glitter of his eyes. The memory of fear returned to her, an icy trickle of warning. Warning what? That this man, her rescuer, was a danger to her? Utter nonsense, of course.

But still, she was unable to relax as he continued down the row of minuscule buttons.

When the last of them gave way, Louis turned back the edges of her collar, exposing the supple whiteness of her throat. It was the intensity of his focus upon that naked curve as much as the familiarity of the act itself that flustered her.

Then he spread his hand wide, cupping her chin between the vee of thumb and forefinger. And slowly, with mesmerizing leisure, he stroked down the sides of her throat, his fingertips coming to rest over the anxious pulse points.

"Louis."

A quiet call from the doorway had him rearing back from his almost intimate pose. Released from the spell of his proximity, Cassie found herself gasping for breath. He stepped away from her bedside as Arabella wheeled herself in to extend the lawn nightdress she'd carried across her blanketed knees.

"Here you are, my dear. This should serve quite nicely." Arabella smiled as if she wasn't aware she'd interrupted something . . . intense between her grandson and their lady guest. Even Louis seemed to dismiss it as his features adopted a distant neutrality. Only Cassie was affected. Her heart was hammering out a frantic rhythm as even now the feel of his touch burned against the fair flesh of her neck. What had happened in that brief instant when time and place had narrowed to fill the space of a heartbeat, when she'd felt him on the verge of asking something of her? Or taking what he pleased.

Perhaps she would never know.

"Are you certain you can manage on your own, dear?"

Cassie clutched the gown in shaking fingers, bringing it up beneath her chin as if to cover the suddenly all too bare expanse of her neck. "Quite certain," she managed, along with a tortured smile.

"If there's anything else you need—"

"Thank you, but I'm sure I'll be fine.

You've been so kind with all you've offered already."

And what had Louis Radcliffe been about to offer with that seducing touch?

Paradise, her fluttering emotions sighed.

"She is very lovely," Arabella commented as Louis pushed her along the hall. When he made no reply, she continued in calm summation. "I quite admire her forthright attitudes, don't you?"

"It's not wise that she stay here."

Arabella was unruffled by his gruff tone. "Why?" she probed gently. "Because of what happened to the men who attacked her or because you are attracted to her?"

His stride broke, then he continued on with a feigned lack of concern. "Don't be ridiculous. I would never harm a guest under our roof. Please give me credit for that much self-control."

"I don't blame you, Louis," she went on as if she hadn't heard his dismissal. "She's lively and challenging. Actually, she reminds me of myself when I was younger. She's smitten with you, you know. That's not hard to understand. It's only natural that you respond with similar feelings."

The chair jerked to a halt. "Bella, what are you talking about?"

"I was merely suggesting that you not feel

ashamed if you find yourself falling in love with Miss Alexander."

"What?" He circled around to face her, his full of thunderous upset. "How could you speak to me of such things? How could you doubt my devotion to you?" He dropped down upon one knee so that their eyes met. His hands scooped hers up and held them with a cherishing care.

Arabella's gaze touched upon their joined hands, his so smooth and elegant, hers withered with passing years. Then she looked up at him to smile with a maddening calm.

"I do not doubt you, Louis. You have given me more wonderful years than I could ever have hoped for. But those years are almost gone—"

"No!"

"They are almost gone," she restated firmly, not unmoved by the anguish and panic brightening in his stare. "I have not been much of a companion for you of late. I am old, Louis. You deserve the love of someone young, someone who can care for you—"

"Stop! I will not listen to this, Bella."

"You must. When I am gone, it would break my heart to think of you alone."

"You're not going to die, Bella."

She laughed softly for his face was so in earnest. "Louis, now who is being ridiculous? Of course I will."

"You don't have to. I could—"

She placed her fingertips upon his mouth, stilling the words. "No. Would you have a crippled old woman be a burden for eternity?"

He gave a gasp of horror. "Bella, you would never be a burden to me!"

She caressed his taut cheek. "But I am already. And I love you for your patience and your care."

He caught her hand and pressed a hard kiss to the bony ridge of knuckles. Above, his eyes blazed with an angry fire. "You make it sound like some martyred duty, like something required but not enjoyed. Why are you treating me like this? What have I done to make you feel less in control of my heart? Forgive me, Bella, if I have in some way hurt you."

Her smile was serene. "Oh, Louis, you are being quite silly. You've done nothing."

"Then why do you accuse me of no longer loving you? Is it that woman? She is nothing to me. Nothing! Had I known that my bringing her here would upset you so, I would have left her there on the street."

She made a chiding sound. "No, you would not have. It is not in your nature to callously disregard someone in need. And that is why I love you so. I am not upset. In fact, I would like to see you spend more time with those your—"

"Age? Bella, there are fewer than a handful who can claim my number of years and none of those I would have in my house."

"Nevertheless, it seems morbid, you hanging about the house when you should be out enjoying life."

"You are the one I chose to spend my life with. You!"

"I never asked you to play nursemaid for me, Louis. It is a cruel fate that casts you into that mold."

"Have I ever complained?"

"No. No, of course you haven't." And her gaze softened with a limitless affection. "But you should. I never meant for your love to become shackles upon your heart. How could you not yearn to look upon a face that is unlined by the years and seek an energy to match your own? I am old, my love, not you."

"What are you suggesting? That I turn from you after all the years we've shared? That I hold my vows so cheaply as to pretend I did not mean 'until death us do part' when I spoke those words? I promised you my fidelity. Have I ever faltered in it? Have I?"

"No."

"Then no more of this."

He was wildly agitated and that hadn't been her intention. "I know you love me, Louis. I know you vowed to love me for a lifetime. My lifetime, not yours."

He looked so stricken, she was tempted to

end the conversation. But for the same reason, she could not.

"We must talk of this, Louis. I've not much time left and there are things we must discuss."

His expression shut down behind an impassive mask. "No, we will not. You are tired. That's all. That's why all this morbid talk of— of death. Tomorrow— "

"Tomorrow, I will not be any younger. The fact of my mortality will not go away just because you wish it to."

He made an anguished sound and abruptly dropped his head down upon her knees. "I wish it to, Bella. I wish it to!" His hands convulsed about hers.

"Louis, you're hurting me."

It was a soft complaint, a reminder of her frailty and he instantly gentled his hold. Arabella slipped one hand free so she could stroke it over his hair in a soothing gesture. And her tender mortal's heart broke at the sound of his jagged breathing.

"I will not go on without you."

That sudden, impassioned vow struck terror into Arabella's soul. "You must."

He shook his head vehemently. "No. I gave myself to you for a lifetime. Mine need not go beyond yours."

"But I want it to." She cupped his chin in her palm and angled his head up so she could see the torment reflected in his glistening eyes. So he could read the sincerity in her own. "I love you, Louis Radman. Did you think that love so selfish, I would demand that you surrender all future happiness because I cannot share in it?"

"Bella, I—"

"Hush. Listen to me. Humor an old woman." When he didn't smile, she sighed and offered a gentle one of her own. "I will die soon." She halted his protest with another press of her hand upon his lips. "If you follow me by bringing about your own death, will our souls be together?"

She hated the pain those words brought him, knowing well how sorely his own damnation weighed upon his heart and mind. But she wanted him to understand and there was no easy way to enlighten him.

"You must go on, Louis. You must live long enough to find an escape from the curse you suffer. You must save your soul from darkness before you join me. Then we can have our eternity together. I want you to give me that promise."

He was silent for a long while. She could have reached out and touched upon his troubled thoughts but she didn't want to intrude upon such a private moment. To do so would have implied doubt and she didn't want him to think she had less than total faith in his word when it was reluctantly given.

"You have my promise."

Arabella's breath sighed from her, and in

her relief she felt positively ancient. "Thank you. Now, I am very weary. I would like to rest for a time. Would you see to our guest for me, Louis?"

Because her voice sounded so suddenly thready with exhaustion, he could deny her nothing.

"I will watch over her."

She smiled at him and let her strength wane. With her head resting against the back of the chair, she let her eyes close as he pushed her in silence toward her room. Purposefully, she closed herself off from him, unwilling to let his misery change the direction of her plans. She had his word that he would go on but it wouldn't hurt to secure his vow with a reason for living.

And Cassie Alexander was going to supply that reason.

Three

She was sleeping soundly. Strands of fair hair fanned across the stark white pillow cover, making a wispy embroidery where it ended in gentle curls. She was lovely. In repose, a soft blush of slumber warmed creamy skin and lightly parted lips allowed the shush of her breathing to escape like beckoning sighs. A large purplish bruise marred the perfection of one cheek. A second discoloration was covered by the wave of her hair across her temple. A fragile mortal, so easily damaged, so easily destroyed.

Louis didn't need the light from the lamp to watch over her as promised. His vision was all too clear through the room's heavy night shadows. He kept himself at a cautious distance but it wasn't far enough to alleviate the pull of temptation.

The temptation of what she was to what he was.

He could feel the lure of her living warmth a room away. The rhythm of her breathing was a fainter echo of the pulse that drew the darkness from inside him. That steady human heartbeat, hypnotizing in its sameness, enticing in its purpose. He'd felt the stir of it beneath his fingertips when he'd touched her throat, the mesmerizing strength of it throbbing with the normal life denied him. Still sated from his revenge upon her two attackers, he shouldn't have felt such a chafe of hunger. Nevertheless, it burned through him as he watched her sleep. It coursed through his veins like liquid fire and writhed against the iron of his will, whispering of how easy it would be to take from her while she was unaware. His instincts urged him with gnawing little pangs of appetite. Desires dark and never fully controlled rumbled like massing thunder. But he wouldn't act out these compelling savageries. He was too civilized. He was too afraid.

Something about the woman, Cassie Alexander, moved him beyond the basic hunger of his breed. And he didn't want to recognize it as anything else.

He liked her. That was the problem. He was charmed by her intelligence and crisp wit. She filled a hunger of loneliness within him, that yearning for vitality and enthusiasm he so admired in humankind. He was grateful to her for providing Arabella with companionship during the times when he could not and he longed for the laughter she brought into the big dark house when the shadow of death had begun to hover far too near.

Arabella was right about the woman's interest in him. He'd known of it from the first but was sure he could discourage it with his continued coolness. She made it hard to remain distant. He was drawn into her conversations by the lure of Arabella's youthful sounding laughter as her own rippled around it in playful harmony. She brought a certain zest back into the woman he loved so he could never deny her access to their home even when her visits grew more dangerous.

Dangerous because he'd begun to anticipate them far too much.

It was impossible to hide anything from Arabella. She could read a fleeting thought upon his most impassive face. It did no good to lie to her. She was a lot better at seeing the truth in his heart than he was at admitting to it. She knew he loved her. He did. But their love could not stop the advance of years any more than he could halt his own restlessness within the rooms of the big dark house. It felt as though he was haunting the halls, waiting for her to die. Helping Cassie through the sorrow surrounding her father's passing had made him all too aware that such grief lay in his near future. That, too, was something he didn't wish to face.

Arabella had accused him of seeing her love as selfish when in truth it was the other

way around. After three centuries of lonely
hell, the fragile mortal presence of Arabella
Howland had made his last sixty years a
heaven in comparison. She had wed him
with promises of undying devotion and had
remained with him when the rest of the
world would turn from what he was in horror. She'd given him a child, a daughter he
adored. She had given comfort to his soul
and contentment to his heart, and for decades they'd shared an exquisite intimacy
while she aged and he did not. Finally, ad-
vancing years and the plague of an injury
sustained long ago— one she'd accepted will-
ingly in order to save his life— confined her
to a chair with steel wheels and put an end
to the physical side of their relationship, but
the emotional bond remained strong, untouched by time's passage. And it would remain strong as long as they both lived. All
he had to do was look into her eyes to see
the woman who'd captured his heart and
that vision was unchanging. The thought of
life without her was a waiting void. A plunge
back into hell.

He had to wonder if his marriage to Arabella was his only claim to humanity. He was
terrified of the loss of that tie. He knew what
kind of a demon dwelt within him. It had
roared to life when he'd answered Cassie's
cries. It was a seething fury, as primal as sin
and just as old. The lust to kill, the thirst for
life. With Arabella he could pretend to certain

sophistication. He could walk as the man he once was without any being the wiser because, briefly, she had known that man and could still coax him out. She was all the good that was in him, his link to the mortal world. But inside beat the beast, ever greedy, always hungry, constantly trying his resolve. And he feared without Arabella's influence, it would be all too easy to succumb.

He was shaken by the violence of his response to Cassie's peril. And it wasn't, as Arabella surmised, because of his decent nature that he'd swooped down to her aid. The thought of her in jeopardy had quickened a passionate rage, almost as if the threat had been to one of his family. It was most disconcerting.

It was the glimpse of a youthful Arabella that drew him to their pretty neighbor. That was all. A nostalgic yearning for what time had taken from him. The vigor of a young woman. The ability to indulge carnal passions. What kind of monster would he be if he betrayed the woman he loved to pursue such superficial desires?

An all too human one.

Upon the bed, Cassie stirred and moaned restlessly within her slumber. Her breaths began to deepen, growing fractured with dismay as dream slipped into nightmare.

"No, please!" Her hands rose up to form an ineffective barrier against whatever haunted her mind. Was it the men who'd thought to harm her or the repressed memory of what had come to her rescue?

Her whimpers moved him to compassion for her. Soundlessly, he approached her bedside. With a feather-light touch he placed the tips of his fingers against the flutter of her closed eyelids.

"Let go of your troubled thoughts. Let peaceful slumber overtake you."

And instantly she quieted at that soft command.

His fingertips lingered, drawing a leisurely path down one silken cheek. Such smooth, unlined flesh she had, warm and clear like fresh cream. Finally he withdrew his hand, aware he'd allowed it to linger for far too long, murmuring, "Sleep well and unafraid."

And she did, deeply, dreamlessly, until the pastels of dawn crept between the loosely closed curtains to tease upon her eyelids.

And she sat up in confusion with his name upon her lips.

"Louis?"

Hearing her own voice brought an immediate rift between dream and reality. Her handsome host hadn't been in her room, speaking with mellifluous tones, caressing her cheek with a gentle touch.

But this wasn't her room.

Remembrance returned with a shock. And with a persistent ache to brow and jaw. Concern prompted her on tottery legs from the bed to see the worst for herself in a small glass perched upon the dressing table. She groaned aloud at the sight. Puffiness and a wealth of colors distorted her face.

"Are you all right?"

Cassie turned to smile ruefully at her hostess. "I was just trying to think of how to explain away these rather obvious reminders of last night."

Arabella frowned slightly as she wheeled in from the hall. "The truth won't suffice?"

"Not in this case." She sighed heavily. "I walk a very tenuous line around my male relatives. If they thought for a moment that I couldn't take care of myself, they'd pull up on the leash of my independence."

"Then you're not going to the police? What about those men who attacked you?"

"The police have enough to worry about without adding another act of random violence. No real harm was done, after all. I'm sure they won't be back to bother me again." And she repressed a slight shiver when she thought of Louis's fierce declaration that they'd gotten what they deserved.

"Then you've remembered nothing more about last night?" Again, that edge of anxiousness.

"Nothing. I must have lost consciousness when I hit my head. If it hadn't been for Louis . . ." She held to that thought, savoring it within the embrace of her heart with a guilty pleasure.

"Are you so sure the act was random? Perhaps you should consider staying here with us for a few more days, until your strength returns and you feel more confident."

How could she feel confident under the same roof with Louis Radcliffe? He even disconcerted her dreams.

"I'm fine. The sooner I get on with my regular routine, the better I'll feel. I couldn't stand languishing about like a frightened victim."

Arabella pursed her lips in mild disapproval but Cassie caught a glint of just the opposite in her keen gray eyes. It was just the encouragement she needed to overcome her bodily complaints.

"Now if I'm to catch the el, I'd better hurry."

"You should take your own carriage this morning, my dear. I don't think you're quite up to the stresses of rapid transit."

"I'll have to be." Pride prevented her from confessing that she'd had to let their carriage driver go the day before. She hadn't the means to pay his wage. What was good enough for the masses would have to be good enough for her this morning.

"Then promise me you'll be extra careful and that you'll come dine with us this evening, if for no other reason than for me to assure myself that you are, indeed, fit and fine."

Cassie flushed with pleasure at Arabella's mothering. It was the closest she could recall to what she'd missed in childhood. "I wouldn't want to impose."

"Nonsense. What else have I to look forward to?"

"All right then, I accept and I thank you. But now I must run."

"That's the trouble with this generation. Always running somewhere," Arabella muttered to herself as she backed from the room, giving Cassie her privacy to dress. Cassie smiled after her with the feeling that Arabella Radcliffe had done her share of running in her earlier years.

And all too soon Cassie was running, up the three tiers of steps to the elevated train, wedging her way into one of the four crowded cars as the life's blood of the city flooded toward the downtown area. As usual, all the seats were taken and she was forced to grab for a strap or be dumped into the closest lap as the green-painted train jerked forward and quickly steamed up to its thirty miles per hour pace. They sped toward lower Manhattan, bumping and jostling with a thunderous noise. Ash, oil and sparks were distributed impartially over luckless pedestrians and awnings and filtered into upper windows as the train came out of the gray morning mists bearing the working class who carried the keys to the city on their belts. They would be followed after the next few runs by the leisurely class, who came into the city with pleasures on their mind to shop the Ladies' Mile between Fifth and Eighth Avenues. Cassie had never traveled in their company. She had always been part of the first wave in and the last wave out, missing the confusion of six o'clock when thousands surged along the transit systems like a panicked populace fleeing a doomed city. Such was the pulse of Manhattan life, flowing on a great tide of longitudinal tracks in and out, day after day, like the regular pull of the sun and moon upon the flow and ebbs of the seas.

The *Lexicon* was located in Printing House Square at the junction of Nassau and Park Row across from City Hall Park. This bastion of press offices for the *Sun,* the *Tribune,* the *World,* the *Staats Aeitung* and the Associated Press was presided over by Ben Franklin in effigy, while a block to the north the Pulitzer Tower rose in tribute to the city's ever upward growing skyline in twenty-five impressive stories topped with a golden dome that could be seen in all directions. The *Lexicon* was one of over fifty newspapers, literary papers, magazines and book publishers who communally used a monster engine occupying a basement in Spruce Street and powered some one hundred and fifty high-speed rotary presses. Her mother's money had bought a second floor lot of office spaces and there her father's dream, and now her own, was operating at full steam by the time she pushed open the front door.

Cassie paused there on that threshold to absorb the structured chaos around her. It was her favorite time of day, when the machinery of their weekly publication was gearing up for production. Typewriters were clattering as beleaguered reporters hurried to meet deadlines. Junior editors were shouting over banks of cluttered desks and harried office clerks were trying to wind through the maze of confusion without spilling their cups of coffee. She'd been passing through these same frosted glass doors since childhood, weaning her way into the business under her father's wing. And now it was hers.

A mixed blessing, but a blessing nonetheless.

The moment she was spotted at the door, the focus of energy swamped her way.

"Miss Alexander, about that piece on Ellis Island—"

"Miss Alexander, I couldn't arrange for that interview until Friday afternoon. Is there any chance of holding up the edition for a couple of hours—"

"What does the other fellow look like?"

That last comment caught her attention. She frowned, not understanding until the reporter made fists and sent a mock punch toward her swollen jaw. Her grimace sent a jolt of misery as a reminder.

"They're waiting for you in the conference room, Miss Alexander."

They? Waiting for what?

Then it dawned on her and she groaned mightily. She'd completely forgotten the editorial staff meeting her uncle had called for this morning. And she was late by a good twenty minutes. Not good, since her Uncle Fitzhugh checked the time with at least three sources before setting his watch. Punctual should have been his given name.

She started stripping off her outerwear as she trotted for her office, taking time only to throw her wrap over the back of her desk chair and to snatch up one of the files littering the mahogany top.

"Coffee!" she yelled as she burst out into the newsroom and darted around the corner into the solemn corridor her uncle claimed as managing editor. Neither daylight nor conversation above a hushed reverence ever penetrated the hallowed hall. Today, it echoed the hurried staccato of her heels.

"Sorry, I'm late, gentlemen," she said, bustling into the conference room, which already hung thick with blue cigar smoke. Avoiding her uncle's glowering stare, she headed straight for her seat at the right side of the long table's head. At the end, the chair still stood empty. She couldn't think of it as other than her father's spot in the crowded boardroom.

"The meeting was scheduled for eight," began Fitzhugh's frigid reprimand. "The rest of us were here so we started without you."

Cassie paused in the act of assuming her seat, duly chastened and at the same time annoyed by his presumption. She gave the graying man a long, leveling stare and said, "Good. All of our time is valuable. I would hate to think it wasted in idleness." Calmly, she settled into the chair and contrarily took her leisure in opening her portfolio and arranging the pages on the desk before her. "How far had we gotten?"

"McWilliams just finished with the international report," her cousin Quinton told her and affected a yawn behind the back of his hand. She smiled but noticed his father did not. Then the young man's gaze riveted to her in horror. "My God, Cass, what happened to your face?"

Now was not the time for fiction to fail her. With an embarrassed laugh, she said, "My own fault. I wasn't watching where I was going and someone bumped me in that terrible crush on the el steps. I couldn't catch my balance and took quite a knock on the head. I don't believe I even slowed traffic. Commuters were more than willing to step over my prostrate form so they wouldn't miss their train. Unfortunately, I did miss mine." There, let her uncle feel just the slightest twinge of guilt over whatever curses he'd been calling down over her tardiness.

"Are you all right?"

"Fine, Quinton," she dismissed easily. "I just look as though I went a few rounds in a pugilist's ring, is all. Shall we get on with business?" She gave her cousin a warm smile in appreciation of his concern and turned her attention back to the running of the magazine.

The rest of the meeting went predictably and Cassie's aching head wasn't given much to strain over. She jotted down notes as each of her key employees was given a turn to speak about his section of the periodical. There was the usual grumbling over the rivalry between newspapers and magazines and the colorful epithets directed to Misters Hearst and Pulitzer, and glum mutterings about the drops in circulation numbers and the growing threat of midwestern publishing centers. After ruminating upon such grim topics, she smiled along with the others as the flamboyant city editor, Walter Rampling, who was always looking for a startling way to present the obvious, suggested several murders of the prior evening had a link to vampirism.

"Oh, come on, Walter," Quinton scoffed good-naturedly. "You don't seriously expect us to consider such nonsense."

The balding editor grinned. "I don't expect you to, but the readers will gobble it up. Just look at the evidence, or rather the lack of it. Two big, burly men slain with no obvious signs of struggle, their throats cut, their bodies emptied of blood." He didn't pause or apologize out of respect for Cassie's feminine nature, knowing she was used to such graphic description. "Not a witness anywhere who saw or heard anything. What doesn't that sound like to you?"

"It sounds like you've been eating too much spice in your food again, Walter, and it's caused you to have fitful dreams," Quinton chuckled. Then his gaze settled on Cassie and he frowned. "Are you all right, Cass? You look awfully pale."

"I'm . . . fine. Walter, where were these two men found?"

"Don't humor him," her cousin groaned in warning.

"Just north of the park," Rampling confided, grateful for the chance to pursue his idea. "Near where they found that poor murdered woman killed in almost the same manner."

"What woman?" she asked.

"The one who took an unfortunate turn through the park last night," her uncle summed up impatiently. "The one you would have heard about had you been here on time."

Cassie was too distracted to take offense. It was a coincidence, surely. It couldn't be the same two men who attacked her. The two men Louis Radcliffe dealt with.

"I can blow it up big," Rampling went on, gathering momentum and enthusiasm. " 'Vampire Killer Loose in New York.' We'll scoop all the other editions."

"Of course," Quinton put in dryly. "They'd be too sensible to run such drivel."

"What do you really think happened to those two men?" Cassie asked faintly.

Rampling shrugged. "Who knows? Some kind of ritual slaying in one of those immigrant religions."

"Find out before you print anything."

"Cassie, that will take—"

"Work?" she supplied for him. "Then work for it. You want vampires, prove they exist. Have sources you can quote. Then you can run your story in the *Lexicon.*" Her tone firmed with her commitment to the integrity of her father's legacy. "Until then, all you've got is two men dead of undetermined causes and that's not news to anyone here in Manhattan. We are not publishing a pulp magazine and I do not employ penny-a-line scribblers. News is news and fiction is fiction. Do not confuse the two. If there is nothing else, gentlemen, I suggest we get on with things."

The other editors snuffed out cigars, gulped the last of their cold coffee and ambled out until only Fitzhugh, Quinton and Cassie remained. She began to gather up her papers, purposefully keeping her eyes lowered out of uncharacteristic cowardice. She didn't feel up to a confrontation with her uncle this morning, not when her concentration was fractured at best.

"Rampling's idea is not without merit," he began reasonably.

"I have no intention of lowering the standards of this magazine to that of carrying— " She was at a loss for the word and glanced to Quinton.

"Drivel," he supplied cheerfully.

"Yes, drivel. My father— "

"Your father would do everything possible to keep this publication afloat. Cassie, you're over your head. I don't know what Brighton was thinking when he placed you in his office."

"Well, I do," she snapped back at him. "He was thinking that the *Lexicon* should go to someone who shared the same visions he held."

"My brother was a fool!"

Her back went rigid. With supreme control, Cassie rose from her chair and gathered her papers tightly to her breast so he wouldn't see how badly her hands were shaking. "My father was a brilliant newsman. He saw the *Lexicon* as a reflection of the people, not as an exploiter of them."

"The people of this city don't want reality, girl! They want sensation. They want the bizarre. They want to be taken in by fantasy. I could have a whole staff of fiction hacks here at the snap of my fingers, working eagerly for next to nothing. The *Lexicon* could be a profitable holding instead of this sinking ship of righteous values. Your father didn't understand that."

"My father understood more than you give him credit for, which is why he chose me for this position instead of you."

They faced one another. The veil of civility that had hung between them since Brighton Alexander's funeral was rapidly falling away. Cassie understood her uncle's hostility. He'd given eight years of sweat and creativity to the magazine, expecting to take over its helm if anything happened to its founder. However, though they were brothers, there was little Brighton and Fitzhugh could agree upon and the direction of the *Lexicon* was one of them. Cassie had hoped it wouldn't be perceived as the supreme insult, passing the reins over his head into his young niece's hands. She'd hoped they could work together. Perhaps those were naive hopes.

"You're not fit for this job, girl. It's a man's world. It's my world."

"It's everyone's world and I have a right to establish my place in it. Now, if you've nothing else constructive to discuss with me, this meeting is over." She spun from the table before he had the chance for rebuttal and stalked to the door, letting it slam behind her.

Quinton gave a low chuckle. "You handled that well, Father. You've got her on the run, quaking in her fine kid shoes."

Fitzhugh glared at his indolently lounging

son. "I'm glad you find this so amusing, you young wastrel. See how great a laugh you get when she drives this magazine under and you have no way to indulge your many vices."

Quinton immediately sobered, his head assuming a haughty angle. "I earn a fair wage on my own merit."

"Merit? That tripe you write is scarcely fit to print. If our copy editors didn't practically build it back up from your scribbled nothings, you'd be laughed out of the industry. Face the facts, boy, for once. Without me, you'd be forced out of your pampered and privileged lifestyle. You'd have no one to pay for your gaming, your whoring, your drinking and . . . and whatever else you do that I do not care to know about. You are a weak and spineless creature, Quinton, and I quite despise you for your reckless dissipation. That girl is more of a man than you can claim to be."

Quinton stared back at him with an air of insolence before drawling, "I am what you made of me, the perfect reflection of your society world."

Fitzhugh made a disparaging sound and turned away from the ironic truth of those words. He didn't see the way his son's features hardened into a sullen snarl behind his back.

"Can you do nothing right? What happened to those useless buffoons you found for me? They never showed up to collect the rest of their pay."

"I thought the plan was to scare her. You said nothing about her coming to any harm. I will not allow you to hurt her."

"Not allow?" Fitzhugh gave a great booming laugh. "And how are you going to stop me, boy? You, who cannot even face the day without clouded eyes and a cloudier mind. You will do as you are told if you don't want to be out on the street. This magazine should be mine! I will not let her run it into bankruptcy. I will take control from her no matter what means I must employ, and you are going to help me, you worthless, whining pup or you'll see every last one of your accounts closed this afternoon."

Quinton had no reply, nor did his father expect one. The air of defiance had all but drained itself dry beneath the harshness of Fitzhugh's summations.

"Now make yourself useful and find me a couple more men of immoral character. It's time to show your little cousin exactly how foolish she is to compete where she doesn't belong."

Four

A smattering of soft applause brought Cassie's attention up from the pages on her desk.

"Bravo, Cousin. An admirable performance. Perhaps I should feature you in the drama section."

She gave Quinton a small closed-lipped smile that didn't hurt too badly. "I would hardly call it an unqualified success. One doesn't win over your father's ambition."

He smiled wryly. "Ah, tell me something I don't know. He's a dangerous man to cross, Cass. I know. Count yourself lucky for the small victories."

"The skirmishes won't matter if I can't win the war." She sighed and let her shoulders slump momentarily.

"Is it as bad as all that?"

Rubbing a hand across her eyes, she allowed a brief truth to escape her. "Worse. My father left things in a financial disaster. I don't know how I'm going to pull anything out of it. Our circulation numbers are slipping. Advertisers aren't exactly beating down our door. And now I have this conflict with your father. I don't want to lose."

"One good story, Cass. That's all you need. One piece of outstanding journalism to set the *Lexicon* back upon its feet."

"One good story," she echoed heavily. "And a few miracles."

"There you go." And he smiled wide, coaxing her to join him. She could always count upon him to lift her spirits. Her cousin was the one true friend she could claim in the competitive business of publishing.

With his delicate, careless good looks and social pedigree, Quinton was a natural for the arts section of the magazine. He looked at things through a dreamer's eyes and a cynic's soul. His reviews on books, theater and music were acerbic, insightful and entertaining to read. He had a flair for the poetic himself and had once recited some works he'd done. When she'd suggested he get them published, he'd laughed, saying his father ridiculed his efforts, calling them sentimental pap. He hadn't needed to spell out how much that summation hurt him. His father's approval was something he strove for in vain. Fitzhugh Alexander was not a man easy to please.

She'd always held a place in her heart for the often woebegone and moody Quinton. Like herself, he'd found himself motherless at an early age, his lost through a physical failing, hers through a mental one. He inspired Cassie to protective feeling with his purposeful self-neglect and tragic yearning for affection. He'd have more luck wringing it from a stone than finding it in his father. She had a soft spot for a sad story.

Then Quinton shook the secure foundation of their relationship by coming up beside her and letting the backs of his fingers stroke over the sore side of her face. It wasn't a brotherly gesture, nor was the sudden intensity that came into his eyes. The intimacy it implied startled Cassie.

"You take better care of yourself, Cass. These can be dangerous times and I want you to remember that you have a friend in me."

"I— I've always known that, Quinton, but I thank you for the reminder."

And when he was gone, she puzzled over the strange change in him. He'd never displayed a preference for her as a woman, not that she could remember. He liked an entirely different type of female, if her uncle's grumblings could be believed. Women who could be bought cheaply and discarded at will.

And besides, Quinton quickened no healthy stirrings of attraction in her. She couldn't work herself up into a passion over a man she saw as too weak of resolve and too intimidated by the bullying shadow his father cast. She wanted a man like— no, not like— she wanted Louis Radcliffe. And there was simply no comparison between the two.

Thinking of Louis made her once again ponder the odd murders. Dare she ask Louis what he'd done with the two men who'd attacked her? Had he merely chased them off? Or had he dealt with them severely, as his manner suggested?

Did she want to know?

Her musings were interrupted by young Tim with a stack of morning mail.

"Nasty bump you have there, Miss Alexander."

She covered the bruise self-consciously. "So I've been told. Anything of interest in that lot?" She nodded toward the pile of envelopes, praying they weren't all bills.

"Just odds and ends, ma'am. Was I right about it being from an admirer?" At her blank look, he prompted, "You know, that package I brought up here last night?"

She'd forgotten all about it. It was probably still at the Radcliffes', unopened. But she smiled at the boy and told him, "I'm afraid not."

He gave a manly sigh and shook his head. "Can't understand that, you being such a fetching female, if you'll pardon me for speaking my mind, ma'am."

She smiled wider, ignoring the rekindled ache in her jaw. "You're forgiven." And she reached for her letter opener to dismiss him before he made any other grand declarations.

Bills and unsolicited pleadings for her to

buy story ideas. Nothing looked promising until she reached the bottom of the stack to find a plain envelope with just her name scrawled across the front. She turned it over in her hand curiously. No postmark, no stamp. No sign that it had gone through the postal system at all. Then how had it gotten into this pile? She craned her neck to see over the partial paneling of her wall into the room beyond in time to catch a glimpse of the boy disappearing out the front door. She would have to ask him tomorrow, if there was any reason for a continued curiosity.

She broke the seal and took out a single sheet. The message was short, penned in broad aggressive strokes.

Why didn't you follow through? I did it for you. Don't let me down next time if you know what's good for you.

It could have meant anything, but a shiver of response trickled through Cassie. Some kind of prank? If so, it wasn't funny with its vague implication and dire innuendo. She was much too tired and yet unstrung from the violence she'd met with the night before.

Probably foolishness.

Probably nothing.

Yet the tremor of uneasiness clung to her all day like an unpleasant chill upon the skin. And for the first time she could ever remember, when the work day ended for her staff, she left with them, comforted by the rush of humanity that carried her along like an indifferent reed upon a tide. Her tension didn't relax on the journey uptown. Anyone who bumped up close to her set her heart leaping into an anxious gallop. Each approach contained a concealed threat. She could feel the prickle of eyes upon her but each time she glanced about she caught no one showing an undue interest in her. By the time she reached her stop, Cassie was drenched with apprehension and eager to flee the close quarters where an attack could be hidden in the sheer crush of bodies.

As she hurried along the walk, agitation followed close upon her heels. Her glance was constantly covering her retreat for signs of possible pursuit. She refused to feel silly in her caution until she was safely upon her own front stoop, fishing in her new bag for her keys.

A slight brush of movement at her elbow sent a scream hurtling up into her throat to catch upon a knot of panic. She stumbled back against her still-locked door, bracing for another brutal confrontation— and was met by the polite bow of her neighbor's Asian servant. With a bland smile upon his impassive face, Takeo extended a folded note. She took it from him with a shamelessly trembling hand and by the time she glanced down at it in question and up again, he was gone as silently as he'd appeared.

Clutching the note in one sweat-slicked hand, Cassie opened her front door and slipped inside the cool reception of her family home. Emptiness was her only greeting. The woman she hired to keep her house had long since gone to be with her own family after leaving an efficiently prepared meal for one wrapped in the kitchen. That solitary plate held no appeal. Gratefully, Cassie turned her attention to the note from next door.

I hope you haven't forgotten our dinner engagement. I'll be waiting upon your convenience. Arabella.

Silently blessing the lonely old woman, Cassie was quick to change from her soot-dappled work attire into a pretty visiting dress of striped changeable silk which enticed with shimmers of rose, green and brown. The inward-facing vandykes of white Irish lace drew the eye down a snug form-fitted bodice, accentuating her female shape. As she surveyed the effect in her mirror, Cassie wondered if Louis Radcliffe's gaze could be made to detail along those flirty points from the ample curves of her bosom to the tiny span of her waist. She was unfamiliar with this new desire to please and attract the opposite gender. It made her giddy and fretful at the same time. And nearly light-headed with anticipation.

But Louis wasn't home.

"I don't expect him to return until later this evening," Arabella told her young visitor, noting the disappointment upon her face. "We can make use of his absence by sharing a little woman-to-woman chat. I do so enjoy our talks."

Cassie smiled, trying to appear enthusiastic. It wasn't that she didn't value Arabella's company, for the elderly woman was always a delightful surprise of intelligent converse. She only regretted that her careful toilet and fluttery expectation would be for nothing.

"I thought we might enjoy a supper alfresco. We have so few mild evenings left us and I do so love the out of doors."

They traveled by luxurious brougham to the south end of Central Park where its gentle landscape reminded Arabella of the pastoral beauty of her native English countryside. There they abandoned the carriage, and followed the bench-lined path down to the tranquil pond, Takeo pushing Arabella's chair and Cassie toting their supper basket. When the elderly woman decided upon a likely stretch of grass near the inviting tree-fringed edge of the pond, Takeo spread a heavy blanket and effortlessly lifted the fragile woman from her chair to settle upon it. Cassie joined her and watched as the Oriental man laid out an elegant feast before them, topped by a sparkling vintage that Arabella said was bottled near her chateau in France. They dined and sipped in companionable silence while Takeo saw to their every need with the briefest communing glance from his mistress.

When all was packed away but the wine and Takeo vanished to return the leftovers to the carriage, Arabella gave a heartfelt sigh and claimed, "It's so beautiful here, like a more peaceful slice from my childhood."

Cassie had to agree with her there. The very layout of the area guaranteed privacy, the paths ever winding in a cunning pattern to provide the utmost seclusion. The sounds of water, of nature quieting, of the city muffled and seemingly far away, acted in tandem to soothe Cassie's frayed senses. She wasn't aware her disconcertion was so obvious until her companion remarked, "Would you care to discuss what had you so agitated earlier? Takeo said you were in a rare state of fright when he came upon you."

Takeo said? The statement struck Cassie as odd, seeing as how Takeo was mute. But perhaps after being so long in her service, a silent communication had developed between them.

"I must confess that the events of last night still have me shaken. Then I received a rather disturbing note at my office. I could not shake the sense of being watched and followed on the way home tonight. Nerves, I guess." She gave a sheepish smile but the other woman was not so quick to dismiss her fears.

"Perhaps not, my dear. Instincts are best attended. If you sense a threat, it could be very real."

"What would anyone have to gain by frightening me? Coincidence, that's all. Products of an over-active mind."

"Products of a lonely heart," Arabella corrected. "Might I ask something of a personal nature?" At Cassie's guarded nod, she queried, "How is it that a woman as lovely and intelligent as you lives alone in that big old house? Why is there no young man in your life?"

Cassie flushed but took no offense at the direct questioning. After sipping her wine, she leaned back on her palms and tried to explain. "It was more important for me to make my own way than to have a husband pave it for me. I guess I wanted to stand upon my own merit rather than lay claim to a pedigree and cite my only accomplishment in how well I ran my household and entertained above my means. A rather fanciful wish for a woman of these times."

"For a woman of any time, but I do understand your want of independence. But now that you have achieved it, does it bring you the satisfaction you desired?"

"Yes."

"What about happiness?"

Cassie paused. She could find no pat answer for that. She felt professionally fulfilled, but beyond that was a distressing emotional void.

"You needn't answer," Arabella said gently. "I can see it upon your face."

"I wanted more for myself than the role

of fluffy chattel, tending hearth and nursery. I wanted to build my own security so I would never have to be at the whim of the man I married."

Like her mother. That revelation took her by surprise as did her realization of its truth. She had seen her pampered society mother's light blaze then fade with a purposeless flicker. Her own would not be so fragile. Her fate would not be decided by some dominating man, the way her mother's had been. And though she'd loved her father dearly, she'd never forgiven him for taking her mother away from her. She never wanted to have that vulnerable a hold on her own future. Never.

"Oh, I completely understand that yearning for freedom. It was my own when I was your age. I saw no need to clutter my life with the demands of some petty tyrant who all but owned me legally and morally."

"Then what happened?" Cassie asked, intent upon her study of the wizened face with its sharply animated gaze.

Arabella smiled. "I met a man."

"Ah!"

"Yes, ah! A man who haunted my dreams and held my heart. Not the wisest choice by any means but the only one for me. And there was nothing I would not sacrifice for him. He made all my other reasons for existence pale in comparison."

"And you didn't regret that loss of freedom?"

"Oh, on the contrary. With Louis, I could fly if I chose."

"Louis?"

Arabella glanced at her, baffled for a moment, then she smiled. "My husband's name, too."

Cassie leaned upon her elbow, fascinated. "What was he like, your Louis?"

"Strong, noble of spirit, tender of heart. There were no shackles within our marriage vows, only an exquisite release from convention. Our love is eternal." Her eyes grew misty with past dreams and Cassie could see a glimmer of the beauty she must have held to in her youth.

"And what happened to that love?" Cassie asked softly, caught up in the reverie.

"Time. Time was our only enemy in the end," she said a bit sadly, then smiled. "But I regret none of it. The years we had were wonderful. I would like to see that love reborn again in another who is close to me." And her thin, birdlike hand slipped over Cassie's, squeezing with a surprising strength.

It took Cassie a moment to realize Arabella was speaking of her and her own grandson, Louis, the namesake of her loved one. And then she was speechless.

"You are not fond of Louis?" Arabella's teasing tone made it clear that less than the truth would not be believed.

"I— he— "

"Yes?"

"He is an exceptional man. But I don't believe he has any feelings for me." Her eyes lowered at that humbling admission.

"But if he did, would he find them returned?"

"I don't think there is any point— "

"Would he?"

Cassie's flush deepened. "Yes," she confessed at last. "Yes, I believe he would."

Arabella exhaled in relief. "Good. You see, it is very important for me to know that Louis will have someone to care for him when I am gone."

"Gone? Oh, you have many years left— "

"No." That was said firmly, in a tone that said the truth of when was no longer a mystery. "I count my time left in days, my dear, and there is much I would see settled before I relinquish the last of them. Oh, please don't look sad. I have lived my life fully and well. I've known a spectacular love. I've borne a child and seen a grandchild. I've seen the ways of my youth disappear to make room for the future and I know I have no reason to hold on to what I cannot change. The only thing I can do to defeat the inevitable is arrange what I can, selfishly, while I am still here. Then I can surrender all in peace."

Cassie stared at her with tears standing in her eyes. She'd never heard anything quite so moving. Selfish? No, that's not what she would call it. Considerate. Caring. A self-sacrifice to assure the happiness of those she loved.

Arabella was giving her Louis. Her every dream.

But that didn't mean Arabella's will would be his.

"I have waited a long while to find a woman worthy of Louis. He requires someone of strength and character, someone who is not afraid of adversity, who will not fail before a challenge. Louis's circumstances are unusual. Not any woman would be equal to them. I think you are."

Cassie was a bit disbelieving. What woman wouldn't fall prostrate for a chance to wed Louis Radcliffe? Surely there were no circumstances that would limit the line of the eligible to just one. To her. He had no imperfections that she could see. And what she could imagine certainly wouldn't scare her off. "I am flattered by your assessment but what makes you believe that Louis shares your regard? Won't he have something to say about your matchmaking?"

"Louis will see that what I've done is in his best interest and out of my love for him. He may resist for the sake of principle but I don't believe he will have any objection to you. You are, after all, very much like me. What could he take exception to?"

Cassie smiled faintly at that bit of logic,

but though her heart was scurrying in its want to believe, her more analytical mind was not convinced that Arabella's wishes would sway a man as self-assured as her grandson.

And she wasn't sure she was the type of woman to sway his desires, as much as she wanted it to be so.

"What is it you wish for in a mate, my dear? We must consider your feelings in this as well," Arabella asked as though the end was all but inevitable already.

Cassie thought a moment, then stated the requirements she'd never dared hope could be met by any man. Until now. "He would have to wish for more in a wife than window dressing. I would not care to be no more to him than the vessel for bearing children for his immortal vanity nor would I want to be a mere slave to his whims."

"You have no wish for your own children?" Arabella couched carefully.

"I like children, but I cannot pretend that I think I would be the best of parents. Are you scandalized?"

Arabella smiled. "No. You should not be ashamed of how you feel. Too many feel honor bound to bear young than harbor no affection for them. Better you be honest about the state of your heart up front. Do go on."

Cassie hesitated, amazed by the elderly woman's acceptance of her unconventional stand but unconvinced that any other would be. "But what if Louis desires a large family?" Now she was speaking as if the matter was settled. Madness. Delightful madness.

"I believe if there is enough love, only two are necessary— man and wife. I think that arrangement would satisfy him. You are still a candidate, my dear, so don't look so apprehensive. Go on. What else do you require?"

Somewhat heartened, Cassie continued with her list. "He would have to understand what my work means to me and not be threatened by the time it takes me away from home. I wouldn't want to give up my sense of being my own person. Does that make me selfish?"

"No. It makes you strong and unique. Those are not bad qualities. Do you think this man exists?"

"I think he's the kind of man you married."

"Traits passed down to this current generation," Arabella confided with an encouraging smile. "I think you would do well for each other."

Cassie's heart leapt at that but she forced herself not to get carried away by what was yet unproven folly. "All well and good but he has yet to see me as anything beyond a neighbor and companion for his grandmother. You can't force magic to appear when none exists. And I have no idea how to kindle it." There, she'd laid it out simply.

Now Arabella would recognize how futile her plan was. Cassie was no coquette, no seducer of the male gender. She hadn't the slightest notion of how to guide Louis's attention in a man/woman direction.

As if empathic to the line of her misgivings, Arabella patted her hand once more and said, "Be patient and be yourself. He will be free to seek your favor soon."

And after that cryptic phrase, further conversation was ended by Takeo's return. He gathered the old woman up and placed her gently in her chair, wheeling her back toward the waiting carriage as evening shadows spread outward from beneath the underbrush to steal upon the path. Cassie followed, pensive, until they were both seated on well-sprung seats and on the return home.

"Is it age that confines you to your chair?" Cassie asked in concern, having wondered before but never having had the opportunity to ask such an intimate question. Considering the topic of their recent discourse, she felt close enough to ask now.

"Partially. But the main reason is a piece of lead I carry near my spine and have for over half my life."

"A piece of lead?" Cassie gasped in astonishment.

"A bullet from an assassin's gun meant to take my husband's life."

"And you were struck by mistake?"

She smiled. "No mistake. As I said, there is no sacrifice I would not have made for my Louis. I considered the consequences fair payment for the protection of his life. I still do, even after the pain has crippled me into this nearly useless shell. That is love, Cassie. Use it as a gauge before you claim undying devotion."

"It's a harsh guide to follow," the younger woman murmured at last.

"Yes, but if you cannot bend your will to it, do not look to Louis as an answer to your need for affection. Loving him will exact a cost and you must be willing to pay. Without question. Without hesitation. If you can't, continue to be what you are now, a neighbor and my companion."

Those words weighted the silence that took them to the Alexanders' door. Takeo leapt nimbly down to assist Cassie to the walk and escorted her to the door, where he waited until she was safely inside. Then, with a courtly bow, he returned to the carriage and the withered-looking woman who huddled within.

Cassie was putting away her outer wraps when she felt an odd unsettling in the house. As if something had been disturbed in the natural order of things. She looked about intently, trying to discover what had her suspicions quivering and saw that the doors to her father's study were left open. She'd made a point of keeping them closed since his death and her housekeeper knew well enough to concur with her wishes. So why were they standing agape as if any second she would hear his boisterous voice calling to her from within?

The sound of the door knocker startled her from her deep thoughts. She hesitated with her hand upon the knob, a rivulet of remembered fear delaying her on the threshold. Finally, she got control of her trepidation only to find Louis Radcliffe on the doorstep, his arms full of the belongings she'd left behind after the attack. For a moment all she could do was stare, sure every hint of her conversation with his grandmother was imprinted upon her face.

"Bella asked if I would bring these over to you," came his low, liquid drawl. She no longer thought it odd that he would call his grandmother by her given name, though it had taken some getting used to at first. "You dropped them last night and I thought there might be something important amongst them."

She took them from him numbly and he paused as she remained mute.

When it seemed she would say nothing, Louis bowed slightly and murmured, "Good evening." Then her trance state ended.

"Please, won't you take a touch of brandy with me? It's a habit my father and I enjoyed each evening and it seems like forever since I had someone to share it with." Did she sound as foolishly desperate to his ears as she did to her own, she wondered in horror. She didn't care. She couldn't force herself to enter that room alone. Louis merely smiled politely.

"I would like that but I can only stay a moment."

"Of course," she stammered on gracelessly. "You must have had a tiring day." And then she realized she had no idea what it was he did to occupy his days. Some sort of importing business, she remembered Arabella saying.

Before she could disgrace herself further with her nervous ramblings, she led him into the dark-paneled study she'd inherited from her father but had yet to use. There, she placed the papers on the corner of the desk, very aware that all was there just as he'd left it, very aware of Louis's presence close behind her in the dimly lit room. And absurdly glad for it.

"Would you mind pouring while I assess the damage to these things?"

"Of course," came his fluid reply. And she was surprised as the breath gushed from her as he stepped to the sideboard. She hadn't known she'd been holding it suspended in the clench of her lungs. Anxiously, she busied herself with the stack of work to distract herself from the intoxication of his company and the odd disconcertion she felt.

The sheafs of paper were badly stained

from the street and the shuffle of dirty feet over the tops of them. The pages were out of sequence and she determined to spend the rest of the evening sorting and salvaging what she could. Once her unexpected guest was gone, of course.

Then she came across the parcel Tim had delivered the night before and all her curiosity regarding it returned. She gave it a shake and again felt the subtle soft shifting of its contents. Unable to wait a moment longer, she slipped off the twine. The bold script on the front looked familiar enough for her to instinctively preserve it as she tore into the package.

A scarf. She unfolded it and saw to her dismay that the pretty yarns were discolored with rust. What kind of admirer would send her damaged goods? Frowning slightly, she opened the card found tucked into the stiffened folds.

For you, it said in that aggressive hand, then it gave a location near the cliff in Central Park North.

She considered it and the soiled gift for a long second, trying to piece together why she should feel there was some consequence tied into one or both. The park. What had she heard just today about the park and why did that arrogant scrawl seem so recognizable?

The murder of a young woman. Now she recalled it being discussed briefly at that morning's meeting, the coincidence of her body being found near that of the two burly men.

A sudden shiver took hold of her in a relentless grip that wouldn't abate until her teeth were chattering.

"Miss Alexander?"

Louis Radcliffe's worried voice seemed to come from miles away.

The significance curdled in the bottom of her belly; the vaguely ominous message she'd received in her office that morning matched the penmanship on the note she held now. Clues to a heinous crime.

Those weren't rust stains on the scarf.

It was dried blood.

Five

The scent of old blood reached him where he stood on the other side of the room, the aroma rushing to his brain, clouding his senses in a way the dark amber liquor he poured never could. It was like the stroke of a blade along a whetstone, bringing a keen edge to his hunger.

As he turned toward the intoxicating lure with a brandy in either hand, Louis saw Cassie's shoulders sway. Her back was to him so he couldn't see her face as he called out her name in concern. The article of clothing she held in her hands fell to the floor as the intricate waterfall of fabric that bunched into a bustle at the back of her gown began a side-to-side swish. And Cassie went down, legs melting within the pool of her skirts.

With a blur of motion, Louis set the drinks aside and stepped to catch her within the circle of one arm. She slumped against him, seemingly boneless inside the hard construction of her corset. Her head rolled back along his shoulder, giving him a glimpse of pale arched throat and the flutter of golden lashes upon skin all but bleached of color. He could feel her heart beating at an impossibly fast tempo, a chafe to his already heightened appetite.

"Cassie?" There was no response as his free hand cupped the side of her face. She was alarmingly cold. Worried, he steered her toward the sofa with the intention of leaning her back upon the slant of its single cushioned arm but the moment he eased her down, her senses began to return enough for her to fix a life-or-death grip upon his coat. The instant he sat beside her on the couch, she was burrowing against the wall of his chest, her fingers clutching in rapid spasms of fright as her swoon gave way to a terrified awareness. He could feel the shallow quiver of her breathing warming his skin through the starch of his shirt front. And the frantic patter of her pulse invited more from him than this rather reserved offer of comfort.

Louis moistened his lips as his hunger rose, momentarily confused between the lingering scent of stale blood and the enticing rhythm of heat and life channeling through the woman pressed too close to him for safety's sake. His mind was dazzled with the rich, luring sensations as his hand rose unbidden to curl about the back of her neck, his fingers testing the pattern of her pulse beats as their smooth tips rested lightly beneath one ear. He was lost to that basic thrum of existence; hers, his, and the need to overwhelm it, to take and combine it, clouding reason in lieu of the reality of what he was. He was hungry. He was more dangerous than any of her fears, real or imagined. Yet she clung to him unaware of the threat, tempting the very fate that could crush her.

Controlled by the dark instinct of his kind, Louis bent his head over her, letting his cheek brush against the pale silk of her hair, letting the soft pant of his breath stroke exposed flesh as his mouth hovered above the beckoning throb of her life force.

Gradually, fatally drawn, he lowered to touch the side of her throat, his lips moving upon the supple satin in a whisper-light caress. He was too absorbed in his own rapidly altering state to notice the shift in hers from fear to a burgeoning desire. She tilted her head innocently, allowing him ready access. One of her hands rose to tremble in uncertainty before shyly clasping the back of his head. Her heart continued its frantic beat, urged by a different sort of distress. Her body, no longer passive in his embrace, woke with a seducing press and not-so-subtle shift against him. A faint sound escaped her, vibrating beneath the seal of his lips in a low moan of his name.

Not knowing what tragic circumstance she

courted, Cassie turned her head to scatter a fluster of brief kisses along the strong angle of his jaw, and that unexpected display of awkward passion startled him from the pull of his own lethal desires. Suddenly she was no longer a nameless, formless victim for his vile lusts but a woman of admirable strength and tender feelings. Agitated by the bewildering juxtaposition, he went completely still then slowly drew back from the unspeakable liberties he'd been about to take from a woman who didn't deserve such callous disregard.

Cassie's eyes flickered open when she felt him pull away. She was still leaning upon him, his hair threaded between her fingers, his coat balled up in one small fist. Their faces were so close together, she could see herself reflected in the dark centers of his eyes. Eyes that were curiously gold in color with centers that sucked at her soul like a relentless whirlpool. She wanted to see the heat, the insistent urgency of moments before mirrored in his steady stare but there was nothing beyond those spirit-draining pupils and the cooling change of his irises from hot gold to chill green. There was no emotion whatsoever. As if she'd imagined the passion sparking between them only seconds earlier.

"Are you all right?" he asked quietly.

She wasn't sure if he was asking about her recovery from his embrace or her reaction to the horror she'd discovered delivered into her hands. Either way, she could see he was trying to pull back from further involvement. So she forced her fingers to uncramp from their hold on him. She made herself lever back from the unyielding pleasure his hard chest afforded. And she tried to sound equally unaffected.

"I'm fine now." She took a deep breath to reinforce her claim. The sound of it shivered noisily through the clench of her teeth. "Please forgive me. I'm not usually given to such vaporish behavior. I don't know what came over me. I'm quite all right."

He wasn't in the least taken in. "You're not fine now any more than you were when you answered the door. What's wrong?" His tone was crisp, almost impatient as he stayed a cautious arm's length away. As if he feared she was about to fling herself upon him for another emotional display. As if the very idea was abhorrent to him.

"It's nothing you need be concerned with," she murmured, inexplicably hurt by his reluctance to give aid. For a moment . . . for a moment, he'd provided paradise within the wrap of his arms and now he was denying her the most meager glimpse of his compassion. Did he regret his impulsively offered passion? Or was it her response that thrust the distance back between them? Whichever, she wasn't about to burden him with the confusion in her heart.

"You were frightened when you came to the door and terrified just now. Has this to do with the other night?" he prodded tersely, giving her no chance to make up any fancy fiction.

His insistence wore her down. The magnitude of her fear was too much to contain inside, unspoken. He may not have been the most responsive confidant but he was all she had. With a sigh, she confessed, "Yes . . . and no."

He stood and her gaze rose hungrily with him. Thinking he was going to leave, she clutched her hands together in her lap to resist the want to reach out and stay him. But he only went to fetch her brandy, and passing it into her shaking hands, he settled once more on the sofa beside her. But not quite as close.

"Explain yes and no."

Cassie took a bolstering sip and savored the rich burn of the liquor as it scorched all the way down. Rather hoarsely, she began, "Yes, I was still upset by the other night. I felt as though someone followed me home again this evening. And then I had the feeling that someone had been here in the house. I have no proof of either thing. Perhaps it was just nerves."

"Perhaps," he agreed with a studied neutrality. He took the empty glass from her and gave her his as well, waiting for her to bolt it down with an expert flip of the wrist. That practiced vice brought a slight smile to the chiseled sweep of his lips. "And what else so distressed you just now? Is it the contents of that package?" Purposely, he didn't look toward the scarf where it curled upon the parquet floor like a deadly serpent.

She swallowed down the coil of sickness to tell him. "It was delivered to me at work last night, a special delivery I didn't have a chance to open then. Today, I received another message asking why I hadn't acted upon what I'd been sent."

"And what had you been sent?" he prompted quietly. His arm was resting along the back of the sofa. His hand had dropped down slightly so his fingers could begin a gentle massage of one rigid shoulder. She trembled beneath a touch that wasn't quite as calming as he'd intended.

"It was that scarf and a location in the park where a woman was killed last night. I think the scarf belonged to her and I think it's her—her blood that's on it."

He glanced at the discarded scarf then and his nostrils flared as if he was testing the scent. "It's blood, though whose I cannot say. You think the murderer sent it to you? Why?"

"I don't know." She rubbed her brow with a shaky hand. "Unless I was meant to find the b-body before the police."

He said nothing for a time, then asked, "Will you go to the authorities now?"

Now it was her turn to observe him carefully as she answered, "I don't know if I should. I wouldn't want to be entangled in the other matter they're investigating."

His reply was low and brandy-smooth. "What matter is that?"

"The police found the bodies of two men in the same general area. If they begin checking into my link with the woman, they might wonder about those two men as well."

"So, what if they do?" His gaze was opaque, his poise unflappable. If he was hiding any guilt from her, she couldn't detect it.

"They sound like they might be the same two men who attacked me. I-I remember seeing one of them clutching at his throat. I remember blood on his hands."

Louis's eyes narrowed ever so slightly but his voice never lost its inflectionless calm. "And you were wondering if maybe I killed them."

Faintly, she asked, "Did you?"

Neither moved as a subtle beat of tension built between them. Then Louis met her question with a question. "If I did, would you turn me in to the police?"

Was that a confession? An admission of guilt? Cassie was reminded then of Arabella's warning of the sacrifices to come.

Had the elderly woman known of this? Had she been doing nothing more than trying to pave the way to protect her grandson? Had the purpose of their heart-to-heart talk been a means of manipulating her emotions?

Was this man seated beside her on her sofa a killer?

She was aware of the stillness of his fingers where they remained pressed upon her shoulder. Such strength he had in those hands. Had he used that strength to slay the men who'd harmed her?

Then other fleeting images returned: the cruel leer of their expressions, their brutal immunity to her pain. And she told Louis, softly, meaningfully, "They hurt me. They were going to do— worse. You saved my life. And I owe you for that."

The slight relaxation of his form condemned him the way no amount of circumstantial proof could.

"I must go now," he said at last. "Bella will be worried. Are you certain that you'll be all right? If you are afraid to be here alone . . . you could return with me." How gingerly he offered that suggestion.

"I'll be fine."

And he must have seen the anxiousness, the turmoil in her eyes and felt her cringe away from the pressure of his fingertips for he gave her a flat, concluding smile and stood. She was aware of the threat he posed to her now. That was good. It was safer . . . for both of them.

"If you are in need, Takeo or I can be here in an instant."

She smiled to herself at the unwillingness of his offer and murmured a simple, "Thank you."

He started to see himself out, feeling the intensity of her eyes upon him, when suddenly he turned back to claim, "The one thing has nothing to do with the other." Then he was gone.

Cassie stayed where she was until hard tremors of shock racked through her body. Then, slowly, she rose and went to pick up the crumpled scarf with its stains of death upon it. Why? she asked herself, echoing Louis's question. Why had the killer thought to send her this grisly gift and the notes that accompanied it? What did it mean? She had evidence in her hands the police could use to catch the killer, but she was reluctant to give it over.

Because though he had denied it, she had to wonder if the woman had been slain by the same man who'd killed her attackers. Had the poor creature seen Louis disposing of the bodies? Had she been an innocent victim of a man desperate to protect himself?

If so, how great did that make her own danger now that she alone knew Louis's secret guilt?

* * *

"Louis?"

The frail call brought him to his wife's bedside. The shape of her aged figure scarcely caused a ripple in the covers. The gaslights were dimmed to reflect only shadow but she didn't need to see his face to read the disturbance in his mind.

"You're troubled, my love. What is it?"

"She knows I killed those two men. Not how, of course, only that I ended their miserable existence."

There was a long pause, then Arabella prompted, "And? What does she mean to do with this knowledge?"

"Nothing for the moment. So she says."

There was an edge to his voice. Fearful of what it meant, Arabella struggled to lift up off the too-soft cushions. A feeble moan escaped her. She cursed her inability to disguise her pain. The last thing she wanted was pity from the man she loved.

Louis came to her quickly with a soothing, "Lie back, little one. Let me come down to you." And he stretched out on the bed beside her, his weight making no discernible difference upon the mattress as he edged in close along her narrow form. His gaze never touched upon her age-puckered countenance but affixed with hers in a timeless communion.

"Louis, you can trust her," Arabella insisted.

"There is only one being I trust completely, and that is you."

"She will not betray you."

"You are so sure of this?" His doubt carried in the twist of his tone.

"Yes. I'm sure. Trust her, Louis. She will keep this secret and in time, can be trusted with others." When he had no reply, her worry for Cassie's safety escalated, well knowing how strong her husband's instinct for self-preservation ran. "You won't do anything to— to harm her, will you, Louis? You must promise me you won't."

"Bella— "

"Promise me, Louis. She is not a danger to you. You needn't treat her as one. Louis? Promise me."

"You have my word I will not harm her."

Arabella gave a thin sigh. "I'm not wrong about her."

"I hope not, my love." He still didn't sound convinced but he was moved to rest his head upon his wife's sunken bosom, careful not to let her feel his full weight as he gathered one of her tiny hands up beneath his chin. Her other moved in a fragile caress through his hair and along his face. A soothing gesture she'd used since the first days of their long history together, one meant to quiet a troubled mind with the healing strength of love.

"Louis, I should like to have Nicole home for the holidays."

He shut his eyes tightly. "Whatever you wish, Bella."

"I should like to have my family near."

He could only nod, unable to answer through the emotion clogging up thick and hot in his throat. She didn't have to spell it out to him. She wanted them to be with her so she could say goodbye.

"Of course, they may be loath to leave the tropics to visit us here in the cold of the north," she chatted casually.

"They will come," he assured her in a husky voice.

She felt the dampness on his cheek but made no mention of it. Instead, she continued on almost happily. "It will be good to see them all again. It's been too long. Time doesn't have the same meaning for you that it does for me. You say 'I'll see you soon' and you might mean a decade later."

"I love you, Bella," he vowed with a sudden intensity.

She stroked his face with a loving hand. "I know you do." Then she rambled on lightly. "We should invite Cassie to join us in some of the celebrations. No one should be alone over the holidays."

"She has her own family, Bella. Her own kind." His words were sharp, carrying his resentment against the woman's intrusion into the affairs of his family. Into this very bedroom where he curled close to his wife with the fragrant scent of young skin still teasing his senses. "What would you have us do? Invite her to dine with us? Accompany her to evening mass? Her kind and ours do not mix well. You know that."

"Her kind. You mean my kind, don't you?"

He was silent for a moment, then apologetic. "I ofttimes forget we are not the same, you and I."

"We are not so different," she soothed.

He answered with a brittle laugh. "Only you would see it so."

"I had thought about being buried near my father in London," she said abruptly, much to Louis's distress. He said nothing but she could feel his resistant tension. "But I think I should like to be laid to rest here. I think of New York as my home now."

"Your home is with me, Bella," Louis chastised gruffly.

"Yes, my love, I know." Then she went on matter-of-factly. "Woodlawn, I think. I should like it there. It's peaceful, don't you agree?"

"Yes." A ragged whisper.

"I will make the arrangements."

"Whatever you wish, Bella," he agreed, his heart breaking.

"Are you sure you want to do this?"

Cassie stood under the cold wash of lights

in the city's morgue, not sure at all, but her voice was firm as she said, "Yes, quite sure, Danny."

"I don't know how you talked me into this," the young sergeant grumbled as he led her to one of many in several rows of tables. A white sheet draped its motionless inhabitant. "It could mean my career, letting you in here without authorization. If I didn't owe your father the shoes on my feet . . ." He let that familiar phrase trail off. They both knew well what he owed Brighton Alexander. The then reporter had taken in a half-frozen waif off the street one night after he'd tried to pick his pocket, had given him a meal and a warm place to stay the night, then saw to it that he had all the warm meals and places to stay he needed from then on. Daniel Hooper considered himself reborn after that meeting and dedicated his life to serving others as selflessly as he'd been served. That gratitude only wore on him when Brighton and now Cassie came to him for an occasional favor.

But they weren't usually as grim as this one.

"Have you ever seen a cadaver, Cassie?" came his cautioning as his hand lingered at the edge of the sheet.

"No," was her wavering reply, but then her tone steadied. "I have to see. Pull back the sheet."

One glimpse was enough to inspire a lifetime of nightmares. Though gray and missing the better part of his throat, there was no mistaking the identity of one of her attackers. She swallowed hard and Danny took that as a sign that she'd seen all she cared to.

Assuming the other man was in a similar state, Cassie had no curiosity left where he was concerned. She girded up her courage and whispered thickly, "Now the woman."

Scowling fiercely, Danny redraped the victim of Louis Radcliffe's wrath and searched through a number of toe tags to find one small ashen foot. Resolve not as steely in this case, Cassie studied that forlornly bare sole and jerked her head in a nod. Danny peeled back the sheet slowly, his own face puckering in distaste at the sight of a woman so young and lovely coming to such a tragic and lonesome end.

Cassie worked up the courage to raise her stare, edging it up along the pristine covering to where it ended at the woman's bare shoulders. Above that was the gruesome cause of death, a slash across the arteries similar to the other body. While sickness roiled and threatened all the control she'd promised to have, Cassie's gaze lifted to the eternally still features for a sudden jolt of recognition. The woman looked somehow familiar but Cassie couldn't place her among any of her acquaintances.

Then Danny made the unfortunate tie. "Why Cassie, she looks enough like you to be your sister!"

Six

"You look as though you'd seen a ghost."

Cassie looked up from the note clenched in her hands to see Quinton leaning against her door frame. It took her a moment to even smile.

"Where were you this morning? Miss your train again?"

Something in his tone hinted that he hadn't believed her the first time. Something in his drifting manner suggested that he was still floating on whatever numbing balm he sought in his evening hours. His eyes were pure black and a half-smile played about his sensitive mouth, bending it into a less amiable angle. His shirt collar was open and askew, his blond hair in a rumpled disarray and his chin hadn't seen a razor for at least two days. His was an attitude of studied neglect. If his father saw him in this obviously intoxicated state, the offices would be ringing with words she had no desire to hear on this particular morning.

"No, I didn't miss the el," she told him

carefully as she folded the first note and tucked it into her desk drawer. "I had some leads to follow up on."

"Ah, the great magazine-saving story."

She did smile then, rather wryly, at his mockery. "Perhaps. Did you want something, Quinton?"

He approached her, his gait loose and rolling like a drunk's only she caught no scent of alcohol upon him. She was frowning by the time he reached her.

"I see such censure in your pretty face."

"What have you been doing to yourself, Quinn? It's not just drink anymore, is it?"

His lopsided grin increased, bringing a hard glitter to his opaque eyes. "Just a little something to inspire the creative juices."

"Neither of us believes that," she told him sharply. She'd seen her mother often enough when she was so pumped full of calming drugs her mind couldn't latch upon something as simple as recalling her name. And it scared and angered her to see her talented cousin choosing that same false avenue of escape. "You'd better go home until your head clears. If Fitzhugh sees you— "

The mask of careless indifference faltered for just an instant and something unpleasant gleamed behind it. "My father doesn't care what I do as long as I don't interfere in his plans." Then a slow, sly smile crafted his lips. "Which is why I've come to see you this morning. I thought you might enjoy a look at this." He placed an envelope on her desktop.

Cassie stared at it warily. "What is it?"

"The dummy copy of our next edition. You might be amused by his changes." His smile became a sardonic twist. "Then again, maybe you won't be."

Fitzhugh Alexander regarded the folder Cassie slapped down in front of him, then looked up with an impassive face.

"Explain this to me, Uncle. 'Vampire Killer Stalks Manhattan'? And the rest, all second-rate pulp fiction. There's not one decently written piece in the lot. Who authorized you to do this? You must know that nothing of this shoddy caliber will ever go to press under the *Lexicon* banner."

He waited patiently for her tirade to run down, then casually remarked, "I wanted to give our advertisers a glimpse of what the *Lexicon* could become."

"What advertisers? Our regular sources would cringe in horror if they got a glimpse of that trash."

"New advertisers. New money. New blood."

Cassie gave a harsh laugh. "Who? Peddlers of mail-order junk? Remedies for piles? Correspondence courses for private detectives? Physical love manuals and quack medical cures? Those kind of advertisers? The *Lexicon* has worked hard to earn its brand-name sponsors. Do you think they'll care to compete for space next to your odd-ball services? I think not. You will not degrade everything my father stood for. The *Lexicon* name will not be featured above some terrified female caught in mid-scream with half of her clothes torn away. Not while I'm in charge of it." And she took the envelope and let it drop with a satisfying clump into the bottom of her uncle's waste can.

Fitzhugh's smile never altered as he fished the material out and stashed it away in his top drawer. "Just doing a little test of a potential market. Your father always allowed me that much freedom. I had thought you would be as open-minded but perhaps you don't care to practice what you always preach about creative initiative."

Taken aback by his smooth chastisement, Cassie eyed him suspiciously. "I have no intention of hampering your creativity, Uncle Fitzhugh. All I ask is that you clear such ventures through me before they go out into the public arena."

"Of course. As I planned to with this package, but now that I know your feelings on it, we will consider the matter closed. For now."

Cassie tried staring him down, not believing his smooth capitulation. But he returned her challenging glare with a bland one and even smiled.

"Cassie, I am not your enemy. I have a good portion of my life invested in this magazine. I'm not about to jeopardize that. You are being entirely too sensitive in this matter. Relax, dear girl. You wouldn't want to suffer from the same high-strung symptoms that plagued your mother, now would you?"

Cassie froze. A threat? Or just an attempt to further unsettle her? Either way, she was determined not to bend in her composure. "I assure you, I inherited none of my mother's weaknesses."

"Good," he drawled. "Because, should you have that same flaw, a position fraught with as much stress as this one could well be your undoing. I am just concerned with your well-being."

"Of course," she replied with an acid drip of her own. "I'm glad we had this little discussion. I think we understand each other better now, don't you, Uncle?"

"Oh, yes. I think we understand each other just fine."

And when Cassie left the room, it felt for the world as though she were stepping out of the lion's mouth.

She spent the rest of the day brainstorming ideas with several experienced members of her staff and had no further opportunity to think of Quinton, his father, or any of the other troubles that preyed upon her the moment she turned down her desk lamp and readied for the journey home. Once again, she'd let time slip away from her and the hour was later than she would have liked.

Remembered anxieties crowded close as she traveled uptown. She tried to focus her attention outward to repress her fears, concentrating on the strange beauty of nighttime transit. As the train rocked by with a rattle and cough of cinders, riders were afforded an intimate glimpse into the homelife of those second- and third-floor dwellers who lived alongside the line. Scenes flashed by in rapid cameos while the track ahead flickered in and out of concealing shadows. Electric lights cast a fleeting, moonlike glow punctuated by the reddish dabs of gas lamps like feral eyes agleam in the distant darkness. That dance of light grew almost hypnotic and she was reminded oddly of the brilliance of Louis Radcliffe's gaze.

Several dozen people descended the stairs at her stop. A few followed in her direction. Several were rough-looking men. As Cassie hurried down the walk, all fell in behind her, dropping off one by one as destinations were reached. Until it was she and one other. One other set of very heavy footfalls closing in with every stride.

Cassie's breath began to hitch in escalating panic, pressing hurtfully against the snug bite of her corset. She tried telling herself she was in no danger, that it was just lingering apprehension that made every stranger a sudden threat. But her deeper instinct whispered she was in trouble. Feelings she should heed, Arabella had told her. And instinct told her to run.

Then a man's hand formed a firm circle about her forearm.

She stumbled in her surprise, for she hadn't guessed her pursuer was so close. She whipped around to face him, a scream welling up within expanding lungs. But the sound was never issued. For it was Louis Radcliffe who stood at her side.

"Cassie, are you all right?"

What could she have said, staring as she was through eyes full-moon round and white-rimmed with fear? She could barely say his name without a frantic stutter of agitation.

"L-Louis."

"What is it?"

Her head jerked around so frightened eyes could sweep the sidewalk behind her. It was empty. "I-I thought I heard someone following me." Then she looked up at him and her tone firmed with conviction. "Someone *was* following me."

Louis took a moment to examine the uninhabited street himself, providing her with a glimpse of his exquisite profile. "It looks as though whoever was there has grown discouraged. Come. I will see you home."

And he curled her cold fingers into the crook of his arm, holding them there with the covering press of his own. He had to have felt the way she was shaking but he didn't comment on it. He began to walk and she fell in beside him, taking comfort in his presence even though she wasn't sure she ought to. Louis could prove every bit as dangerous to her as her unseen stalker.

"So once again you become my rescuer."

His teeth flashed white in the darkness. "So it would seem. Fate has cast me in that mold. Have you an objection?"

"No," came her faint reply. Her grip on his arm tightened and she stepped in closer to his side. He was hatless, wearing only his suit coat against the chill, as if unaffected by the bite of evening air that cut right through her own woolen cloak and left her grateful for his shelter. She was surprised to note that he was of no great height and that only several inches separated them from a level meeting of their shoulders. He seemed bigger, more impressive, but perhaps that was due to his overwhelming sense of presence. He was a man who would command attention in a crowd, the one servants would defer to without question. He was a man of power and Cassie admired that. And she feared it as well. He made her feel safe with him, but that could well have been an illusion. The same illusion that woman lying naked in the morgue might have felt.

"You're still shivering. Are you cold?"

Cassie's gaze leapt up to his with a guilty

start. "No. I-I'm fine. Really. Just jumping at shadows after all that's happened."

"Any more notes?"

She shook her head.

"My business requires me to be downtown for the next couple of days. Would you take exception to sharing the ride home with me?"

She hesitated.

"I will be a perfect gentleman, I assure you. And we would not be unescorted."

Her reputation was not the worry teething upon her will. She was dangerously infatuated with a man she feared to be a killer. How wise would it be to accept a ride with him anywhere?

Then she considered the claustrophobic panic she'd felt on the train and the fear stalking behind her down the walk.

And she heard herself saying, "If it's no trouble, I appreciate your consideration."

"It is no trouble," he assured in the fluidly accented drawl that quite undid her sensibilities, but she could feel an undercurrent of tension in his posture and the slide of steel beneath his congenial tone. He was equally cautious where she was concerned. He didn't know how far he could trust her either. And she guessed that made them even.

He paused suddenly and she was surprised to see they stood at the end of her entry walk. He slid open the wrought iron gate and held it wide so she could pass. "Until tomorrow evening then?"

She hesitated once more, eying the facade of her home, wondering fretfully if any unpleasant surprises lurked inside. And for a moment, the thought of inviting Louis in with her flirted through her mind. Madness, of course. He would not come even at her request. She could feel that self-imposed reserve within him again. As if he were both shy and wary of her. As if he were anxious to be on his way home. To what? Had he any attachments? She didn't know. Arabella had spoken of none. How odd that a man so breath-stealingly handsome should not have a bevy of beauties clutching at each arm. But it was obvious he did not want her as one of them.

"Yes," she answered his hanging question rather stiffly. "Until tomorrow."

She didn't dare linger there with him any longer, for the urge to stretch up and steal a kiss had come over her like moon madness. She'd reached the door before she was brave enough to look back and he was still standing at the threshold of her property, his hand upon the gate, his eyes upon her with an intensity that was both burning and oddly lonely. And she wondered over that look, over what would make him seem so sad, this handsome, wealthy and powerful man who could have the world if he wanted it. She raised her hand to him as she opened her door, giving him a wave he acknowledged with the nod of his head. Then, after she'd closed and locked the separating portal behind her, she peered through the lace covering one of the sidelights, watching him move on toward the next house, to the home he shared with an old woman and a mute servant. And she was overwhelmed with a sudden sense of kinship, that he was just as needy as she and just as eager to connect with a little warm, human companionship.

But not from her.

She turned away with a sigh.

Arabella sat in silence watching Louis pace the floor like a restless tiger. He was so distracted by the turmoil of his thoughts, he didn't acknowledge her there in the door to the parlor. She reached out gently along the mental link they shared and tried to soothe his agitation.

Louis.

He came about so rapidly, he had no chance to erase the distress tightening his exotic features. Then, with the flex of his monumental control, his expression was wiped clean of all but care for her.

"Bella, how are you this evening?" He came to drop a soft kiss upon her brow. She delayed him with the hook of one thin arm about his neck, holding him close for another long moment so she could savor the feel of his cool, smooth cheek against her own time-ravaged skin. Love for him rose with an engulfing magnitude to the point where she no longer worried about her own exit from the world but rather about his remaining in it.

He eased back at last, settling onto his heels in a crouch so they were still at the same level. He smiled at her and the emotion glowing in his eyes was an unchanging constant from over the past sixty-odd years. Those jewel-like eyes slid closed as her leathery palm caressed the side of his face.

"Have you dined yet this evening, my lord?" she asked quietly.

He turned his head slightly so his lips brushed her hand. His eyes didn't open. "Not yet. I will attend to it presently."

"And Cassie? Did you see her home safely?"

His gaze snapped open and the taut edges returned to his features. "Yes," he growled. "She is tucked in next door. And I will be her escort for the next few nights. Just as you requested."

"Thank you, Louis."

He pushed up to his feet and began the prowling once more. "I do not see how she suddenly became our problem. If you fear her life is in jeopardy, she should contact the police. They are supposed to see to such things, are they not?"

She was unshaken by his querulous tone, understanding its cause all too well. "I do not think it wise to involve the authorities. Considering."

He paused in his pacing. "You are right, of course. Still, I do not see why we need to concern ourselves further."

"She is our friend, Louis."

He made an uncharitable noise.

"Can you deny that you enjoy her company?"

His gaze flickered to her uneasily. "She is your friend, Bella, not mine."

Arabella only smiled at his over-pronounced protest. "Then do this for me."

I would do anything for you. That projected thought caressed her mind with the warmth of a summer breeze.

"Then take care of Cassie. See to her with the same care that you would have for me."

She could feel him beginning to balk at that, so she exerted a little pressure of her own. *Louis, remember your promise to keep her safe.*

He turned away from her with a rumble of objection but she was content with the degree of his acquiescence. Her control over him went no further than the emotional bond they shared and she knew enough not to strain that tether. For now, he would do as she asked. He might not like it, for reasons of his own, but he would do it.

A fine mist seeped beneath the casements, spilling down to the dark bedroom floor where it massed and roiled and finally gave way to a form that looked human but was not.

Louis regarded the woman asleep upon the bed. His features were dispassionate, his tone a low dangerous growl.

"You are complicating my life, Cassie Alexander."

The blonde head tossed restlessly upon a lace-edged pillow. He went on, knowing she could not hear him, at least on a conscious level.

"I don't know what you have planned between you, you and my clever wife, but it will not succeed. I am not looking for someone to replace the woman I wed. I will not have you pushed upon me. You are not my concern."

Cassie made a small sound and shifted beneath the covers. Her movement tugged the quilt and linen down so they tangled about her waist. The thin nightdress she wore pulled taut across full breasts, tempting his gaze to linger there, then at the demurely tied neckline. And because he was not unmoved by the sight, Louis's mood darkened.

"You do not know what I am, foolish girl. You do not understand the danger you are courting. You have invited me in with all the blackness that accompanies me. Unknowingly, you have placed your fragile life into my hands. These hands have the blood of centuries upon them. Yours could mingle there as well."

She sighed with a quiet contentment in her dream, oblivious to his dire warning. Then her body arched against those frail bedclothes almost as if she were entertaining a lover, and a single name escaped her in a husky purr.

"Louis."

He stood for a moment, shocked by the confusion of desires her sultry plea called to. And more distressing was the sudden want that arose in response.

She didn't know what she called to. He was no man who could sink into the heaven of her embrace, to take from her kisses and savor the supple human warmth of her body. He was no lover to woo her in the way she deserved. All he was free to give her was the demon inside him. All he could share was the vileness of what he really was, drawing her into the same shadow of the damned that surrounded him.

The temptation rose, hot, swirling, unbearably enticing. So easy to excuse his weakness by saying he couldn't help acting upon the instincts of his kind. If that had been all it was, he would not be lingering still, chafing with forbidden longing. He would take from her without conscience, without care and be gone before she was aware of him.

But that wasn't the way he wished to possess her—fleetingly, anonymously—in the night.

And because he recognized his darker motives, he resisted the pull.

Then, realizing that he was the one now courting danger, he made his figure shimmer and thin to a vaporous impression, finally collecting into a phantom fog and slipping out as silently as he'd come.

Seven

Cassie stood for a long moment staring at the brown paper-wrapped parcel placed upon the center of her desk. She'd been gone from her office for less than ten minutes, to wash her hands and dot her face with cold water in hopes of revitalizing her flagging spirit before making the trip to her lonely home. When she'd returned for her cloak and her papers, there it was.

She approached it carefully, as if it were some new and deadly breed of snake. One glance identified the handwriting. Common sense told her it was a matter for the police to handle, that she should call them before disturbing the parcel.

But professional curiosity was like an itch she couldn't reach— maddening, compelling— goading her beyond the limit of her will.

As carefully as she could, she slipped the twine from the bundle and unrolled the heavy paper. Inside was one ladies' glove, a black and tan eight-button of taffeta jersey for the right hand. Only this particular length of silk and linen was unnaturally colored. And she knew it wasn't with rust. A piece of clothing from the same woman? She could only pray it was.

Slowly, she reached for the folded note and lifted it with quaking hands. She opened it gradually, hating to learn what it would tell her yet unable to ignore the message.

It was blunt.

Don't let me down again. Baxter Street and Bottle Alley, third floor.

Louis was settled back in the anonymity of his brougham when he was surprised by the sight of Cassie Alexander bursting through the front door of her magazine's building. She never so much as glanced about, but headed directly down the walk at a harried pace. He frowned slightly. Had the woman forgotten he was to be her escort? With a sigh, he swung down from the carriage and followed rapidly in her wake, earning startled looks from several pedestrians as he brushed by them with a stir of air and a blur of undefinable motion.

"Miss Alexander?"

Her gaze jerked up and the anxiousness he saw in her dark eyes multiplied upon recognizing him. As if she were afraid of him.

"Did you forget our arrangement?"

She looked fearfully blank. He could feel the pulse of anxiety pounding in her throat, a wild, erratic beat. He gentled his tone accordingly.

"I was waiting to give you a ride home."

"Oh. Oh, yes. I'm sorry. I-I had some last minute business to attend and it slipped my mind. I didn't mean to inconvenience you."

But as she spoke that polite prattle, she was backing away from him, the fear in her eyes continuing to mount until it was a black sheen of unreasonable alarm. Whatever was wrong with her? Louis had no patience with her hysterics. He placed a hand upon her arm and gestured back the way she'd come.

"My conveyance is there."

And instantly she began a subtle pulling, twisting against his grasp.

"I appreciate your kindness but it really is not necessary. I have an important appointment to keep— "

"I will take you there."

His calm insistence seemed to overwhelm her objections. She stood trembling within his grip, her huge, panic-glazed eyes fixed upon his, her breath rushing in tiny gasps of fright. He gave a slight, compelling tug upon her arm.

"Come. You can give the direction to my driver."

She walked tame at his side, her every step a bundle of tense readiness to flee some imagined threat.

"Baxter Street," she told his man, her voice hoarse with strain. There was no mistaking the driver's recoil of surprise and reluctance.

Cassie sat in the comfortable seat beside him, her body reflecting a stiff posture of distrust. Louis could not fathom what he'd done to earn it— she'd not been of that mind when last he saw her. In fact, if he was correct in reading the all too blatant signs of human emotion, she'd been ready to cast herself into his arms. Though this cautious distance was preferable, he was annoyed by the ability of her slight to disturb him. He had no desire to court the woman's confidence, after all. He was simply complying with Arabella's wishes.

But as the fearful pattern of Cassie's breathing didn't lessen with the miles, he began to take a deeper exception to them.

"What takes you to Baxter Street? I was under the impression that it was a rather unsavory part of the city."

Her glance darted to him suspiciously. "My work takes me to many unsavory spots. I go where there's a story to be had." Her tone was sharp and defensive. It pricked his curiosity even more.

"And what story do you expect to find there upon those unwholesome streets, beyond that of timeless poverty and neglect?"

"I'm not yet sure," she admitted gruffly. Her gaze lingered on him for a moment as if she were searching for some meaningful truth. He had no idea what kind of reassurance she was seeking so he returned her stare impassively. Finally, she looked away and their carriage sped on.

Manhattan could boast of an impressive roster of wealthy philanthropists whose mansions anchored upper Fifth Avenue, but in doing so it would also have to claim the extensive areas of hopeless poverty contained in the city's Lower East Side. There, crowded in tenements and squalid shanties, huddled the city's poor and preferably forgotten, there near the docks and railroad yards amid saloons and slaughterhouses, where the names Five Points and Mulberry Bend equaled the shiver conjured by the mention of the Westside's Hell's Kitchen, places so bleak pauperism was a permanent lifestyle. Places so stark, sunlight never reached them.

Cassie hadn't traveled this far into the Bowery after dark. Passing under the black shadows of the elevated train, she suffered from a chill of guilt and distaste, pitying those forced into such depressed straits and fearing them for the violence of which they were capable. On summer nights, the sidewalks provided a free bed for the inebriated, forcing the passersby to step over row upon row of them as if they were battlefield dead. But now that winter cold had begun to settle, they crowded into recessed doorways, bottles cradled in their arms with the loving fondness of a child with a cherished doll. Litter and spoiling garbage from pushcarts filled the mouths of countless dark alleyways, contributing to the pervading stench of human misery.

"A street of lost souls," Louis commented quietly, and she had to agree with that cruel summation on this avenue where the parade of gin mills and indifference led a straight line to Bellevue. And suddenly, despite her cautious suppositions, she was very glad to have Louis beside her.

When the glossy carriage came to a stop and the driver called down, "Are you sure this is where you want to go?" Cassie's first impulse was to say, "No, keep going," and to urge him on until she reached the clean streets and comfort of her own home. But she couldn't give in to it.

"Yes. Here is fine."

Louis stepped out and offered up his hand.

"You needn't come with me," she was saying even as her fingers gripped his tightly. "I'll only be a moment."

"A moment here could prove to be an unpleasant eternity. I'll go with you."

An unenthusiastic statement. She didn't argue.

The world she descended into was made up of back alleys, stable lanes and concealed byways through which police and rent collectors couldn't follow. Homeless crowded against filthy walls to share ramshackle shelters pilfered from the dumps. It was the haven of tramps and rag-pickers, a maze of darkness and festering criminality. Cassie tucked in close to Louis's side, fighting against the want to cling to the one who might yet prove responsible for her peril.

She couldn't dismiss the possibility that Louis Radcliffe was involved in the mysterious message killings. He'd been present to interfere with her stalkers. He'd dumped them near the same vicinity that the first victim was found. He was there outside her office building when the second parcel appeared upon her desk. She didn't believe in coincidences. She could well be stepping into dreadful danger beside a maniac.

But she didn't want to believe Louis guilty, either.

The typical tenement house had a stairway passing up through a dark well in the center. There, no light or open air could penetrate and it was pitch black even at midday. In this evening hour, it was a tangle of upward reaching shadows, all sinister to one of Cassie's sheltered breeding. The smell was atrocious. There was no ventilation in the slum buildings and noxious gases accumulated in those desolate stairwells. Taking a deep breath, Cassie started up.

Tiny flickers of light showed from the open doorways on either side, creating a gruesome dance of silhouettes stretching out over the dim stairs. Pale and unhealthy children played listlessly upon the steps, survivors of the horrendous death rate. From the flats opening off either side, bloated, hostile faces peered out at her in her fine coat, with her elegant escort. Cassie knew a growing fear for her well-being as well as an overwhelming pity for these hollow-eyed inhabitants. She continued upward around the first floor bend, wishing she had the means to see all these wretched souls away from this place of sinking futility.

"Where you going, missy?"

A sturdy leg clad in torn and dirty wool made a brace across the stairs in front of her. From out of the shadows, Cassie could see several gaunt shapes.

"I'm visiting a friend."

"Yeah? And who might this friend be? One of the almighty Vanderbilts?"

There was a chorus of coarse laughter and the sense of menace mounted.

"We're not here looking for trouble."

Louis's soft-spoken statement brought an instant stiffening to the three men who had hoped she was alone. They separated from the darkness and came to make a solid barrier on the second-story landing. There was a scuffling below and Cassie looked behind them to see two more threatening figures coming up to block their exit. Louis came up to share the same step with her, using the broad expanse of his shoulders to shield her.

"We're not looking for trouble," he amended in the same quiet tone, "but if you don't move aside, you may have more than you can handle."

"From you?" one of them sneered and that sound was instantly choked off as Louis's hand forked under his chin and squeezed. The man's eyes bulged as his feet left the littered floor.

There was a swift movement from the left and a glint of bared steel. Louis pivoted so that the man he held suspended became the target of the arcing blade. As the victim screamed, Louis shoved him away, knocking both down into the dirty corner. Almost at once, Louis was kicking out to the side, his instep catching another luckless assailant in the throat and sending him gasping, end over end down to the first floor landing. A one-two blow from his elbow and the back of his hand sent another tumbling behind him.

The remaining attacker stood with knife poised when Louis locked stares with him. Cassie watched dumbfounded as the filthy fellow seemed to crumple from the sheer strength of Louis's will until his pock-marked face went slack and his eyes were vacant.

"Drop your knife." It was a low, forceful order.

There was a loud clatter.

"Pick up your friends and be gone before we return this way. Otherwise, you will need someone to carry you away with the rest of the refuse."

The sole combatant grabbed up his two stunned and bleeding partners and dragged them into one of the dank rooms. The two on the landing below had already disappeared.

Having dispatched the threat without even laboring for breath, Louis turned to Cassie with the offer of his hand. She stared at it for a long moment, through eyes wide and frankly amazed, then back up at him for an explanation.

"I've never seen fighting like that," she whispered.

"You don't come to places like this without knowing how to defend yourself." His tone was curt, suggesting she was a fool because she had been ready to do just that. She was chafed into a temper because she couldn't deny it. Had the men confronted her, she would have had no recourse but wit and will. And from what she'd seen, both would have proven woefully inadequate.

Slowly, she slid her hand into the palm he'd extended. The wrap of his fingers was strong and engulfing. A current of confidence swept clear to her toes. This was a man ready to meet any odds. But was he her enemy as well as her savior?

Taking another deep breath, Cassie continued upward toward the pitch blackness of the third floor. The sound of a baby's hungry cries mingled with a domestic fight in some language she couldn't understand. The want to turn back, to give everything over to the police, rose within her once more as she regarded that bleak unknown. But after all the heroics Louis had shown in her defense, how cowardly it would seem to run away without discovering what she'd come to learn. She made herself take another step.

Abruptly, Louis's grip tightened and he hauled her up short, causing her to bump into the rigid plane of his body. Startled by his roughness, she cast up a questioning gaze and was riveted by the dark intensity of his expression. There was no way to explain the hot gold luminescence of his eyes. There was no light in the narrow corridor to reflect within them. They simply glowed, coalbright, with a cat-like gleam.

"There's death up there."

His words were so flat and absolute, a tremor shook her fiercely in response. "How do you know?" she demanded faintly, not doubting him despite the challenge.

He held himself perfectly still and seemed to be scenting the stagnant air. The strangeness of it had the hairs along her arms prickling.

"Wait here," he ordered. That was growled from him with a thick huskiness. He released her and started up the last few steps to the third floor landing, his familiar form gliding upward to blend into the waiting darkness.

Cassie waited. For all of three seconds. Movement scurried on the stairs below her and unknown danger lurked above. Better the unknown beside Louis, she decided, and hurried up behind him.

He was standing with his hand upon the knob of a half-opened door, his posture stiff and unnatural. The hiss of his breathing cut through the impure gases hanging heavy in the hall.

"Louis?"

Her whisper had no effect upon him.

He pushed the door all the way open and stepped inside with Cassie treading in his shadow. With uncanny instinct, for Cassie couldn't see a thing, he found a simple oil lamp and coaxed a small flame to penetrate the filthy blackness. The blackness had been better, Cassie decided almost at once.

They stood in a small parlor, the main living area of the flat where rags were heaped high in the corner and the smell of spoilage and musty paper was suffocating. A broken stove dominated the tiny room, its crooked pipe rising up at odd angles and most likely leaking at every joint when lit. At the moment, there was no fire and a still cold pervaded. A dented tea kettle sat on the charred burner waiting to do double duty as a wash boiler. The only other item even to resemble furniture was a table made from rough boards propped upon boxes. The closeness and the odor was appalling, for the door and windows opened into the stairwell where no fresh air could be found.

"Wait here," Louis instructed a second time as he started for one of the two pitch dark coops that only a stretch of the imagination could deem bedrooms. There was little space for anything but the heaps of old boxes and foul straw that served poorly as a place to sleep but not rest.

And as she crowded up close behind Louis, Cassie could see a single shape that had managed to find the latter. Only it was a rest one didn't rise up from.

"Cassie, get back. It is nothing you want to see."

The very grimness of Louis's voice sparked a defiant curiosity, a *need* to know. She went back into the filthy parlor and carried the smoke-clouded lamp to the bedroom door. The weak light wavered wildly in her hand as she beheld the room's interior.

There was a young woman sprawled out across the bed, her eyes staring like vacant marbles toward a cracked and stained ceiling. Blonde hair fanned out upon a dirty blanket. She was wearing a nearly threadbare chemise and an elbow length glove on her left hand— the mate of the one still wrapped in its delivery paper upon Cassie's desk.

Both were liberally stained from the gash opened across the woman's throat.

And despite the pinch of hunger and the still of death, there could be no mistaking the resemblance.

The dead woman bore a striking similarity to Cassie Alexander.

Sickness came over her in a wave too intense to ignore. Louis caught the lamp as it tipped precariously but he made no attempt to stop her when she reeled from the nasty little room with its stench of poverty and death. She staggered down the dark stairs to burst out into the open air, sucking great lungfuls of it in an effort to purge the thick taste of decay. Shock had her knees banging together by the time Louis eased up to envelop her within the wrap of his arms.

"I'll take you home."

She didn't object, not to his statement, nor when he bundled her up into the waiting carriage. She sagged against the plush squabs and struggled for perspective. It was hard to attain when the film of ghastly murder clung like cold sweat.

Finally, as the carriage spun beneath the civilized glow of electric light, the tremors eased and rational thought returned. With it came an awareness of her escort.

He was leaning back against the seat, as shaken as she was, if his pallor was any indication. His face was all dramatic hollows, sculpting a portrait that, like fine art, was hard to interpret. He'd killed, so she couldn't believe him squeamish, but there was no denying the torment echoed in every ragged breath he took.

Having felt her scrutiny, Louis looked her way. Traces of hot brilliance still lingered in his eyes, giving them an eerie incandescence, but his voice was as cool and urbane as ever in contrast.

"What made you choose to visit this particularly unfortunate female? Surely not coincidence, as I don't subscribe to that theory."

"Nor do I," Cassie answered with a helpless shudder. "I received another message from the killer." She waited for his reaction. It was smooth and only mildly curious, the arching of one haughty brow.

"Oh?"

"A piece of the woman's bloodied clothing was delivered to me at my office along with that address. I was hoping I would find something other than what we did."

Louis was looking at her intently now, the fire in his gaze becoming a dark, compelling whirlpool of emotion. "You knew what you could be walking into and would have gone alone anyway? Why?"

She stared at him as though he were being obtuse. "I am a journalist. That's what I do. I was looking for a story."

"And what of the danger?"

"That's what makes it a good story. My father would not have run from that room

as I did. He would have remained to ferret
out clues. I fear I will never be the same
caliber of reporter."

"And perhaps you will live longer."

That curt conclusion brought tears of anger to her eyes. Her father had died investigating under similar circumstances. He'd
been willing to give his all in pursuit of the
truth. She hadn't been. She hadn't been able
to stomach the sight of one more corpse.
And she'd let the story elude her.

"I should like to go back."

"Are you mad? Whatever for?"

"To find out what I might have missed in
my timidity."

"Nonsense. You'll do no such thing."

His autocratic command had her squaring
her jaw tenaciously. "And who are you, sir,
to say what I may or may not do? Let me
out of this coach."

"No."

"Let me out, I say!"

And when he sat, unmoving, refusing to
honor her demand, Cassie reached for the
door handle. It was an impulsive gesture.
She had no plan to cast herself from the
fast-moving brougham. But that didn't stop
her from squirming furiously when Louis
grabbed her about the waist to prevent her
from impetuous suicide. One hard backward
jerk ended with her sprawled across his
knees. Before she could scramble up, spitting

indignantly, he had her by the shoulders, meaning to shake some sense into her.

Then, as if awareness struck like a double dose of lightning, they both went completely still.

Cassie stopped her floundering when she realized that her position upon his lap, within the steel bands of his embrace, was nothing she wanted to escape. She could feel the rock hardness of his thighs beneath the bend of her spine and was aroused by the strength of his hands where they restrained her. Both of them were breathing heavily, the exertion of passionate expression altering from anger to something altogether different. Desire for him spiked hot and high as their gazes mingled in a clashing interplay. Her heart was pounding madly as potent and potential tensions rose.

"You are the most aggravating female," Louis began in an unbearably condescending tone.

So she shut him up.

She caught the lean angles of his face between her palms and, before she could consider the brazenness of what she intended, Cassie pulled his head down. Their mouths met and mated with a flash of urgent fire, a flame fed by the intensity of what they'd just shared, fueled by the pressure of what was long repressed beneath a cordial surface. And Cassie gave herself over to the volatile sensations, so deeply, wildly, impossibly in love, she didn't care what he'd done or might yet do.

But Louis minded, very much.

At the first crush of their lips, he'd known a jolt of regret and a twinge of shame. Because he wasn't free to enjoy the pleasures reaped through Cassie's compliance nor was it right to encourage what could never be. But it was hard to draw away when she supplied such surprising sweetness it seared to his immortal soul. She tasted of boldness and bravery, of capriciousness and youth— things he admired, things he hungered for. Things he hadn't been willing to admit were lacking in his life of late. Her willing warmth woke needs in him that circumstance had forced him to deny.

And deny them, he must.

When he started to withdraw, her fingers sank further back, twining in his hair, holding him fast while she feasted upon his kisses.

"Cassie—"

"Oh, Louis."

Her sigh of submission stirred another type of need, one that was strong and dark and nothing she'd intentionally call to. But awake it did, a growling, twisting thirst for the vitality she could bring him, an appetite four centuries deep.

His resistance gave before it. His mouth gentled upon hers, becoming wooingly seductive as he layered on the magic of his kind until she was weak with longing and ripe for his purpose. Hunger, heightened by the scent of death, blocked out everything that made him able to pass as human, warping compassion into cunning and desire into deadly necessity.

Entranced and obeying a command never spoken aloud, Cassie let her hands move mechanically to the fastenings that held her coat closed over her throat, working them loose then the buttons to her bodice as well, until creamy skin lay bare and gleaming beneath the brush of his kisses. She arched up with a beckoning moan, coaxing him to greater intimacies without understanding how fatal they might prove to be. She only knew how much she wanted him, wanted this seething passion, regardless of time or place or propriety.

Then the brougham rocked to a halt and Louis lifted up in a ravenous glaze to see they were stopped between their two houses. Hers was dark and empty. His held a single light from above, a light calling him back to reason.

Abruptly, he righted Cassie and pushed her to an arm's length. He could see her confusion as the spell of his enchantment released her into mortal turmoil. When she tried to return to his embrace, he blocked her with the brace of one hand against her shoulder.

"Louis?"

Her eyes were soft and vulnerable, drowning eyes. Trusting eyes. Pleading eyes, asking for what he could not, should not, give.

"Go home and lock your door," he instructed softly, letting a hint of his power coerce her unguarded mind. "Forget your cause for this night and sleep safely, soundly until morning."

She was stronger than he anticipated for even after he opened the door, she lingered to exert a little tempting magic of her own.

"Come in with me?"

Such an innocent request made to man, not monster.

"No, I cannot."

Disappointment registered in her dreamy expression but she didn't argue. He watched her make her way down the walk, letting herself inside and closing him out. Only then did he dare exhale and chastise himself for what he'd almost allowed to happen.

Once inside his own abode, the magnitude of his time with Cassie settled in to taunt him. He'd been so close to surrendering all his promises, all his decency, to claim a moment's paradise. He thought of the woman who waited upstairs, the woman who held his allegiance and his love. The woman he'd almost betrayed in an instant of weakness.

He couldn't tell himself it was only the blood that drew him to Cassie Alexander. Not anymore. He'd allowed her a kiss and he'd allowed his emotions to run rampant.

He'd wanted to make love to her.

And that damning knowledge pierced through his heart with a single thrust of torment.

He paused at the foot of the stairs to lean his forehead against the cool wood grain of the newel post, needing to calm his thoughts before going upstairs. The last thing in the world he wanted was to bring the taint of his treachery up to his wife.

"Louis?"

There was a hum of machinery as the banister vibrated beneath him. He lifted his gaze to follow Arabella's descension in the elevator chair built into the side of the stairs for her ease in mobility during daylight hours. He tried to bring an impassive mask to bear, but the compassion that softened her features told of his failure. She could read his guilt upon his heart, and yet she still forgave him.

"I love you, Bella," he began in a tortured rush as he dropped to one knee beside her chair. "I— "

Her hand touched his lips, over the dampness left by Cassie's kisses, the light pressure halting the rest of his confession. "May we talk of this another time, my love? I've been waiting up for you, but now I find myself too weary to converse. It is I who must apologize. I have so little stamina of late."

Without a word, he gathered her frail body up in his arms and carried her upstairs. He would have taken no relief in her small smile nor in the turn of her thoughts had she allowed him to see them.

If he was racked by guilt, it meant Cassie had secured a place within his heart.

And that left Arabella free to do what she'd been planning.

Eight

Her name was Lainie Potts. Neighbors said she'd been pretty in life and had hoped to marry out of her desperate straits. There had been hope for it, too, when a sharply dressed uptown man began courting her with expensive gifts.

Neighbors, who looked much less sinister in the daylight hours, were more than willing to do a little talking at the flash of Cassie's coin. One of them was the man Louis had tossed down the stairs. He moved stiffly, favoring his shoulder, and pretended not to recognize her. And he was a wealth of information once the right amount had crossed his palm.

Lainie had been a whore, plain and simple. A lot of men went up and down those dirty stairs. But only one of late, and only one brought her pretties. Like the pair of fancy gloves she was so proud of— one she was wearing when the coroner came to take her away. The other was locked in Cassie's bottom desk drawer. He'd never gotten a good look at the dapper swain, who always came at night, took great care to keep his face well hidden, and always came by hired rig. He'd told the same details to the police an hour earlier but didn't mind repeating them to the lovely reporter and her portly friend.

Had he happened to mention that Lainie Potts had another pair of visitors shortly after her death? A pair that several gentlemen of the neighborhood had tried to assault and rob? No, the fellow said a bit worriedly, he'd never seen anyone go up those stairs until the police came. And he was certain all his friends would be willing to agree to that story. Then he closed his fist around the batch of silver placed in his palm and, with a slight bow, faded off into the grimy alleyways.

"What do you think, Walter?" Cassie asked.

The stocky city editor was busy jotting down impressions in his battered notepad. "Hmmm? Oh, about this? I think you're right, that it's related to the other slayings. And I think if I hurry, I can get it into this edition before it goes to press this noon. It smells of a good series and from the look of it, none of the other papers or magazines have picked up on it yet. How did you happen to hear of it so soon?"

"I-I have a friend on the police force. He tips me off occasionally."

"Well, send his tips my way. And thanks for this one."

Cassie didn't return his smile. She was still bothered by the information she was withholding from the authorities. Her father would have pooh-poohed the twinge of moral conscience. He would have said to play out the hand she was dealt. A pot couldn't be won without risk and a few bluffs. If she could use the clues she'd been given in an exclusive exposé, the sales of the *Lexicon* would soar as high as the New York skyline. All she had to do was suppress her uneasiness and pursue the leads she'd been handed. And she could prove to them all that she had what it took to sit in her father's chair.

"What did you mean when you asked that fellow about the deceased's last visitors?" She'd hoped Walter had missed that interchange, but he was all shrewd reporter. "Are you holding out on me, Cass?"

"Just something I heard but can't verify. Let's just stick to the facts for now. All right?"

"The facts. Sure thing, boss."

As he read those supposed facts, a cold fury rose in Louis Radman. The headline of Walter Rampling's story screamed for attention.

Vampire Killer Goes on Rampage in Manhattan.

That shocking claim was followed by a series of equally startling innuendoes. All lies, but enough to alarm Louis. Hysteria was a terrible tool of the ignorant. He'd witnessed it more than once in his unnatural lifetime. It was usually the innocent who suffered. And he did not care to be involved in this particular witch-hunt.

"That damned woman," he growled with enough threat to catch Arabella's attention.

"What is it, Louis?"

"Our supposed friend has published the most entertaining piece of fiction under the guise of fact." He passed his wife the latest issue of the *Lexicon* and watched as new wrinkles appeared over old.

"I don't understand," she murmured. "It's not like Cassie to allow such foolishness in her magazine. It must be some mistake."

"Yes. A mistake you convinced me to make in trusting her. It's incendiary garbage like this that brings unwelcomed focus back to my kind. I am not pleased, Bella. Not in the least."

"This is the city, Louis. No one believes in superstition here. No one will believe such exaggerated folly. These are people who ride in elevators and use telephones. They are not going to scurry about brandishing sharpened stakes in search of the undead asleep in their coffins." She noticed her husband's wince at that graphic image. "At least give her a chance to defend herself."

"What defense can there be against such negligence?"

"Ask before you condemn."

He scowled but made a quick summons for Takeo. The Oriental appeared silently in the doorway and sketched a bow.

Master, how may I serve you? It was an unspoken question, one heard in both Louis's and Arabella's minds along the psychic link they shared.

"Takeo, I want you to fetch Miss Alexander from next door. Be polite, but accept no excuses."

"Louis . . ."

"Do not harm or frighten her," he added to placate his wife. "But impress the seriousness of her immediate response upon her."

The Asian bowed again and slipped out to do his bidding. Within minutes, Cassie arrived. There was no need for Louis to broach his indignation. She was fairly seething with her own.

"You've seen this week's edition, I presume," she began in a smoldering rage. "How could they have done such a thing with my express disapproval? Please be assured I'll in no way allow your name to enter into this— this ludicrous travesty."

"The question now is what do you intend to do about it?"

His penetrating words forced her to stop and think. The damage was done. Her uncle had circumvented her authority to allow the inflammatory article to run in full lurid glory. Now she would have to scramble to recoup the respectability of her publication. And her own name. The only way to overcome fantasy was with hard fact.

"What I should have done in the beginning. Go to the police with the evidence I have. That should eradicate the image that we are out to sensationalize the truth and will prove this killer is no supernatural folly but a real flesh-and-blood maniac who requires serious measures if he is to be caught. I have a friend on the force I can go to. He'll believe me if I tell him I had no part in this circus stunt."

"Louis, go with her."

"What?" Louis looked sharply in his wife's direction.

"It is late and Cassie should not be out alone."

It was Cassie who made the first protest. "Really, Arabella, that isn't necessary." The memory of the last time she was alone with Louis had her cheeks heating with discomfort. Or rather, her lack of memory. The details were sketchy at best. She had kissed him. She had invited him in to do more and he'd turned her down. Politely, of course, but it was rejection nonetheless. And there was only so much bruising her pride could stand. She couldn't allow Arabella to push her at her grandson any longer. Not when Louis had made it clear he wasn't interested.

But Louis's interest was the reason for his restraint. He was attracted to the youthful Cassie and aggravated by Arabella's insistence that he pursue it. He was having a hard enough time hanging on to his flagging will without additional interference from both women.

"I'm sure Miss Alexander will be fine. She has stated on many occasions that she is more than capable of handling her own affairs."

The cool dismissal was a further cut to Cassie's confidence but Arabella, instead of backing down and allowing her some dignity, persisted in thrusting them together.

"Louis, as a favor to me." *Remember your promise.*

He was uncomfortably caught. What could he say? To protest louder would invite unwelcomed speculation. "Miss Alexander, I would be happy to escort you down to the precinct house."

Cassie frowned. That was about as sincere as an alcoholic's morning-after oath. "How very— kind of you, Mr. Radcliffe. I would be grateful for your company."

And he smiled grimly to acknowledge her cynicism. "I'll go have the carriage readied."

When they were alone, Cassie turned to the older woman with a sigh. "Arabella, please. He has no feelings for me. You are making things awkward with this insistent matchmaking."

Arabella gave her a gentle smile. "How wrong you are, and soon you will realize it."

Cassie was about to argue further when she noticed how frail and wan the old woman appeared. "Are you all right this evening, Arabella?"

"It's been a bad day for me, I must confess. My doctor has given me something for the discomfort."

"Are you certain you wouldn't rather have us stay with you?"

"What a dear and thoughtful child you are, but no, I am weary is all, and I will have an infinite time to rest. You and Louis see to what you must. I have plans of my own this evening." And again, that serene smile.

"What can I do before we leave to make you more comfortable?"

"You can make me a promise."

"Anything."

"Nothing so simple, child. It concerns Louis. I want your promise that you will love him."

"I beg your pardon?"

"Love him as I have loved him, without limits, without judgments. Can you make me that promise?"

Cassie was momentarily lost in the feverish intensity of the elderly woman's gaze. It wasn't madness, it was determination. She hesitated, suddenly afraid of the commitment asked of her. What did she know about

Louis Radcliffe, really? She didn't know how or where he spent his days. She didn't know anything about his past or any of his future plans. All she knew was what appeared within her lonely mind's eye— a man of melting charm when he chose to use it, of searing sensuality he chose to resist, of compelling looks and dangerous secrets. She couldn't trust him, yet found her life repeatedly in his hands. Hands that had protected her, hands that woke a stirring need in her with the slightest touch. And Cassie heard herself reply with a quiet certainty. "Yes, I will love him."

The breath sighed from Arabella and with it went much of her strength. "I think I should like to lie down now." She glanced up at Louis who had just reentered the room. "Would you take me up now?"

Louis bent to lift her out of the chair with an infinite tenderness and bore her up the stairs as if she were a delicate child. She circled his neck with thin arms and pillowed her gray head upon one wide shoulder, enjoying the pulse of ageless power flowing through him. She had known when she'd made her choice a lifetime ago that it would not be easy to watch herself grow old through his eyes. He'd been true to his vow to love her and if he'd ever chafed in the bonds of their unusual marriage, he never let her feel his dissatisfaction. He'd always made her feel beautiful even as her hair silvered and her skin grew seamed. But it had become an unfair bond for both of them. He was denying her the dignity of death and she was withholding him from the joys of life. His love, his strength, his passionate nature had sustained her beyond the limits of her frail mortal body. She was old, worn out, and ready to seek a world without pain. She'd hung on so long for Louis's sake, worried about his will to continue without her. Seeing him torn at heart over his devotion to her and the temptation Cassie presented had decided it for her. She had suffered silently for too long to wish the same upon the man she loved.

As he settled her upon the downy bedcovers, she held to his hand a moment longer to say, somewhat wistfully, "I have always loved you, Louis, from the very first."

And he smiled, looking so unchangingly handsome her heart ached all over again.

"And you know that you have always been first in my thoughts and in my deeds."

"Yes," he agreed, brow furrowing slightly as he wondered over the direction of her speech.

"Please don't be angry with me."

"Angry? Whatever for?"

But her gray eyes, always her best features, were clouding up emotionally. "For not being as strong for you as I would have liked to have been."

He carried her frail hand to his lips, then

pressed his cool cheek into the well of her palm. His tone was rough with feeling. "You have been my rock, Bella, my strength. You have never failed me. You have given me a chance at humanity that I would have never known, a chance to experience the world through mortal eyes. You have given me the best years of my— " He smiled with sad irony and concluded. "— of my life. If anything, you have given me a better appreciation of what it means to be alive."

That seemed to satisfy her for she sank back into her pillows with eyes closing, looking very much at peace. "Go with Cassie, Louis. Be good to her, for I sense she's not had the luxury of much affection in her life. Strength has a way of creating its own vulnerability— the inability to show when in need. She needs you even if she is too proud to say as much. Now go, be of help, and guard her well. Then I will be happy."

Louis pursed his lips, wanting to protest at the way Arabella pushed the degree of intimacy between him and Cassie higher, but he didn't because she looked too fatigued. He would have to have a long talk with her, soon, to shake her from the notion that he would ever abandon her for another. His thoughts might play with the idea, his heart might stir with possibilities, but never would he stray in fact from the loyalty of a vow made long ago. Not as long as Arabella

Howland Radman had breath left in her body.

"Rest, little one," he murmured with a tender concern, then bent to brush a kiss upon her brow. "You exhaust yourself with the unimportant. I will be nice to Miss Alexander and when I return, I will be very good to you."

Arabella smiled at the hint of passionate promise in his eyes. Oh, if only that promise could be met. If only she wasn't too weary to consider sampling from the bountiful pleasures they'd shared in their lengthy past together. The memories she held, so sweet and searingly sensual, could never have been equaled within a so-called normal relationship.

Lucky Cassie. She had no idea what wonderful things awaited her.

"Good night, my love," she whispered with a last caress of his exquisite features. But when he was halfway to the door, she found she could not let him go that easily. "Louis?"

He turned and in the failing light he was . . . beautiful.

"I look forward to that eternity we will someday share."

Perplexed by her odd mood, he smiled and said, "I, too, await the day."

And then he was gone. Arabella waited until she was certain they had left the house, until she was sure Louis could not pick up on the mental call she sent with the last of her strength.

You promised you would come if ever I should call. I'm calling you now. Please don't forsake me.

There was no betraying sound, just a subtle shift in the heavy current of air hanging within her closed-up room. The hairs stirred on the nape of her neck in a recognition of her peril and a shiver of fear troubled her, as it did whenever she was confronted by one of Louis's kind. She could sense him long before she could actually see him occupying the darkest shadows of the room.

"Gerardo?"

"Buena sera, cara mia."

With that familiar croon, he advanced into the room, graceful, sleek and deadly. Blackness surrendered him into light by slow, almost reluctant degrees: a portion of one smooth white cheek, the momentary dazzle of pale eyes, a twist of his bland smile. Then he was there, standing like a dark angel at the foot of her bed, Gerardo Pasquale, her husband's once dear and unquestionably oldest friend. And, without a doubt, one of the most unpredictably dangerous beings she'd ever encountered. One didn't summon him without the feeling of having conjured a demon.

Louis had killed him in the early fifteen hundreds in a sword duel over a treacherous woman. Only Gerardo had never been buried. He haunted the world of the living with his wicked paramour, Bianca du Maurier, feeding off it with an amoral abandon at the side of the beautiful ghoul who had stolen both his and his young friend, Luigino Rodmini's souls. He had no care for humankind and treated them with the indifferent contempt of one far superior. Perhaps he was superior in many ways, but in others he was sorely lacking. He suffered from none of the guilty torment that tortured Louis. He killed with a careless pleasure, toying with his victims with the ruthlessness of a cat. And he'd never felt a tug of remorse or a moment of regret. Nor did he harbor a sense of affinity for any other creature . . . with the exception of Louis and his wife, Arabella, and their daughter, Nicole. Toward them, his heart could never completely harden, and though Arabella was rightly cautious, she had no real terror of her visitor.

After all, a demon was exactly what she needed.

"It has been . . . long," he purred in his luxuriously accented voice. "I have thought of you often in these passing years, but no longer flatter myself into hoping you have held any thoughts of me." His cool gaze assessed her. "The color is gone from your hair but not the fire from your eyes. It is good to see you again, Bella. And Gino, how is he?" He could try to conceal it but Arabella saw a touch of bittersweet affection creep into his expression, as if he were sorely aggrieved by his estrangement from his friend.

"He is well."

"And Nicole? I have not seen her since the child was born. Her husband has no fondness for me after that unfortunate misunderstanding we had over your injury." He gave an elegant shrug as if it was of no consequence. "I suppose I cannot blame him for certain ill feelings, but *Dio mio*, he has the look of one who will hold a grudge for centuries. *I* didn't make him what he is so I am at a loss to comprehend his animosity."

Arabella smiled at his typical narrow focus of thought. "Marchand wants only to protect his family."

Black brows soared in indignation. "Well, I have never harmed Nicole, nor was I the one who slew his silly brother."

"Perhaps it is guilt by association," Arabella suggested silkily.

"Hmph. Perhaps, but I am no less offended. It's not as if I had no feelings at all, though Bianca accuses me quite regularly of having no heart. Perhaps she is the one who is right." Then he smiled, a charming tease of a smile that hid the evil of what he was. Even knowing him as she did, Arabella was not immune from it. But she had learned to lessen his lethal appeal.

"And how is Bianca?"

Gerard gave a haughty toss of his head. "Why spoil our reunion with talk of that one? I would rather talk of us." With a movement that managed to appear both languid and too fast to follow, he was stretched out on the bed beside her. His words became a husky rumble. "Say you have decided to have me over Gino and make me the happiest of men."

Arabella laughed at the absurdity of his plea. "What would you do with an old woman?"

He was close. His jewel-like eyes dazzled her. "Time means nothing to me, *cara*. I see you as I saw you on your wedding day. Remember?" And he lifted her hand to his lips, only the hand that bore Louis's ring was no longer withered with age and tracked by spidery blue veins. It was fair and full and soft; a young woman's hand. Arabella drew a startled breath as he vowed, "You are still beautiful to me."

She put her other hand to her face and felt the taut skin of a twenty-year-old instead of roughened parchment. "What have you done? What trickery is this?"

"What? Gino cannot alter time?" He gave a sly smile. "Ah, yes. I forgot he is a . . . half-breed. He has only a portion of the power I possess."

Arabella pulled her hand away, upset and confused. Then she remembered whom she was dealing with. "You have no power," she challenged flatly. "You wrap lies in the illusion of truth, that's what Louis told me."

A soft chuckle. "Louis. Yes. I cannot think of him by that name. They are not all lies, pretty Bella. I can make this illusion last a lifetime. Can he do the same? I can make you young again."

"You can make me *believe* I'm young again."

"A minor point of semantics."

"I think not."

Then he leaned forward until the smooth chill of his lips brushed over hers. His eyes stayed open. It was a gesture for effect, not a display of genuine emotion. Arabella wasn't sure he had the capacity for more than half-remembered mechanics. She turned her head slightly. "We have had this conversation before."

He pursued her determinedly, with his cool kisses, with his sultry whispers. "Ah, but never have I had so much to give. Come away with me, Bella. Let me know a little of the dream you've shared with Gino. Surely you must know that I have always lo— "

"I'm dying, Gerard."

He reared back slightly. There was no flicker of anything in his gaze. "How sad. I am so sorry." His voice was inflectionless. She had no way to know if she'd touched upon any true emotions. "Is that why you have called me to you, so you could say goodbye?"

"No."

"Then I am confused."

"Your illusions cannot save me, but perhaps you can."

He was all attention and instinctive caution. "And how might I do that?"

She laid it out for him quickly, clearly, so there could be no mistake. "I would like you to take my life for me, Gerard. Now, tonight."

Nine

Gerard gave a soft laugh. "Surely this is some jest."

"No."

He edged back even further. "You want me to kill you." His eyes narrowed into glittery silver slits of suspicion. "Why should I do this thing?"

"Because of the love you have for Louis and for me."

He considered this impassively for a moment, then said, "Gino, he would tear me to pieces."

"I thought you said you had nothing to fear from him, that he was inferior in his powers."

His supple mouth crooked in a half-smile. "You feed me my own words as if they were poison. You have said you were dying. Why the hurry to get it done this minute?"

She was touched by his reluctance but had no time for patience. A demonstration was needed, one that would make her case for her, one that might sway the cynical vampire to the desperation of her request. "This is what I live with daily." Arabella put a hand to his brow and let him feel the brunt of her pain, the grinding misery that even the best medications of science could not control. He gave a startled gasp and winced away. When he looked at her again, his eyes were still cautious but his voice was far from unaffected.

"I am sorry, Bella. My heart breaks to think that you suffer. How could Gino allow such a thing? He is supposed to care for you."

Arabella let her fingertips trail down his angular face, calming the flare of fury. "I have hidden it from him. But now I ask you to release me."

He squirmed uncomfortably and hid it behind pretended insult. "Why do you choose me for this task? You would not share your life with me, yet you turn to me when it is time to seek your death."

"You are the only one I can trust, Gerard. The only one who is . . . hard enough to do what must be done."

"You wound me, *cara.*"

"No, I don't. You are flattered that I thought of you. You have always wanted to take me from Louis, yet now you protest when I am ready to go."

"This was not what I had in mind, *cara mia.*" His tone firmed decisively. "You are Gino's responsibility."

For once Arabella's panic was plain. "But he will not let me go and I fear he will not be strong enough to— to do what must be done so that I can rest peacefully. Please, Gerard." She touched him, hoping to touch him deeper, to move those long-buried emotions that lay at the heart of the man he'd once been before centuries of death had blunted him to care. "I beg of you not to let me linger. I have only a matter of days left me. I had hoped to see Nicole and her family again but fate is against it. Allow me the dignity of choosing my own time. Set us both free, Louis and me. I cannot bear the pain in his eyes any longer nor the pain in this frail mortal shell. Release us both if you love us."

Gerard was silent for a long while and completely immobile with a stillness only his kind could affect. Arabella could not guess what moved in his heart or mind, uncertain of the first and wary of the second. When he spoke, it was with a bitter drawl.

"You ask much yet give little. A selfish request, *inamorata.*"

"What I ask is not without reward." And quickly she nicked one of the swollen blue veins in the skeletal wrist he hid behind his illusion of youth. She heard his hiss of breath when blood beaded up at the site of the small cut. Deliberately, she smeared it on her fingertip, then rubbed the slash of crimson off along his lower lip. Instinctively, the tip of his tongue swept that tease of life away. He moaned softly as his eyes gave a rapturous roll and closed. When they opened again, his gaze was bright with icy fire. And Arabella's courage faltered when she viewed what she'd awakened. She'd known what he was when she brought him to her: a vicious predator led by his vile appetite. It was a risk to rely upon what might be a nonexistent mercy. Yet what choice had she?

"Try to make Louis understand." It was a tender plea.

"If he does not behead me first." Arabella knew with that gruff grumble that she'd won him over— and that her time was a heartbeat away. So many things rushed up then, important things, minor things, all needing to be said and settled but only one mattered in the end.

"Tell him I love him."

And Gerard eased up for another of his passionless kisses, letting his mouth slide from hers in a chill path to her bared throat. Fright leapt for an instant and she was pushing at him, but he was immovable, drawn to the rich scent of her sacrifice.

"Gerard?" Anxiousness echoed in that call, but not true resistance.

"Ummm?" It was half purr, half hungry rumble.

"There's a letter on the dressing table. Would you see it is delivered? Just delivered, no more than that."

"*Cara*, you don't trust me?"

"I know you."

His chuckle brushed over the exposed flesh of her neck. A shudder raced through her and she forced her thoughts to fix on Louis and upon the memories she would carry with her.

"Be kind, Gerard, and be quick."

Arabella felt his smile, slow and full of lethal charm. "I am not kind, my love, but I do promise you a most pleasurable end."

Louis let himself into the dark house, musing over the interview at the police precinct. When he'd been asked what his involvement was, Cassie had interrupted with an outrageous lie, telling the police sergeant that he was her driver, her non-English speaking driver. He'd been impressed by her want to protect him and by her calm refusal to shift any of the culpability from her surprisingly strong shoulders. She made no excuses for her failure to report her contact with the killer and to come forward with evidence. She bore up under the bullying and threats of incarceration and, in the end, she bent them around to her sincerity with a promise to cooperate fully in the future. A strong woman. An interesting one. She faced down consequences with a brave nobility, and that he admired.

There was a lot about the plucky mortal he had to respect.

He was smiling slightly, lost to his thoughts of her when suddenly the quiet of the house nudged him into a state of alarm.

"Takeo?"

"He is— resting."

Louis's head jerked up toward the source of that accented drawl. Gerardo Pasquale was perched upon the stair rail on the second floor landing, one foot swinging negligently, his manner inscrutable. A dark bird of death hovering over choice carrion.

"What are you doing here?"

"Gino, amico mio! What kind of greeting is that between old friends? Come. Embrace me. Say you are glad to see me."

Louis advanced up the stairs warily, keeping a close eye on his old and occasionally treacherous friend while reaching out into the shadows of the darkened house with his sharpened senses. He received no response to his summonings, not from his wife, not from his servant.

"I was invited, if you must know," Gerard continued, "by your lovely Arabella."

"Why would she ask you here in my absence?"

"She had a favor to ask and she knew I would not refuse her."

"What kind of favor?" He was closer now and could feel the just-fed warmth emanating from the other, just as he could hear the

smug tease of satisfaction in his voice. But
he wasn't truly afraid until Gerard relin-
quished his taunting pose and became un-
characteristically somber.

"Her last words were of you."

"Her last—" That thought trailed off into
an incredulous understanding. And he could
only stare at one who was of his kind but
nothing like him.

"I am sorry to be the bearer of such sad
news," Gerard murmured with an affected
sigh. No trace of feeling showed in his flat
stare. He could easily have been speaking
about the failing of an investment or the loss
of some treasured memento. His attitude was
detached from personal involvement. "She
did not suffer, not as she did in life. I saw
to that for you."

"No!" Louis's breath left him in a rush of
disbelief. "No. What are you saying? What
have you done? *Bastardo! Demonio! Omicida!*"

Louis's hand flashed out, but he didn't
pause after feeling the solid contact of palm
to cheek. Nor did he wait to watch as Gerard
toppled backward off the railing, somer-
saulting, only to right himself slowly in mid-
air and rise back up effortlessly to the
second floor hall. Louis was reeling toward
the bedroom where only hours before he
had tucked in his beloved. Where he had
left her to accompany another woman, a
woman who had filled his heart and mind

when he returned unaware of what had happened in his absence.

Louis staggered to a stop in the doorway, momentarily stunned by the sight that greeted him.

"I thought you would like to see her this way once more."

Louis didn't acknowledge Gerard's comment. Instead, he went to the bedside where a vision of past loveliness lay as if frozen in time. His beautiful Bella, as sweetly enchanting as she had been on their wedding day, her features seamless, ageless, her eyes closed frailly as if in sleep. The sheet was drawn up over her motionless bosom and left to pool beneath her chin. He reached an unsteady hand toward the edge of that sheet.

"Gino, don't—"

"Mi lasci in pace! Leave me alone!" And he shook off the staying grip of Gerard's hand to tug down the sheet. Even the severing of Arabella's head could not disguise the cause of her death, the twin punctures on her throat through which her life had been drained away. Even so familiar a sight horrified Louis beyond rational comprehension. "How could you? How could you do such a thing?"

Gerard's reply was coldly matter-of-fact. "Because she asked it of me. Because you would not do it for her."

"Non capisco," he moaned brokenly.

"What is to understand, my friend? She

was a vampire's bride, a slave to his kiss. She did not want to die alone, afraid no one would perform the necessary rituals to see she remained at rest."

"So you— you killed her."

"*Si.* Who else could she turn to? Who else could she trust to slay her without conscience?"

Louis hit him. The blow would have shattered the bones of a mortal man but Gerard fell back, stunned, unhurt. Not surprised. He held his ground, not seeking a wiser retreat as his grieving friend's fury mounted to surpass his shock.

"I am going to destroy you for what you've done," Louis vowed fiercely.

Rubbing his jaw, Gerard shrugged philosophically. "I guessed you would be of that mind."

"First I see to her, then I come for you."

"You will not have to look far, *amico mio.* I told her you would not be of a forgiving nature."

Yet he'd done it anyway, without concern for consequences. Rage, blacker than any he'd ever known, boiled up inside Louis.

"Get out. Get out of my house, away from my— my wife." And as he turned back, Louis was confronted by the true Arabella, a woman who was nearly ancient, withered and racked by suffering and advanced age. The woman he had loved beyond life. And he couldn't deny her expression was one of infinite peace.

Then, carefully, Louis lifted an oil lamp from a side table and consecrated his bride with its perfume. The strike of a match set all to flame.

"*Arrivederci,* little one. We will have that eternity together," he whispered as a final goodbye that was not farewell.

And as the fire grew higher and hotter, Gerard became uneasy. "Gino, we must leave this place." Flames were beginning to leap up the bed curtains and consume the wallpaper in a rush not unlike vampiric hunger. In moments, it would seal them into its eager embrace. And even for an immortal, that caress would be fatal.

"You go. Save your own miserable life. Let me be."

"I do not think this was what your Bella had in mind." He settled his hands upon Louis's upper arms. "Come away. Let her go."

When Louis would struggle to free himself in a wild agony of grief, Gerard wrapped him in a tight hold, carrying him bodily, cursing furiously, from the room.

"Put me down! Let me go! I will kill you! I will see you in hell!"

"Probably, *amico mio,*" Gerard said agreeably, "but not tonight."

With that, he bashed Louis's head into the edge of the door jamb, causing his friend to go limp in his arms. And there, he was momentarily cradled with tender care.

"You will survive this, Gino. Our kind always does. They always die and we go on. It is better not to love and live alone than to let them break your heart with their mortality." He hoisted Louis up over his shoulder and bore him down the stairs where they were joined by a groggy Takeo, only now waking from the spell of sleep Gerard had cast over him. The Oriental's gaze flew upstairs in alarm as smoke curled down the hall.

"A burial pyre," Gerard explained. "See to your master. Get him outside and do not leave him alone."

Takeo nodded grimly, his black eyes filling with tears.

"When he wakes, tell him . . . tell him I will await his pleasure." And he shrugged his friend's weight from his shoulder so he could see to the rest of his promise.

Cassie woke with a start then was certain she yet dreamed, for at the foot of her bed was the most wickedly handsome man she'd ever seen. Fear fell away as she was lost in the pale brilliance of his gaze.

"*Buona sera, signorina.* Please forgive the intrusion. I have a message to give you."

At the word "message," Cassie sat up in alarm. Was this the mysterious killer? Right

here in her bedroom? Before she could think
of an adequate defense, he came toward her
and it was then she was sure it was all a
sleeper's fantasy. Because no one could move
the way he did, without any obvious effort,
without taking a single step. He simply
glided around the bed with the ease of a
phantom, without a sound, without disturbing the air.

"I'm dreaming," she said aloud.

He smiled, the serene and beautiful smile
of an angel. "I could show you a dream, one
you would never wish to wake from. Perhaps
I will, another time. *Buona notte.*"

She realized something had fallen upon
her covers. It was an envelope with her name
penned on the front. By the time she
glanced up from it, she was alone in the
room.

The messenger may have been a passing
dream but the letter was real enough. She
picked it up and took out the single sheet.
It was covered with a spidery scrawl, some
of it barely legible.

*Cassie, my dear friend, I must ask you now to
attend your vow. Take care of Louis and love him
well. He is sure to be inconsolable when he finds
what I have done and will need you desperately
despite any claims he might make. In time, when
he is no longer angry with me over the action I
had to take, he will see the two of you are meant
for one another. Until then, have faith and keep*

your strength and wits about you. To you I entrust my greatest treasure. I await my love in paradise.

It was signed simply, *Arabella.*

Cassie sat blankly for a long moment trying to discover some significance in the cryptic words. She blinked once, then several more times. At first she thought it was fatigue and eye strain that filtered all she saw through a searing glare. Then she started to tear against a harsh burn and happened to glance out the window.

To see the entire upper floor of the Radcliffe estate on fire!

"Oh my God!"

She was out of bed and racing down the stairs without thinking to pause for a decent wrap. The night air was a cold snap to the senses that was quickly overpowered by the intense heat of the neighboring blaze. She ran down the walk, oblivious to the fact that her feet were bare and her hair unbound. Her heart was wild with panic. Arabella! Louis!

As she struggled with and finally managed to push past her front gate, she joined in the small crowd of the curious banding together on the walk.

"Has anyone called the fire department?" she yelled as she shoved her way through. "I have a telephone inside my house next door. Would someone please make the call!"

Then she wobbled to a stop. For there on the edge of the fence line stood Louis. Uttering an unconscious prayer of thanks, she rushed toward him only to pull up short again at the sight of his face. His expression was stark with sorrow.

"Arabella," she whispered hoarsely. "Oh, no." And her stricken gaze lifted to the blazing upstairs rooms.

"I did not arrive in time to save her," came his leaden confession.

Without a care to propriety, Cassie wrapped him up in her arms and hugged tight. He didn't move as her tears were lost in the smoky wool of his jacket and from someplace too far away to do any good, fire bells began an impatient clanging.

An ocean and a continent away, Gerardo Pasquale stood watching the as yet unseen sun brighten the peaks of the distant Alps.

"Do you want daylight to catch you dreaming, pretty one? Close the drapes and come away from there."

He didn't turn or respond to the mild chiding. Instead, he shut his eyes and lifted his face toward the far horizon. "I was thinking how good it would feel to have the sun warm my skin."

An unkind laugh sounded behind him. "Yes, right up until the moment you went up like a howling torch. That you would not enjoy, I can assure you. Come away, fool. You literally play with fire."

When he didn't move, his lovely companion reached past him to jerk the heavy curtains together and give him a firm push. When he remained docile to her rough treatment, she scowled at him suspiciously.

"What is wrong with you this evening? You've done nothing but mope about as if you'd lost your last friend." Then she gave a gasp upon hearing her own words. "Not Gino! Nothing's happened to Gino, has it?"

He shook his head.

Her sigh of relief was audible. "Thank goodness. I was afraid that—" She issued a small laugh, unwilling to betray her feelings further. "You frightened me, Gerardo. I have only known you to carry on in such a shamelessly human manner when it concerns our dear old friend or his puny mortal bride."

"She's dead," he said flatly.

"What?" Bianca du Maurier rounded on him in a frenzy. "What did you say?"

"She is dead."

Bianca's mind gave a fevered leap, then caution caught her. "Are you sure? Gerardo, are you sure?" She had him by the shoulders, her fingers curling into talons that pierced his unnatural flesh.

"I'm sure," he mumbled.

"How do you know? How are you sure?" she ranted.

Angrily, he flung her off and shouted, "Of course I'm sure. I ought to be sure. I know because I—" He stopped, then after a beat continued. "Because I was there."

"Arabella is dead." Bianca repeated that aloud as if she needed to reassure herself that it was really true. "And Gino? How is Gino?"

Gerard glowered at her. "How do you think he is? He alone among us can actually claim to have a heart. He is devastated. But he will get over it. In time. What else do we have but the advantage of time?"

"Poor Gino," she mused without real sympathy. Her mind was already spinning joyously ahead to ways she could console their dearest friend and her former lover.

"Don't make me laugh, *cara*," Gerardo sneered. "You've not a drop of compassion in your veins. You hated the woman and tried to dispose of her on several occasions so you could have Gino for yourself. You could never stand the thought that he preferred someone else over you. A mortal, no less."

His attack made her testy and spurred her to the offensive. "And what of you, my lovelorn friend? How distraught you must be now that your paragon is no more."

"Don't be ridiculous," he snapped frigidly. "Why should I mourn the death of a mortal? What was she that I should care one way or another about her fate?"

"That I have never known," Bianca murmured as she watched him turn toward the huge mirror above the fireplace. It reflected the elegant room but not his perfect features. He was staring aimlessly, his posture stiff while his hands methodically crushed the delicate spun glass figures that adorned the mantelpiece. Pulverized crystals sifted between his fingers indifferently stained bright with blood.

Moved by his odd behavior and by her own agenda, Bianca came up behind him, creating no more of an image in the mirror than he did. Her arms laced about his neck and she leaned against his back. When he refused to respond to the sensual invitation, she kissed his sharp jawline and stroked him like an anxious pet.

"Please, my love, I cannot bear to see you so upset. What can I do to ease your troubled heart?"

"I have no heart, remember? As for what you can do, you can leave me alone."

He shrugged off her embrace and strode from the room without a backward glance. And when he was gone, he was quickly forgotten. Bianca allowed a small cunning smile to shape her lips.

Now to find dear Gino and offer her condolences.

Ten

"And you were where when this tragic event occurred?"

Louis looked up from where he sat stiffly upon Cassie's sofa to regard the police detective unblinkingly. "I believe I answered that already. I was not at home."

"And you can verify that?"

"If I must. Am I under some sort of suspicion here?"

"Mr. Radcliffe, we're just doing our jobs. Fire breaks out like this, resulting in a death, we have to investigate all the possibilities, you understand."

"I understand that you have been harassing me with the same questions for over two hours now. If you think I am guilty of something, charge me or leave me alone. I have lost someone very dear to me. She was old and ill. My guess is that she knocked over the bedside lamp and lacked the strength to escape the flames. By the time I got home, there was nothing I could do. She was— she was already dead."

And with that hitch in his words, a hint of emotion showed through the inscrutable wall of his defense for the first time since the police had arrived. Tears stood in his eyes, glimmering wetly. He made no attempt to apologize for them or to wipe them away. And as if that was what the detective was waiting to see, that great well of anguish and vulnerability springing to the surface, he folded his notebook closed.

"Thank you for your patience, Mr. Radcliffe. At this point, we'll be ruling the circumstances as accidental. That will of course be dependent upon the autopsy."

"When can I see to her burial?" That came out in a hoarse rasp.

"I'll let you know. And if there should be any further questions, where can I reach you?" His home was gone, a smoldering ruin. Only the heroic efforts of the fire fighters had saved the surrounding properties from like destruction.

"You can reach him here," Cassie put in without glancing at Louis to gauge his reaction. The detective's was subtle but apparent disapproval. She had been wrapped around Louis Radcliffe in her night clothes when they arrived, had shifted them to the comforts of her home, and now was housing a handsome bachelor under her roof without a thought to her reputation. Let them think what they liked, Cassie thought wearily, but let them leave. "I'll see you out, detective."

When he was gone, Cassie leaned gratefully against her front door and wondered what to do next. Inside her pocket was the clue to everything, the proof of what really happened to Arabella Radcliffe. Yet how could she show it? How could she tell Louis that his precious grandmother had actually killed herself in such an awful manner?

She couldn't. She would keep Arabella's secret and she would make good on her promise. Louis was now her responsibility.

When she found him again, he was standing at the heavy parlor drapes, peering out into the softening grays of morning in a posture so aloof and vulnerable, her soul ached to behold it. It was a pain she could understand well, that soul-deep agony of loss. She'd suffered it herself not so long ago. This man and the woman he now mourned had eased her depthless misery and so it was only right that she do what she could to help him over the shock of grief. She wasn't good at dealing with personal pain, having had so little contact with displays of compassion in the past. After the ordeal with her mother's illness, she'd learned to hold emotion in tightly, to suppress rather than express, and the turmoil had seethed, unresolved for years. It was Arabella's kind counsel after her father's passing that showed her how to face death with dignity instead of denial. Those were the lessons she clung to now when confronted with the question of how to deal with Louis.

He heard her step but didn't turn.

"I cannot stay here."

His quiet claim made her heart leap in alarm. That he would go, that he would deny her the chance to offer solace, had never occurred to her. "But you've nowhere else to go. I insist, Louis."

"It's almost dawn." He said that as if it held some significance.

"And you're tired. Rest awhile. I have plenty of room, for both you and Takeo. No one will bother you here. Please. It's the least I can do . . . for Arabella."

He made a soft sound. It snagged somewhere between agony and anger. She crossed over to him without a thought, wanting desperately to provide some comfort for his anguished soul. But when she touched his arm, he recoiled violently.

"Louis?"

"This is my fault . . . and yours." He came about, his glorious features contorted with pain. He was staring at her through wild, feverishly bright eyes.

"What is?"

"She is dead because of us."

Cassie winced at the cruel lash of his reasoning. But he was in shock, so she instantly forgave him. And she tried to get him to forgive himself. "How could we have known something like this would happen while we were away? Louis, no one is to blame."

"I should have guessed she would attempt something so foolish— and brave. Damn her! How could she do this? How could she leave me?" His words trickled off in a forlorn lament.

"I'm so sorry."

Then his gaze sharpened, becoming glittery and gold. "Sorry? That changes nothing. Nothing!" He began to pace in rapid agitation, each movement a stroke of strong, aggressive poetry. Cassie watched him, helplessly drawn by the beauty of him, hopelessly caught in his torment. But she wasn't prepared for the sudden focus of his blame. "She did this because of you. Because she hoped I could turn to you when she was gone."

Cassie said nothing. She couldn't argue what she knew to be the truth. Nor had she any defense for his massing fury.

"Well she was wrong!" he roared and Cassie trembled at the evidence of his rage. "She died for nothing!" He staggered to a halt, his head falling back as he wailed at the ceiling, "Bella, how could you do this to me?"

Compassionate impulse overruled rational caution. Cassie went to him to extend a consoling embrace. He stiffened within her arms and she was sure he would pull away. Then gradually the tension flowed from him and his arms came up in a loose circle and his head bowed to take rest upon her shoulder.

"What am I going to do without her?" he mourned as if in hopes of hearing an answer. "How could she have thought I'd welcome such a sacrifice?" And he let go of the awful anguish, weeping with loss and guilt until his knees buckled weakly and Cassie steered them both back to the sofa.

There she held him, aware of the power flowing rough and ragged through him, malleable for this moment to her tender touch. Did he know how Arabella had chosen to die? Had he somehow guessed? His awful laments made her think perhaps he did, and how terrible that knowledge must be she could only imagine. She was humbled by the strength of responsibility for another's pain and by the depth of her love for Louis Radcliffe. Her promise to Arabella wouldn't be hard to keep, for she was lost to her feelings for him already.

He had quieted in her arms. She could sense the gathering of his control like the massing static in the air before a thunderstorm. He wouldn't be hers for much longer and knowing that gave her the necessary boldness to kiss his brow and savor the sensation of his hair sliding through her fingers. How had Arabella thought she possessed the charm and wisdom to hold a man such as this?

He began to stir slowly. His hands spread

wide along her shoulder blades as his head lifted and turned, the movement bringing his cheek against hers and his lips close enough for her to feel the rush of his breath upon her ear and unprotected throat. A shiver raced through her and her own breathing altered into a scurry of anticipation when she hoped that he might kiss her.

He didn't.

The fingers of one hand rose to mesh in the hair at the back of her neck, twisting, tightening until her head was tugged at an awkward angle. She took a quick breath of confusion, about to protest when he leaned away and she got her first good look at his expression. It was set in cold, harsh lines, his gaze burning from it like hot coals. Cassie thought at once of madness and was terrified to the core. If he was mad, he could well be her stalker. If he was already perched upon a tenuous mental balance, how far off that edge would he plunge at the shattering loss of Arabella?

"Are you happy now?" he hissed softly. "Now you have everything."

"I don't—"

A sharp yank on her hair silenced her and made tears bead in her eyes.

"Louis—"

"So clever to play upon an old woman, undermining her with your youth and your years, making her think her time was past and her purpose served. Well, you got what you wanted, didn't you? Except you had no idea what you were after. And now you will get what you deserve."

"Louis, please! I don't know— "

"No, but soon you will." He pulled harder upon the loop of her hair, bending her head back, arching her neck into a pale curve. He could see the fright glistening in her wide gaze, could hear it in her panting breath, yet he felt no sympathy for her. He felt . . . nothing.

And that's when instinct rose to fill the void of emotion. Hunger, razor-edged and all consuming.

Dawn was approaching and his need to secure a hiding place was paramount. His was destroyed and here was his answer. So many secrets could not be trusted to a woman whose inquisitive nature could seal his doom. Necessity forced his decision and self-contempt overruled objection.

This was the creature who had swayed his loyalty from where it should have stood firm. She was the cause of his fresh despair, the reason his future loomed empty of meaning. Remorse would not allow him to be the man she yearned for. Retribution supplied the beast instead. Now she would learn she could not have one without the other.

Cassie gasped as his mouth fastened fiercely upon her throat. A charge of anxiousness and expectation shot through her system, awareness so acute it sizzled like fire along her limbs and beat like a wild thing within her breast. It was desire, it was madness, it was a lack of control so overwhelming her will ceased to be her own. There was only Louis and she clung to him for stability as her senses soared.

Her body reacted to the shock of his bite but her mind was far beyond the recognition of anything akin to physical pain. Reality raveled into a loosely woven mesh of strange sensations: floating, drowning, fire, and a vast empty chill. That last began to grow, surmounting the rest, that chill that was like dying. A whisper of fear wound through the heavy strands of pleasure and her thoughts groped outward in hopes of solace.

Louis, I'm afraid.

And his voice sounded within her head, a stroke of reassurance flowing like the pulse of her blood from her to him.

Have no fear. You belong to me now. We are one, just as you wished, but not quite as you wanted. You are the slave of my needs, an extension of my will. You sought the darkness and now it resides within you. You wanted me and now you will pay the price of that desire for all eternity.

The confusion of his words, so calming yet so cruel, was too much. Cassie swooned in his embrace.

There was a shrill ringing. It pierced the veil of her slumber, a strident demand. Cassie moaned and thrashed beneath the smothering weight of her covers, reluctant to respond. Finally the noise stopped and she was able to sink into obscurity once more, to awaken hours later to the bright wash of midday sun streaming across her bed. The brilliance of it was like daggers to her eyes and she squinted them up in objection.

Then the brightness abated, closing off into cooling shadows. She managed to turn her head to the side to see Takeo sealing her draperies shut.

It took awhile for her to realize the oddness of the Radcliffes' Asian servant's presence in her bedroom. Then it came back in vague waves of memory. Arabella had died in a fire. Louis was her guest. And she was still in bed at lunch time.

Good grief! She had to go in to work!

But the moment she tried to sit up, dizziness swamped over her in crippling waves. She sagged back into the bolster of pillows, her muscles weak as water, her senses spinning in a sickening whirlpool of confusion.

Do not try to get up. The weakness will pass in time. You should try to eat something. Then you will feel better.

She heard the voice clearly, but as her bleary gaze flew about the room she saw no one but Takeo. And he was mute. Pressing a hand to her temple, Cassie closed her eyes. She was ill and feverish. Some sort of sudden influenza affecting a delirium of the brain.

"Is Louis here?" she asked of his servant. Her voice was a gravelly rasp, her throat filled with the singe of hot ash.

Takeo shook his head and carried a tray to her bedside. It held a carafe of juice and a bowl of some thin hot cereal. She turned away, unable to face the thought of swallowing anything past the agony in her throat. She generally had an iron constitution. Sickness of any kind was practically unknown to her, so the severity of her present condition was doubly upsetting.

"I need a doctor. Could you find someone to call me a doctor?"

Takeo placed a calming hand upon her brow, stroking back the wet strands of hair that clung there. His expression was gentle and reassuring, as if he were dealing with a fretful child. She didn't want to be treated like a child. She wanted to know what was wrong with her.

Irrationally, the solution to all things in her bewildered mind was Louis. He could take the fear away. He could ease the panic in her heart and erase the frenzy from her mind.

"Louis. I need Louis."

He will be with you when twilight falls. Until then you must recover your strength. For him.

For Louis. Yes. She must get stronger for Louis because he would need her. That made sense and she seized upon that purpose, never questioning the rest. Not even the fact that she'd heard Takeo speak so clearly when he'd never moved his lips.

He extended the tray again, and this time she allowed him to prop her up on her pillows so she could force the liquids through the raw channel of her throat. And fortified, she slept, deep and dreamlessly, long into the afternoon hours, stirring only when she felt the presence of someone near her bedside.

"Quinton, is that you?" Her voice was little more than a croak.

Her cousin smiled and leaned closer so he could place warm hands over her own chill ones. "I was worried when you didn't come in this morning. I tried to call but got no answer, so I decided to come see for myself. Your— servant let me in." He glanced over his shoulder at the somber-faced Takeo, who was regarding him through watchful eyes.

"That's Takeo. He works for the Radcliffes next door. They had a terrible fire there last night. Arabella Radcliffe lost her life."

"How awful. What about you? Were you somehow injured by the smoke? I've never known you to come down with so much as the sniffles. Are you all right? Has a doctor been sent for?"

She cast a questioning look toward Takeo and saw him move his head in a subtle negative. An unspoken eddy of caution transferred between them. Then she forced a smile for her cousin.

"I'm fine, Quinton, really. Just exhaustion and a bit of a cold. Nothing bed rest won't cure. I'm sure I'll be myself tomorrow."

"The whole staff is abuzz about the latest issue. You need to take a strong stand or my father will think he can have his way."

"The staff . . . latest issue . . ." Her attention was waning. She had no idea as to what he was referring.

"The *Lexicon*, Cass. The article Walter wrote."

"Walter . . ."

Quinton sighed. "Don't trouble yourself about it now. Get the rest you need and we can talk of it later."

Cassie nodded faintly, her eyes already sagging down, her consciousness already giving way before a blissful darkness.

Quinton turned to the glowering Oriental. "Boy, go downstairs and have my driver bring my carriage around. I shall be leaving momentarily."

Takeo hesitated, then sketched a bow before heading silently toward the stairs.

Alone with the slumbering woman, Quinton lifted up one of her limp hands and pressed his lips ardently to her palm. "You must be strong, Cass. Together we can defeat him. Without you, it is for nothing. All I do, I do for you. For you. You must know that." He shut his eyes and let the madness swirl up to take control. "Do not disappoint me. I would hate for you to end up like the others."

The tease of voices woke Cassie to the muted shades of gaslight. Her thoughts were vaporous at first then sharpened to one familiar tone. Louis.

A desperate urgency overtook reason and weakness. She had to get to him. Had to! Just to see him, to be near him, to let him know she was there for him, that she would do anything for him. Anything.

Compulsion drove her from her bed on feeble legs. She tottered to the door then pulled herself along with hands pressed to the paneling for a fragile balance. Her knees shook. Her head swam. She didn't know where she got the strength to take one step after another but she continued on, shuffling like an invalid. Toward the compelling sound of his voice.

The stairs loomed before her as steep and threatening as a plunge off a mountainside. Her vision was wavering, making the individual steps ripple like the sinister undulations of snake skin. She knew she was too unsteady to attempt such a feat but found herself edging downward in a dangerous tangle of bedclothes. To where he waited.

I must contact Nicole and her family but I cannot make arrangements until the police release her . . .

I understand, Master. I will prepare for their arrival. There is ample room below where we can—

The voices stopped when they saw her there huddled upon the stairs. Voices they had not been using in the normal fashion, but voices heard no less clearly within her befuddled mind.

She was going mad. Just like her mother.

"What are you doing there?" Louis growled. "Spying?"

Cassie cringed beneath the cold sting of his accusation but still the yearning to be close to him prompted her to creep downward. "N-no, I wasn't. I heard you talking and—"

How could she have heard them talking when one of them couldn't speak?

Dizziness, cold and penetrating, seeped through her limbs. She was shaking, close to dropping where she stood, yet she took a few more steps. To be with him.

"I did not call you. Return to your room. I will not have you meddling in my affairs. You exist only to serve me. I will let you know when you are required."

He stared at her with such loathing, her soul shriveled on the spot. And when he turned his back on her, a desolate agony ripped through her heart. She rested her cheek upon the cool wood of the banister, feeling her tears flow unrestricted. What had she done? Why was he treating her so terribly? The hurt of it was crushing. But he'd commanded her to go, so go she must. Slowly she began to drag herself back up the steep flight.

Louis was trying to reassemble his fractured train of thought when he caught Takeo's reproachful look.

"What?"

I have never known you to be so harsh with one anxious to show devotion.

"And I have never known you to push your opinions upon me. I have my reasons for what I do. I gather you do not approve."

I am puzzled, is all.

"How I treat my servants is my business."

Would you treat me as poorly?

"No, my friend. You have shown me only loyalty. She conspired to destroy my love."

Cassie sank down on the steps, aching to deny his cruel words, wondering why he thought she deserved them. She could go no farther, her strength exhausted. She could feel Takeo's pitying eyes upon her but Louis had dismissed her from his mind.

"My only concern is the autopsy. They mustn't discover anything amiss. If only there were some way to be sure," he was musing.

"Louis?" How painfully thin her voice sounded.

He glanced about in irritation. "What do you want?"

"I can help you. Let me help you." It was a desperate entreaty.

And Louis turned her way, offering her the chance to escape his anger. "How?"

It took some time to track down Danny Hooper but he promised he would clear the necessary path for them to see the coroner in charge of Arabella Radcliffe. Cassie felt none of her earlier dread in the cold morgue. She could feel little beyond the paralyzing weariness. Assuming the surroundings were the cause of her faintness, the coroner kindly provided her with a chair then regarded Louis warily.

"I am not at liberty to discuss my findings with you. I don't know what Sergeant Hooper was thinking letting you come down here but—"

"But you will now tell me everything I wish to know."

Louis's forceful demand was met with a moment's silence, then Cassie was astounded to hear the complying mumble of, "What do you wish to know?"

"What did your examination tell you?"

The doctor was staring dreamily into Louis's eyes. "She did not die in the fire. She was murdered. She'd been decapitated."

Cassie made a small choking sound but no one seemed to hear her.

"That is not what you will write in your report." His voice lowered into a soothing, almost hypnotic cadence.

"It's not," the coroner echoed.

"No. You will put down that Arabella Radcliffe succumbed to smoke and subsequently perished in the flames. You will state you see no cause for further investigation."

"No cause."

"And you will not remember this conversation or that we were here at all."

"Not here. Not at all."

"Yes, very good. You may conclude your report now." And he came to put his hand out to Cassie, lifting her to her feet.

As they traveled back to her home, Cassie curled up in the far corner of the seat, quivering with the effects of shock and disbelief. All was like madness to her now. Nothing was real.

"You did well by me tonight. I am grateful." When she made no reply, Louis glanced in her direction. "Why are you weeping?" There was no hint of concern in that question, just a mild annoyance.

"Did you kill her?" Cassie whispered.

That shot past his cold disdain. He flinched. "No. No, I did not."

Cassie turned her head away, failing too fast to even care if that was the truth. "She was my friend."

"She was more than that to me," came Louis's clipped response. Then there was silence.

When they reached her home, Louis aided her down from the carriage then started up the walk at a brisk stride, oblivious to her struggle. Cassie took two steps and collapsed in the pool of the nightdress she still wore beneath her full-length coat. When he didn't turn, she attempted to crawl down the walk after him.

"Louis?" A faint whispering cry, but enough to coax him around. He stared at her dispassionately, at the woman who was the cause of his sorrow.

Then from someplace deep inside the coldness of spirit came a faint flicker of warmth and light. A soft chiding remembrance. *Your promise, Louis.* His promise to keep Cassie safe from harm. A promise broken with Arabella not yet in her grave.

Afraid his return to the callousness of his kind would reach beyond the veil to distress Arabella in her well-deserved rest, Louis backed down from his cruel stance. The last thing he wanted was to confuse his new relationship to Cassie with kindness, but Arabella's memory demanded it of him. How much easier it would be to keep an unfeeling distance where he could have the lovely mortal without endangering his heart. In a way, his conscience could approve.

But that conscience would not allow him to dismiss his last vow to his love, either.

He came to kneel beside Cassie, scooping her up against his chest and standing easily with her in his arms, murmuring all the while, "Forgive me. It was not my intent to lay you so low or to so misuse you." And that much was true. He had no wish to slay her for her foolish treachery.

Cassie was trying to hang on to consciousness, longing to hear his soft-spoken words. Her head dropped to his shoulder but she had no strength to lift her arms and put them about him. It was enough to feel his strength, his heat against her, to sense the power of his heartbeats, the soothing tenderness of his care.

"Love me, Louis," she whispered weakly into the collar of his coat.

"I fear that is not possible. I will never trust my heart to love again. Never."

And with tears gathering in her eyes, Cassie released her hold on awareness, preferring darkness to the empty echo of that truth.

Eleven

It had all been a nightmare. Cassie was convinced of it when she woke the next day clear of mind and possessed of most of her strength. She was shamefully conscious of the strange feverish turns of her delirium over the past twenty-four hours and hoped she had not been a burden.

Takeo appeared with her breakfast and a politely offered smile, assuring her with his nods that Louis had settled in comfortably as her guest and was presently gone on business. No subconscious conversations. She blushed at the very idea. After thanking him, she delved into the hearty fare with a mannerless urgency, as starved as a stray cat. Then she was able to dress herself for work and rehearse what she would say to her uncle. The problems at the *Lexicon* engulfed her, pushing aside the mania of the past hours when she'd heard voices in her mind and believed Louis Radcliffe had the power of the devil. Delirium. She would have to apologize to her houseguest when she returned, in case she'd done anything to offend him during her illness.

And as she thought of Louis, a sizzle of sensation streaked along her veins and a hungry longing surged within her breast. That was harder to dismiss. But she would try.

Takeo directed her into the Radcliffes' private carriage and she would not protest that luxury. What a terror it would be to faint upon public transport. But for all her worries, the day progressed uneventfully. Her uncle was out of the office and all was quiet within; the eye of the tornado, she was sure. She tended what required her attention and found herself daydreaming more often than not about Louis and the puzzle of their relationship. The last thing she clearly remembered was his embrace upon the sofa. He had kissed her wildly, passionately and . . . she could recall nothing beyond that.

Could they have made love?

She squirmed uncomfortably at that thought. Not because she would not wish it to be true, but because she could not bear the thought of not remembering every detail.

It wasn't as if she could come right out and ask him!

Could she?

Too distracted and restless to remain where her heart was not, she left work early, anxious to test out the unfamiliar waters of romance with her visitor. She was not surprised to find he hadn't yet returned but was delighted by a bouquet of stark white roses awaiting her on the hall table.

Thank you for your kindness, Louis.

Not as personal as she would have liked, but it was a start. She was still smiling over his note when she turned in to the front parlor and pulled up short. There before her bow front windows was a brand new coffin.

Arabella, of course. She swallowed hard and worked to restore a normal pace to her heart. Where else could Louis have arranged a private viewing before the services? She placed her hand upon the satin-smooth rosewood lid, fighting the emotion burning inside. It wasn't so long ago when her father had lain here in state. Yet she had gone on as Louis would go on.

"I will keep my promise, Arabella. Rest well knowing that."

"What promise is that?"

Cassie gave a start, for she'd not heard Louis enter the room. She turned and was surprised by the intensity of her response to him. It was all she could do to remain where she was while buffeted with the need to seek out his arms. She felt the blood and heat come roaring through her as her breath began to labor and pant from her in longing. And while she stood a room away, wanting him so desperately she was close to writhing with it, she could feel the cool wood of Arabella's coffin beneath her hand and was shamed by the thoughts that would not stop, by the inappropriate nature of her— lust, for what else could describe that wanton yearning? What else but madness could explain the way her knees went weak and her heart was pounding, pounding until the sound of it thundered between her ears? Trying to appear normal, she managed a strained smile and admitted, "I swore to look after you. She was very concerned in her last days that you not be alone." But even those quiet words sounded husky with her desire. What on earth was wrong with her? The man was mourning a loved one and she was appealing to him like the basest street walker.

It was Louis, himself, who broke her spell of steamy enchantment. There was no mistaking the cold chill that came over his green eyes. "And so I shan't. I have Takeo and soon my family will be here. I hope you do not mind that I have invited them."

"No. No, of course not." What was there about his crisp rejection that made it . . . *hurt* so horribly?

"Her services are for this evening. They will be here within the hour."

Cassie withdrew her hand from the casket lid, struggling against a fierce trembling that rose up inside her— a rattling of weakness and wanting and frustrated need. She lowered her gaze so he would not see her turmoil. And slowly, she said the words that weighed so heavily on her heart. Words that would separate them when the thought of being without him, even for an instant, suddenly seemed worse than the isolating darkness of that big box. "I will retire so you can have your privacy."

She had started past him with a wobbly dignity when his hand cupped about her elbow. And even that slight touch filled her with an ache of desperate desire. "Cassie, I think she would have liked you to be there. She thought very highly of you." A slight pause. "It would not be an intrusion."

She couldn't look up at him, embarrassed by her watery gaze. But she did nod. "I'll go change into something more suitable."

She had mourning clothes in her wardrobe. She'd been properly attired at her father's funeral, but he had expressly forbade her in one of their father-daughter talks to ever linger in sad raven dress for his sake. Though she'd earned her share of shocked disapproval, she'd abided by that wish. Pulling out the drab black costume of Henrietta cloth and crepe swept her up in a familiar sea of sorrow, but because she didn't want to be a poor hostess, she forced herself to get beyond the pain and ready to meet the Radcliffes.

Quiet murmurs reached her as she came down the stairs. Through the double doors of the parlor, she could see the family gathered to pay their respects. Louis had his arms about a young woman who was weeping copiously in defiance of the rules of etiquette which stated it was vulgar to be seen crying over a corpse. His sister, Cassie guessed from what she could see of their similarity through the heavy black veiling. Off to one side stood another young woman, a younger sister perhaps, for the resemblance there was also strong. She held to a stony expression but clung to the arm of the man beside her. He was darkly handsome with a broad rugged build, somberly set features, and flashing black eyes. All attention turned to her when she entered the room. It was not a warm welcome but one of understated reserve. And wariness. Louis had been wrong when he said she would not be an intruder. Cassie forced a stiff smile.

"Cassie, let me present you to my family," Louis began. He hugged the woman in his arms. "This is Nicole and that is her husband, Marchand, and their d—and Frederica. This is Cassie Alexander. She was Bella's dear friend and was kind enough to allow us this time to say our goodbyes."

Marchand came forward to kiss her hand, murmuring a soft salutation in French. The two women regarded her with a mixture of curiosity and caution, obviously wondering what Louis wasn't saying about the two of them.

Marchand tucked her hand into the bend of his elbow and provided a flat smile and an explanation. "I hope you don't think us odd conducting the services at twilight, but this was Arabella's favorite time of day, the time when we could all be together as a family."

"I think it's a lovely sentiment. I always admired her for the way she flaunted convention."

Nicole gave a soft choking sob and Louis hugged her up more tightly, crooning to her in what Cassie assumed was Italian.

About then the funeral bearers arrived to take the casket to the New York, Harlem and Albany Railway for its final ride to Woodlawn Cemetery. The special train was designed to carry funeral corteges to the entrance eight miles north of Harlem Bridge, and there the solemn procession walked amid the shadows and the moonlike glow of tombstones to where a preacher spoke a brief and moving eulogy over the flower-strewn casket. All the witnesses were grimly silent, shedding no tears of goodbye at the graveside.

Struggling to contain her own, Cassie was fishing about up her sleeve for her black-edged handkerchief when she happened to spy a lone figure standing apart from them. She held her gasp upon recognizing him as the mysterious man who bore her Arabella's last words. In the natural darkness, his features appeared gaunt and even more ghostlike. As did the rest of the funeral party, she noted with surprise. It must have been some trick of the lighting that gave them each such a ghastly sheen. Standing so still and silent, they blended beside the marble monuments with their respectfully bowed heads and reverent attitudes.

Until Louis's head shot up and his glistening eyes fixed upon the solitary mourner. Anger twisted his features and he looked about to stride over to chase the interloper away when Nicole placed her hand on his arm and spoke to him quietly. Louis regained his control and stood at rigid attention as Nicole started toward the distant man.

"Nicole!" The sharp hiss of disapproval came from Marchand but, when she didn't stop, he made no move to intercept her.

Cassie watched as the slender woman in black came up to the handsome stranger to enfold him in her arms and kiss his dark head tenderly. They stood for a time in that needy embrace then she stepped back, retaining his hands, tugging on them as she tried to coax him to join the others. He shook his head, pulling to reclaim his hands but Nicole must have been stronger than she looked, for in the end he came along with her docilely.

Cassie thought she'd imagined him and his disturbing beauty, but he gave her a smile and a slight bow of greeting. That gesture was stiffly replayed for a rigid Marchand and Frederica. Then he faced Louis for a long unmoving moment, the air charging with an unnatural static between them.

Suddenly, the dark stranger gripped Louis by either side of the head, holding him anchored for an expressive European kiss upon either taut cheek.

"Amico mio, mio fratello, mi dispiace, mi perdonare."

Louis received that impassioned plea stoically, his resolve breaking only momentarily when he leaned against the other, seeming to go weak within his embrace, a soft moan of despair escaping. Then his hands came up, holding the other's forearms briefly before shoving him brusquely away. Then Louis strode from the cemetery without a backward glance, followed by his family. Nicole lingered.

"Come with us, Gerard."

"No, *cara*. It is not my place."

She didn't argue. Instead, she lifted her veil and stretched up to kiss his cheek, then, more gently, his mouth. "She thought of you fondly, as her friend, as someone whom she could trust."

Gerard drew a fractured breath as if he would speak to that, but he remained silent, saying finally, *"Buona notte, Nicole."*

She stroked the side of his face with tender fingertips, then lowered her veil and joined the others. Cassie was the last to follow, struck by the poignant loneliness of Gerard's stance beside the freshly chiseled marker. She thought she saw a shimmer of movement behind him, a shifting mist that seemed to take human form but then Louis caught her arm, distracting her, and when she looked back again, there was only Gerard in his solitary vigil.

Soft laughter flowed about him, mocking, taunting.

"Ah, my sweet sentimental fool. What a touching scene. For what deed were you begging forgiveness of our dear Gino?"

"Go away, Bianca," Gerard muttered. "You defile this place with your presence."

The beautiful blonde woman was seated upon a nearby tombstone like a fair bird of prey. "And what of you, my pretty hypocrite? Do you think their mortal God will listen to anything you have to say?"

"Not for myself. I am damned and lost my audience with God long ago. But for her, I will say a few words in hopes that He will hear."

Bianca chuckled. "You waste your time and His. Dear Arabella does not need your petition to earn her sainthood. You had elevated her to a deity already."

"Do not speak of her to me. Not now. Not here."

Bianca laughed again, her merriment cruel. "*Caro,* do my eyes deceive me or are those tears upon your face?"

He stared at her, his immobile features tracked with dampness and utterly void of any expression. "You see only what you want to see, *il nemico.*"

"*Au contraire,* I see all. So explain to me why you were begging Gino's pardon. Feeling guilty because you were in love with his wife?"

His glare intensified. "No, because I killed his wife."

"You—" She broke off, plainly and deeply shocked by his admission.

Gerard gave her a bittersweet smile. "So you see, Bianca. You are quite blind." Then he addressed the grave marker once more. "Rest in peace, *cara mia.*" And he crossed himself unconsciously out of a long forgotten habit before disappearing into the rising mists of evening.

Cassie regarded the group in her parlor trying to shake off the odd sense of uneasiness. Something was not . . . right about them. Perhaps it was the way they moved, the weightless drifting that carried them about the room as noiselessly as shadows. Or the hypnotic stillness that settled when they stopped. She wasn't sure which unnerved her more. The four of them—Louis included—seemed so out of place and time in her mother's cluttered decorating scheme, like fireflies brought into the house.

Perhaps it was the way they were all so aware of her, following her with unblinking gazes until a shiver of gooseflesh rose upon her arms. It wasn't hostility or even curiosity she sensed. It was something else, something basic and dark.

Something dangerous.

"Might I fix you some refreshment?" she asked, nervous in her role of hostess.

"What a generous offer," the youngest woman purred in a way that was both mocking and intimidating.

"Rica!" Marchand admonished softly. Then he smiled at Cassie. "You need not go to any trouble for us."

"Some tea might be nice," Louis interjected. "To cut the chill." Then he glanced at the young woman with a hint of sternness. Frederica promptly turned away with a haughty sniff. Then Louis, too, smiled at Cassie in the same condescending manner. "If it's no bother."

"No, no bother," she insisted, eager to exit the room.

The moment she was gone, Nicole turned to her father with a direct, "How did she die?"

"There was a fire," he began gently, then added when he saw his daughter's horror, "I don't believe she suffered." For a reason unknown to him, Louis was reluctant to speak of Gerard's part in it. Perhaps in his heart, he was already beginning to forgive his friend, who, in his own way, had loved the woman they'd just laid to rest.

"This mortal woman, who is she?" Frederica wanted to know. *What is she to you?* was the unspoken question.

"As I said, she was a friend of Bella's. She has offered me shelter for the time being."

"Voluntarily?"

"Rica, your manners!" Marchand scolded. "Forgive her rudeness, Louis. She has had too indulgent an upbringing."

"Does she know what we are, Father?" Nicole asked.

"No, Nicole, and I would prefer she remain ignorant of it. She is nothing, so there is no reason for her to know."

But Nicole was watching his expression and she knew that protest to be entirely false. She just wasn't sure what she thought of her father's interest in another woman . . . a mortal woman, so close upon the time of her mother's burial. Before she could ask any more questions, Marchand came up behind her to offer the support of his strong embrace. He kissed her temple but the censure was there. *Do not pry, cher.* And so she would not. At least, not yet.

Cassie entered the parlor, juggling the tea tray, then stopped in surprise to see only Louis within.

"They had to leave," he explained without turning away from his outward facing stand at the front drapes.

"Oh." She set the tray down, trying to recover from the sense of slight. Never had she felt quite so insignificant and poorly used by guests in her own home. The strain of the situation, she decided in their defense. She was a stranger and she knew she could not expect to be a part of their pain. Yet she felt it, too, that ache of emptiness that accompanied the loss of someone loved. She had cared deeply for the old woman, who had been close as family within her heart.

She watched Louis, thinking of Gerard in his secluded vigil. Didn't men such as these know how to seek an avenue of consolation? She could feel the sorrow emanating from Louis in palpable waves. It played upon her mood like a low, melancholy tune, wringing her emotions with each increasingly mournful note until her heart twisted in anguish and her soul cried out for relief—hers, his.

She went to him then because she couldn't hold herself away and do nothing as he grieved. She touched a hand to his arm. When he didn't flinch away, she chose to see that as a sign of his compliance. Slowly, she fit herself up against him, her hands upon his arms, her cheek resting between his shoulder blades, her body molding liquid along the hard line of his back and the taut curve of his flanks. A strange sense of affinity overcame her, a feeling that they were somehow one. What he was suffering, she endured as well. Her awareness of him was so acute it alarmed as well as stimulated. She absorbed his heat. She was charmed by the rhythm of his heartbeats, a pulse so strong it commanded hers to follow in sync. The well of his loneliness was so deep and dark, falling into it was to give up hope to the swallowing of despair. She couldn't bear the totality of his grief.

"What can I do to help ease your hurt?"

Cassie whispered that impulsively, compulsively, as if the need to offer was something out of her control. She had to give him aid, she longed to supply relief. It was the only purpose behind her pounding heartbeats, the only reason of her being.

"You can leave me to my sorrow. It is not something I can share. Not yet."

Every thread of her will protested the thought of leaving him. She clung a moment longer, confused by the strong, almost desperate need to be near him. It was as if her love of independence was gone, as if the only freedom found was here in his presence, doing for him. Her sense of self was one small fiber caught up in the web of his will, woven so tightly within the network of his being, that her only strength came in the fabric of the whole. And the fact that she could so readily accept that made for a deeper panic. What was happening to her? When had he become her entire world?

Attuned to her distress and not unmoved

by it, Louis lifted one of her clutching hands in his to press a light kiss upon it.

"Go upstairs and prepare for me."

That softly spoken command rippled through Cassie like tongues of urgent fire. *Prepare for me.* That could only mean one thing. He was coming to her bed.

Alone, Louis lingered by that front curtain, battling the squeeze of his anguish, the pull of the night. Then when his spirit was calm, he noticed, as he hadn't before, another presence near him. This one was not in the house, but rather kept to the shadows outside, a stealthy prowler hugging to the foundation. He could detect a heartbeat, could taste its hurried tempo of intensity and fear. Could sense a spice of something else, something bitter. It was rage.

Who are you?

Louis sent out that demand like a bolt from a bow and he experienced the shock of impact. Then . . . then nothing. The intruder was gone as was the impression of danger.

Had it been Cassie's mysterious stalker? A tremor of anxiousness overwhelmed him at the thought of threat to her. His first impulse was to rush upstairs to assure himself that she was all right. But he didn't, not right away. Because as much as he was disturbed by the midnight prowler outside, he feared the midnight predator within himself all the more.

Twelve

Mourning garb was returned to the cupboard, and with that conscious act Cassie said her goodbyes to her grieving for Arabella in order to concentrate on fulfilling her vow. The past had to be put behind in order to proceed with the future. And her future would soon be arriving at her chamber door. Cassie was a-dither with nervousness.

What she was doing was craziness. What she was allowing was scandal. Yet she could no sooner stop it than she could bring Arabella Radcliffe back from the dead. She was five and twenty with no prospects for romance. If she didn't grab at this opportunity, she might never again have the chance to experience the mysteries of physical love. And who better to experiment with than the man to whom she'd already pledged her heart?

She'd listened to lectures on free love, and though her independent mind agreed to the wisdom of a woman's choice, her virginal modesty quailed when confronted with the actual fact. Her relationships with the opposite gender were chastely confined to business, other than those searing kisses with Louis. Those had her eager to discover more. This night she would have all her answers and a live-in lover besides. Even the most liberal-minded females of the day would blush at her behavior. She couldn't let that matter, not now. Not when she was about to be granted her heart's desire. Now was not the time for timid reflections upon a morality she'd always considered single-sided and grossly unfair.

Tomorrow she would be a fallen woman. She was surprised that she should feel such a variance of will. Wasn't Louis everything she wanted? Wasn't this the straightest mode of winning him as a husband?

Maybe not.

A whisper sounded in the back of her mind that men didn't marry women they could have upon a whim.

But wasn't it a bit late to be crying off for propriety's sake? And did she really want to?

Cassie finished disrobing and slid her pristine cambric gown over flushed bare skin. As she tied the dainty powder blue ribbon fasteners over her bosom and at the base of her throat, she wondered if Louis would soon be pulling them loose again. A suspenseful thrill shook through her. Would he find this gown, with its girlish modesty, pleasing? Would he find her pleasing?

And even as she puzzled over those questions, a deeper truth unfolded. She would not, could not, deny him anything. Not because of the strength of her attraction but because of her weakness of will.

And Cassie frowned at her reflection. What had happened to the big claims she'd made to Arabella about her ideal man allowing her her freedom? Louis said, "Prepare for me," and she was scrambling witlessly to please him. Without thought. Without choice.

She had let him into her house, this man she barely knew and scarcely trusted. She'd allowed him to embarrass her in front of his family and his servant, to take control of the premises and of her very life. And she was about to let him take the most personal liberties a man could take with a woman without a word of his regard, without a promise of tomorrow.

Had she gone entirely mad?

Was she slipping into that coma of confusion that ultimately claimed her mother?

A churning fright rose like ice cold water to drown out excited expectation. Cassie stared at her own reflection as if seeing herself for the first time. When had she gotten so pale? When had her eyes become sunken shadows? She hardly knew that woman peering back so wanly from her glass. Somehow, over the last few days, she'd lost the essence of her vitality and with it, just possibly, her grip upon what was real. The long gaps in her memory, the remembered whisper of fear, the strange episode of illness that wasn't like any sickness she'd ever heard of. And now this fading strength of will. What was happening to her? Why was she so complacent about the mystery surrounding her guest? And the danger?

Shivering as an inexplicable weakness followed that numbing chill, Cassie sought her covers and lay there tense and trembling. There was something very wrong in her obsession with Louis Radcliffe. Yet she knew she wouldn't turn him away if he came to her this night. She hugged her blankets about her and shut her eyes, praying he would not come, longing for the moment when he would join her.

But the conflict of her heart couldn't forestall the weariness of body and by the time Louis opened her door, she was soundly sleeping.

"What am I to do with you, *cara mia?*" The fury and self-absorbed misery of the night before was gone as if seeing his Arabella placed in the ground was a freeing catharsis of the blame, if not the guilt. To that point, he'd allowed himself to wallow briefly in the dark basics of his kind, thriving on mindless instinct when reality was too much to bear. Seeing his family had called him back to reason. And made him shamefully aware of how poorly he was treating his sheltering hostess.

He realized now, belatedly, that Cassie Alexander hadn't hastened his wife's death. Time had done that, time and Arabella's devotion to him. And now he was alone again and that thought plainly terrified him. Was that the reason for his attraction to the slumbering beauty? If only it were that simple. Even before Arabella's passing he feared what he wanted from Cassie was more than a reminder of the past, more than the lure of the blood.

Wanting her felt like a betrayal to her who had been loyal for so long.

He walked to the edge of the bed and settled there to watch her sleep. It would be easy to invade her dreams, to fill them with erotic images, to fill her with unwholesome desires. To make her his slave, as he'd boldly claimed below.

What an arrogant, self-serving creature he'd become in the thrall of pain and loneliness. How uncomplicated to take without asking, to control without commitment. How frightening to admit the want to belong again with heart, with soul, with spirit to another woman the way he had with Arabella. Not the same way. There would never be another Arabella Howland Radman. But there could be a future. It was what Arabella had wanted. It was why she'd chosen her grue-

some end at the hands, or rather the appetite, of his obliging friend.

"Bella, I don't want this," he moaned
aloud even as a denying quiver of passion
stirred within him. "I did not ask for you
to find me another and place her irresistibly
in my way. It was not my choice to give way
to temptation, but now that it is done, what
would you have me do? I cannot love this
woman without betraying what I had with
you. But neither can I walk away now that
we are bonded, one to the other. She is my
safety just as I promised you I would be
hers. Let me be strong enough to remain
faithful to your memory."

He was answered by a deep quiet, not an
emptiness but rather a feeling of self, and
with that self was the tentative link he'd
made to Cassie Alexander.

"No. Take this temptation away from me
before we are both destroyed." But there was
no one to grant his plea. Only the soft hush
of Cassie's breathing and his damned awareness of the warmth throbbing in her veins.

It was too soon to take from her again.
He'd been careless the first time and she'd
nearly not recovered. If she was to serve
him, she would have to be strong. If he was
to resist her, he'd have to keep a judicious
distance. Not easy when they both resided
under the same roof. Not simple when he
found himself studying the soft curve of her
lips while his parted in unbidden response.

He could not pledge his heart to another mortal. He could not suffer again as he did with Arabella that knowledge of time's irreversible passage. He could not commit to a future when all that lay ahead was an inevitable end. Nor could he in good conscience bring another over to endure the same curse of midnight that he carried over the centuries. That would be the ultimate in selfishness—damning another to assure a companion for eternity. He could not be as callous to the human right to mortality as Bianca du Maurier had been when she'd taken him for her own.

He had enough souls on his conscience already.

So what then could he do about his feelings for Cassie?

"Dio del cielo." He rose up restlessly and left her to her peaceful sleep. His own was hours away and he needed some distraction. He hadn't much interest in exploring his new surroundings before. Perhaps now would be a good time to get acquainted with more than just the cellar.

Cassie's home was a testimony of wealth but not necessarily taste. It had the latest conveniences: hot water from the taps, a large bathroom, a telephone that was linked to the 9,000 odd in Manhattan. The kitchen was awful and gaslight hadn't yet given way to the mellow burn of electricity. The style of room decoration was years out of date and quite terrible; a heavy mess amusingly called Renaissance. He couldn't remember such gaudy grossness from his own era. Furniture had Baroque weight, rococo curlicues and Oriental flourishes, each with inlays of metal, wood and porcelain, overwrought with arabesques, carved fruit, animal claws and human busts in supports and for ornamentation. Red velvet and burgundy satin masked windows and swaddled plump sofas and chairs. Add to that the suffocating clutter of embroidered footstools and fussy tatting draped upon every horizontal surface and enough stiff brocade to service the Orient and it made for an uncomfortable mishmosh both lavish and offensive. He knew art and recognized a number of costly pieces hung upon the walls, but they were thrown up for effect, not for any aesthetic value.

As he stood staring in disturbed curiosity at a trio of asphyxiated birds arranged upon dead flowers beneath the imprisoning dome of a bell jar, he wondered if Cassie realized just how hideous the whole of her home was. It made him think, not unkindly, of his young Florentine friend, Gerardo Pasquale, whose lust for possessions overwhelmed the proscriptions of good taste. Not born to wealth, Gerardo had loved things the grander and more ostentatious, the better. He'd never cultivated the sensitivity to appreciate a delicate brush stroke or the ear to catch a particularly exquisite arrangement of sound and cheerfully refused to absorb instruction. But Louis had loved him in the way of friends who were blind to one another's faults. He missed Gerard's flamboyance, his simple joy of living. The best part of being alive was having someone to enjoy it with. And now he had no one.

There was a slight stirring of air behind him. He turned into a passionate embrace.

"I came as soon as I heard. Oh, Gino, I am so sorry."

He was so shocked, he didn't protest the hungry kisses that rained down from temple to cheekbone to fasten hotly upon his mouth. Once he'd struggled to fight his lust for the woman feasting off his lips. Had struggled and lost because he'd been a mere man and she a demon incarnate determined to have him. And still was. But he was no longer a mortal under the influence of vile magic. He tore his head back and glared into the face of her unholy beauty.

"What are you doing here?"

"Gino," she purred, "I came to be with you in your time of grieving. Isn't that what friends do?"

"We are not friends. We have never been friends." He pushed away from her clutching hands. But Bianca du Maurier only smiled.

"Perhaps it is better not to have friends when they serve up such treachery as to kill the one you love. What I cannot understand is why you allowed him to live to brag of it."

Brag? Gerard had bragged to his succubus companion of taking Arabella's life? That insinuation cut to the core of his heart. Then, before a new rage could rise and reheat his fever for retribution, he recalled the source of information. It was Bianca. And she never told a complete truth.

"That is between me and Gerardo. And it is an irony that you should bring it up at all. Why are you here? Did you come to gloat and torment me? If so, I am immune to your clever torture."

"Gino, so cruel you have become. Can you not believe that I came out of concern?"

"No."

That blunt reply curtailed the crooning seduction. Bianca observed him through cunning eyes and it was then he could see the flaws in her beauty; small scars yet remaining from the terrible burns she'd received at Marchand's hands when he'd come to wrest Nicole from her sinister influence. She had recovered well but not totally, and to one of Bianca's vanity it must have been a devastating cross to bear.

"So she is dead and you are at last free of mortal obligations. I came to offer you what you have always spurned in the past, a chance to live to the full potential of the glorious creature that you are. Come with me, Gino. Hunt with me. Keep me from an eternal boredom."

"And what of Gerard, your *innamorato?*"

"Gerard has become quite sulky of late. I fear a parting of our ways is imminent. Unless, of course, you would like it to be as it once was, with the three of us, together."

"There was no three of us. There were two friends betrayed by your demonic force. You caused a split that can never heal. I want no part of you or your mock sympathies. I want to be left alone."

Bianca smiled at him with a serenity that made him immediately wary. She'd pursued him for over three centuries. He wasn't about to believe she'd give up on the chase now. But that's what she pretended.

"Very well, Gino. Or do you still wish to go by Louis? I will leave you to your morbid thoughts and when you tire of them, I will return. Perhaps by then you will be of a mood to appreciate what I offer."

"What you offer is an obscenity I will never welcome."

She smiled wider. "We will see. We will see." And, like the Cheshire Cat, she left him with the illusion of her smile and the echo of her laughter.

Broadway north of Madison Square as far as 31st Street was lined with large new hotels and a bustling thoroughfare of progress. But where Sixth Avenue was intersected by Broadway and 33rd Street under the roaring of the el was the metropolitan night town, dingy by day and corrupt by dark. From 14th Street northward, it was a gaslit carnival of vice and depravity, where each shabby side street was packed with houses of prostitution, bawdy saloons and garish dance halls like the Cremorne, the French Madam's and the Haymarket, all vying for titles of evil repute in the district known as the Tenderloin.

In this atmosphere of decadence, no one paid much mind to the weaving figure of Quinton Alexander as he tottered out of yet another saloon. Normally, he would have appeared easy pickings for the cutpurses who roamed the streets, but one look at his expression dismissed the notion that he'd be a simple mark. His features were carved by harsh strokes of cunning, his eyes burned with a crazed inner fire. The thin smile crooking his sensitive mouth was more sneer than amusement and those who knew him steered others clear. He was no one a sane man tangled with. They said he was a fair enough drinking companion, free with his money when he had it, but when he was in the thrall of his favored narcotic haze, he was ruthlessly unpredictable.

If he was aware of the whispering, Quinton didn't react to it. His thoughts, his very being, were all focused on one thing—upon the remembered silhouette of two entwined together, highlighted against Cassie's parlor window.

How could she? Didn't she know how much he adored her? Didn't she realize that she was . . . his everything? He thought of all the sacrifices he'd made, the substitutes he'd sought for her affection. Did she know about the other women? Was she jealous? Was that why she'd fallen into the arms of another man? She had to realize the others meant nothing to him. They were offerings to placate his father, to temper his uncontrolled desires. They had nothing to do with the purity of his feelings for her. She was to be his salvation, his strength! She couldn't fail him, not now!

Just then his glazed stare caught upon a shiny blonde head and unconsciously he fell in step behind one of the saloon singers on her way to work. She was pretty, in a rather coarse way, but that pale coronet of hair, the way she smiled . . . She made him think of another. And he smiled.

She saw him looking and her dark eyes gleamed with a conniving brilliance. "Like what you're seeing, mister?"

"Oh, yes," he murmured back.

She slowed to let him catch up to her and simpered when he curled her arm in courtly deference through his.

"You are a beacon, my sunny miss. A veritable light of goodness that shines to lonely searchers such as myself within this bleak existence we call life."

She stared up at him a bit slack-jawed, then giggled. "My but you talk fancy."

"I make my living with words."

"Guess how I make mine?" And her free hand stroked over his taut abdomen, pausing just below the band of his trousers. Quinton smiled. "Creatively, I hope."

Again, she giggled, a truly annoying habit, but one could overlook it when lost down the spectacular valley between her upthrust breasts. "I'm done at the Canary around midnight." She studied his fine clothing as if visually weighing his worth before suggesting, "If you want to take me to dinner afterwards, I can show you. I have lots of energy after a good meal. And lots of imagination."

"I'm counting on it, Miss— "

"Flora. Flora Landers. Please ta meecha."

"The pleasure is mine entirely." He grinned because he was sure it would be.

And shortly after two o'clock in the morning, when he was wiping his damp blade off on the remnants of her petticoat, he knew it had been.

Thirteen

Cassie's bad mood in the office couldn't be attributed to too little sleep but rather to too much. Louis had never come to her. She awoke in confusion and alone. In a fit of impulsiveness, she decided to find her houseguest and demand an accounting . . . and couldn't find him.

None of the upstairs bedrooms looked as though they'd been slept in. She'd assumed he'd made himself at home in one of them while she was stricken with her odd illness. If he wasn't sleeping upstairs, where on earth was he resting?

Takeo had greeted her with his inscrutable bow.

"Where is Louis this morning?"

He just stared at her blandly.

"Where was he . . . last night?"

Again the unblinking gaze. She knew he understood her, he just didn't choose to communicate. She had no ill feeling toward the man who was simply acting in his employer's interest. Actually, she had to admit a debt of gratitude for his silent attentive care. Her own housekeeper had been pensioned off when Louis moved under her roof. He'd made it seem like a logical action; the woman was a terrible cook, worse at cleaning, and an irrepressible gossip. Did she truly want the goings-on within her house to be broadcast across the working class grapevine? And could she complain if Takeo was willing and better able to see to the same tasks with no expense to her own purse?

No, she couldn't complain. But she could chafe because the decision had been made without consulting her.

Frustrated, she had gone to work in the Radcliffe carriage and had stormed into the newsroom with the latest edition tightly rolled in one hand only to be informed that Fitzhugh wouldn't be in until that afternoon. She left a curt message that he was to come to her office the moment he arrived, then she closed herself up in her office to stew and worry. After her first two cups of varnish-stripping coffee, she sent for Walter Rampling, slapping his copy down upon her desk with a fierce, "Explain this."

He returned her glare mildly and said, "Fitz okayed it. You weren't available and he made the decision to go with it. You wouldn't believe the response we've been getting."

"Yes, probably from every ex-Bellevue resi-

Wish You Were Here?

You can be, every month, with Zebra Historical Romance Novels.

YOU'RE GOING TO LOVE GETTING

4 FREE BOOKS

These books worth almost $20, are yours without cost or obligation when you fill out and mail this certificate.

(If the certificate is missing below, write to: Zebra Home Subscription Service, Inc., 120 Brighton Road, P.O. Box 5214, Clifton, New Jersey 07015-5214

Complete and mail this card to receive 4 Free books!

Yes! Please send me 4 Zebra Historical Romances without cost or obligation. I understand that each month thereafter I will be able to preview 4 new Zebra Historical Romances FREE for 10 days. Then, if I should decide to keep them, I will pay the money-saving preferred publisher's price of just $4.00 each...a total of $16. That's almost $4 less than the publisher's price. (A nominal shipping and handling charge of $1.50 per shipment will be added.) I may return any shipment within 10 days and owe nothing, and I may cancel this subscription at any time. The 4 FREE books will be mine to keep in any case.

Name _____

Address _____ Apt. _____

City _____ State _____ Zip _____

Telephone ( ) _____

Signature _____
(If under 18, parent or guardian must sign.)

LP0595

A $19.96
value.
FREE!

No obligation
to buy
anything, ever.

dent in the city claiming to have sprouted fangs and, after doing the deed, disappearing in a puff of smoke or turning into some big bat or whatever it is your vampires are supposed to do."

"They are not my vampires and according to some of the best authorities at Bellevue, there are those running about who genuinely believe they must have human blood to survive."

Cassie gave a shudder. "Really, Walter. Now you're starting to sound as if you belong in one of those little rooms."

"I'm serious, Cass. Only there are no fangs involved, of course. Instead of finding the literal twin puncture wounds at the base of the neck, they use a thin-bladed knife to sever the jugular and—"

"Thank you for the lesson. Now I want you to learn something of value. I own and run the *Lexicon,* not Fitzhugh. All decisions on copy go through me. Is that understood?"

"But Fitz gave me the go-ahead to do a follow-up article for the next edition."

"On my desk, and I will decide if it has merit."

"You know, Cass, this is turning out to be more than a lark. I've found out some things that—" Suddenly, he clamped his jaw tight.

"What things?"

"Read my next article," he challenged, and with a wave left her office.

Vampires. What nonsense. She sagged

back in her chair and rubbed her throbbing temples where a huge ache of tension was massing. Vampires, demons, disembodied voices, figures that appeared and seemingly disappeared at will. She was weary of it all. Where was her sensible world? What had happened to her feeling of control? She was feeling the pressure of the male-dominated society closing in about her; her uncle threatening her reign at the *Lexicon,* Louis ruling in her own home. One interfering with her business, one playing with her affections. She didn't like it. She wouldn't be ignored or treated lightly as if her opinions, rights, or feelings had no merit. And it was time both of these arrogant and powerful men knew of it.

By lunch time, she was in too great a state of nerves and aggravation to eat anything. By the time her uncle appeared at one o'clock, she was feeding on her own anxiousness. He and a rather ragged-looking Quinton settled in chairs on the other side of her desk. Fitzhugh had a lean, predatory gleam in his eye that bode ill for her confidence, but she launched right in determinedly.

"You have overstepped yourself, Uncle. You put out this issue against my express wishes and in doing so, seriously undermined the chain of command here at the *Lexicon.*"

"If anyone has undermined the line of authority, it's you, Cassandra. The staff is rapidly losing faith in your ability to fill your father's shoes."

"What?" She glanced at Quinton for a confirmation of this, but he wouldn't meet her eyes.

"In fact, while you were abed with your—illness, I called an executive meeting—"

"By what right—"

"—and I presented my ideas for the direction the *Lexicon* needs to take in order to survive. They were enthusiastically received. You're losing your control of the magazine, girl. If you're smart, you'll turn it over to me while we still can afford the presses to run each issue."

"Never!"

"A position of power is no place for a hysterical female."

"I am not hysterical!"

His cold, observing stare refuted that.

"I am not my mother. I do not suffer delusions. I have no intention of closing myself up in my house in a fit of raving paranoia. I own this magazine and I will conduct it in the manner of my father before me."

"You are not your father. His people trusted him even when the times were bad. I see no such following rallying behind your figurehead."

"Quinton, is this true?" she demanded of her sullen cousin.

He canted up a brief glance. "I'm afraid so, Cass."

Though the thought of desertion struck a dreadful fear into her heart, she managed to gather the pluck to say, "I don't believe you. I don't see our writers jumping to other projects like rats off a sinking ship."

"You will," was her uncle's dire prophesy. "And the *Lexicon* will fold or be eaten alive by its competitors. I didn't invest my life in it to see that happen. I will take control, with or without your permission."

"What kind of threat is that?"

He glared at her smugly. "No threat. I already have people working through legal channels to break Brighton's will. We'll see what breaks first, that ridiculous document or your resolve." With that, he pushed up out of his chair and stalked from the room without a civil word of parting.

Cassie sat frozen in her chair. Could he do what he claimed? Could he batter down the validity of her father's will? Panic thickened around her heart, squeezing out a desperate and despairing palpitation. She looked up in a daze at Quinton, who had refused to offer his support when she'd needed it yet was quick to offer his advice now.

"He can do it, you know. Your situation is just unique enough that the single throw of a rock could bring it all down around you."

That hardly inspired confidence!

"There is a way you can circumvent my father's plan," came his soft suggestion.

"Don't keep me guessing, Quinn. Throw me a rope for I'm ready to drown."

"If you want to solidify your claim upon the *Lexicon,* you need to give the court system an unarguable case. Marry and turn the control of the *Lexicon,* at least on paper, over to your husband."

She stared at him, agog.

"Don't you see," he continued with an impassioned fervor. "That way you can have it and no one can take it from you."

"No one except that convenient husband," she muttered resentfully.

"Not if I were that man."

Again, she could only stare, incredulous.

"Marry me, Cass. We could run the *Lexicon* any way you see fit. We could break my father's hold once and for all. Don't you see? It's the perfect solution to everything."

And he came around her desk to press his case more personally. He came down upon one knee, startling her so with his grand gesture that she almost began to giggle nervously. With a hand over her mouth to seal in an inappropriate response, she watched him work himself up into a dramatic declaration.

"It's always been the two of us together, Cass. Always, since we were children. We're different, you and I. We belong together in a world where no one else can appreciate us for who we are."

"Quinn, stop." She placed her fingertips upon his lips to still the flood of words. "No. You mustn't continue with this. I cannot marry you. We will always be friends but nothing more."

Though she made her rejection gentle, she could see the devastation well up in his eyes. And behind that hurt was something more, something she couldn't identify.

"I don't understand," Quinton said. "I thought—"

"What could you have thought, Quinton? There has never been anything romantic between us. Can you honestly say that you love me?"

He was silent for a moment then uttered a staunch, "Yes," much to her dismay.

"I don't think so. Not in the manner of real love."

"And you are an expert in that area, are you?"

The bite of his attack made it easier for her to say the rest. "I know what I want from the man I marry. I want strength and support. Those things you cannot give me. How could I entrust you with my future and that of the *Lexicon* when you couldn't stand up to your father just a minute ago? I need a man who will take a firm position beside me, unafraid. That man isn't you, Quinn. I'm sorry."

The look of wounded loss was gone from his expression. In its place was a glaze of hard belligerence. "And who is? Your new lover, I suppose?"

Cassie was too surprised to respond and he took her silence for an affirmative. Angrily, he climbed off his knees and gave them a brusque dusting.

"Well, I'm glad I could provide you with a moment's amusement anyway."

"Quinn—"

"Oh, please. Spare me the pitying rhetoric. I can take no as no. I'm that much of a man at least."

"Quinton, please—"

He waved off the rest of her appeal on his way to the door and in a moment was gone. Cassie leaned back in her chair, bemoaning how badly she'd handled both confrontations. What could possibly happen to put a darker cast upon the day?

Her answer was soon forthcoming as Tim entered her office carrying another package.

"Special delivery for you, Miss Alexander. And you expect me to believe you don't have a secret admi—"

"Put that down, Tim. On my desk!"

He complied slowly, startled by her abrupt behavior. "What is it? What's wrong?"

The breath jerked from her in painful spasms as she studied the familiar scrawl. As calmly as she could, she instructed, "Don't leave the newsroom, Tim, and don't talk to anyone until the police arrive."

"The police?" he yelped.

"Not a word!"

"Yes, ma'am."

Danny Hooper arrived within minutes of her call to find Cassie paralyzed within her chair, her fixed gaze held by the brown paper parcel.

"Like the others?" he asked softly. Her nod was faint but positive. "Have you touched it?"

"No. Tim, our delivery boy, just brought it to me. Open it."

"Maybe it would be better if I took it—"

"Open it, Danny! It was addressed to me. I have to know!"

Slowly, using his pocket knife, the sergeant cut the binding twine and unrolled the heavy paper. Inside was a lacy petticoat now starched with dried blood. Cassie swallowed hard and looked away.

"A note," she said in a strangled voice. "There should be a note."

Danny lifted the gory contents and found the single sheet.

"Read it."

"Cassie—"

"Read it!"

"It says, 'The price of betrayal is death. See for yourself behind the Canary on Sixth Street.' There's no signature. Is it the same handwriting?"

"Yes." That was a choked out whisper.

"Is this the first time there's been an implied threat to you?"

Again, the hoarse, "Yes."

"Cassie, I want to place you in protective care until this lunatic is found."

"No. That might scare him off. I'm— I'm not alone. Let's go." She began to gather up her cloak.

"Go? Where?"

"To Sixth Street."

"Cassie, you don't honestly expect me to let you go with me."

"Do you honestly think I would stay behind?" Her tone firmed with a professional logic. "This involves me, Danny. I'm supposed to go there. Something— worse might happen if I refuse."

He looked reluctant but finally relented.

Then Cassie was faced with finding the courage to sustain her bold assertion.

To make her father proud and continue her tenuous hold upon the *Lexicon*.

Fourteen

Another bloody gift. Another intimidating note. Another body with a face like her own.

Cassie got through the remainder of the day in a numb daze. Her mind throbbed from trying to make some sense of it. Her heart ached from all its frantic pounding. And her soul was raw from its cry of, *Why me?* The last thing she was prepared for was a confrontation with Louis Radcliffe and all the unanswered questions surrounding him as well.

She settled into the brougham beside him but not looking at him, a task not as easy as it would seem because just looking at him had deepened into a whole new level of enticement. She could feel his gaze intent upon her and the pull of compulsion to respond. She resisted it on principle because she was tired of having no control over the things that had happened to her that day. And she could feel his surprise.

"What has happened?"

The slight of waiting upon him the night

before piled atop all the other stresses left her testy and defensive. "Complications at work. Nothing that need concern you."

Her clipped tone must have taken him aback because he was silent for several miles and minutes. Then she gave a start as his palm cupped beneath her chin to direct her gaze about to meet his. His was dark and oddly intense, the flicker of green-gold lights hypnotic and as impossible to break from as the firm grip of his hand.

"You are not telling me the truth. I sense danger and fear. Tell me everything. You are my responsibility."

That sparked an angry burst of emotion within her, its flare hot enough to burn through the enslaving dominance of his stare. She tossed her head, pulling from his grasp to look determinedly out the other side of the carriage. Her voice was low and frigidly edged. "I am no such thing. I am in control of my own life, sir, and do not care to give it over to the handling of some narrow-sighted man. I've turned down one such offer already today and am in no humor to entertain another."

"What do you mean? What kind of an offer?"

"One I am thinking I should accept if I knew what was good for me and the *Lexicon*. Perhaps I misspoke myself too soon. Perhaps a woman is not meant to control an empire

but can only control it behind the figurehead of a man."

"Please try speaking clearer now, madam."
And the stiff slice of his tone was too much.

Cassie swiveled upon the seat to cut him
with a direct glare of her own. "I am speaking of acting sensibly, of using the regiments
of this unfair world instead of struggling
against them. I am a female on my own,
prey to every manner of male who thinks to
impose his will upon me. Had I the strength
of a married name behind me, none would
dare take such bold advantage."

Louis blinked, his expression totally bewildered. "Married?"

"Does the thought of a man's interest in
me so surprise you? I am not totally without
charm or merit."

"I did not suggest that you were—"

"And I am also in control of a fairly in-
fluential magazine. Not a bad dowry, if one
can support the debt."

Louis's attitude had grown chill, his eyes
aglitter like emerald chips. "And whose generous offer are you considering?"

"If it is any of your business—"

"It is."

She fumed for a moment at his bold claim
and just when she was about to give him a
proper verbal filleting, a wild thought occurred to her. He was jealous. Fiercely, furiously jealous. And the idea of his
possessiveness pleased her enormously. But

of course, she could not let him know that.
She narrowed her eyes and gave her head a
haughty toss. "You are again mistaken. We
are bound together by an old woman's
wishes. Nothing more." Her stare challenged
him to say it was more while her heart battered a hopeful volley within her breast.

"You are wrong, Cassie," came his soft
drawl, as soothing and sensuous as a physical
caress along the heart strings. "What binds
us is stronger than vows and deeper than
eternity."

She was trembling. Her gaze danced nervously away. "You're speaking in riddles."

"No, in truths. Look at me, Cassie."

She couldn't, suddenly afraid— of what he
might say, of what he might see in her unguarded gaze.

"Look at me."

And that command was as hard to resist
as a physical force. She turned toward him,
painfully aware of her flushed cheeks, but
he didn't notice them. He was fixed upon
her eyes. His drew her in with a mesmerizing power, relaxing her denying tension,
calming her anxious fears. Looking into his
eyes was like falling into her soul.

"We are one, Cassie. You can feel that,
can't you? You are mine now. Can you deny
it?"

She sucked in a fragile breath and whispered, "No." Because she *could* feel it even

if she couldn't explain it. "I-I don't understand."

"You don't have to understand. You only have to believe."

And the swirl of his power engulfed her senses, teasing her with strange prickles of awareness— of him as a man, of him as more than just a man. That was where confusion arose. What else was he? What could give him that kind of control over her sensibilities? Because she lived a life of asking questions and seeking answers, it went against her grain to blindly accept what was before her. Even when she was under a smothering pressure to do just that. She blinked hard and struggled against his spell.

"W-what are you doing to me?" she demanded with a gathering sense of self. With it came the scary realization that the emotional chords she was reacting to were being played outside her mind. "Is it some sort of hypnotism?"

He smiled blandly and continued to seduce her with his brilliant gaze. "No cheap magician's trick, I assure you."

"Stop." That was said with a wavering certainty, so she took a deep breath and tried again with more authority. "Stop it!"

"But I am only giving you what you want. Why are you protesting?"

His logic was inescapable and Cassie could feel her will weakening. Frantically, she sought an argument. "It's not what I want!"

"No?" That word was edged with subtle mockery and he began to lean toward her. She meant to draw back, to maintain the distance, but she was unable to move.

"I don't want to be owned by a man. I want to be loved by him." But even as she made that claim, her breath was slowing into long languid pulls and her eyelids were sinking down with a luxurious expectation. And when his mouth touched to hers, reason failed her.

"You wanted me, now you have me. The degree of possession should not concern you."

But it did. That last flare of independence flickered and was momentarily extinguished beneath the consuming rush of her desire as his kiss grew in intensity, devouring, overpowering all protest. She surrendered to it with a whimper because it was a force too strong to reckon with. Arguments of the will could not hold against barriers the heart and mind had already conceded. Cassie closed her eyes and opened her soul, letting the essence of him overtake her. And then she had to wonder dreamily why she had objected at all.

A heavy wave of sensuality washed over her senses, feelings so erotic, so intense, they frightened her with their fierce craving for him. Thoughts as foreign as his mysterious power flooded into her enraptured mind—submission unto death. Anything, anything to please him. A sudden frenzied need to satisfy him, to . . . nourish him.

Mindless of the fact that they were in an open carriage in mid-Manhattan, Cassie threw back her head and loosened the ties holding her cloak together against the chill of the night. She was warm, too warm, and the desire to feel the darkness upon bared flesh was like a madness. She tore open the collar of her stylish gown, exposing the column of her throat right down to the upper swell of her pale bosom. And she moaned in ecstasy as the breeze teased over her flushed and feverish skin.

But it wasn't enough. She needed, desperately, to feel him there. Her hands caught at his head, pulling him to her in an agony of bliss, her soft cries becoming close to orgasmic as his cool lips fixed upon the arch of her neck and a swift, fleeting pain brought her to a soaring pinnacle of release.

She held to him as long as she could, giving to him of her body while he was filling up her soul. Then a fuzzy strengthlessness began to climb, weakening her limbs until they fell useless at her sides, weakening her breath until it came in soft shallow sighs. Finally there was peace, a drifting sense of emptiness as her head rested heavily upon his shoulder and their carriage sped on through the night.

The brilliance of Broadway rushed past her bleary eyes. Dark shapes that were carriages and omnibuses streaked past her, their different colored running lamps dancing down the boulevard like scores of fireflies. Brightly lit shop windows and the glare from huge hotels poured forth a stream of radiance to dazzle her swirling senses. White rays shot from the reflectors outside a line of theaters, making the walks glow bright as daylight as they came alive with people bent on their pleasures. Cheerful voices, merry laughter, entwined with the strains of music and scattered applause that floated out the doorways to hang upon the air like midnight perfume. Restaurants blazed in invitation and upon the street corners, small crowds gathered to listen to the songs of wandering minstrels working for a hatful of coins.

Then as they passed several blocks beyond Canal Street, the world grew dark and silent and Cassie was lost within the vastness of a sensory void.

"She is beautiful, Gino. Who is she?"

Louis betrayed no surprise as the figure of a woman appeared on the seat opposite. She folded back her hood, revealing the haunting loveliness of Bianca du Maurier.

"No one," he claimed as the black stare settled menacingly upon the woman cosied against his side.

"No one, indeed." Her laugh was brittle. "I am to believe that?"

"I don't particularly care what you believe. I am not your business."

"You will always be my business, Gino. You will always belong to me. I will allow no interference ever again." And a cold glitter in her obsidian eyes bode ill for Cassie Alexander.

"Really, *cara,* so dramatic." Gerardo was suddenly seated on the other side of the dazed mortal woman. "Gino is not one of a fickle nature. He would not so soon forget the woman who loved him so well. Would you, Gino?" And his chill, nearly colorless stare pierced right to Louis's guilt-ridden soul.

"She provides me with a place to stay and whatever else I might require. Beyond that, she means nothing." He made that indifferent claim and dared Gerard to challenge it. Bianca sat back to watch them spar with wills, as entertained as she was jealous.

Gerard released a slow, provoking smile, delighting in his friend's dilemma. If Louis displayed an undue interest in the woman, Bianca would slay her in a possessive fit of fury. If he cared for her, he would not try to protect her and that was what Gerard was counting on.

"If she means no more to you than the next mortal, you will not mind sharing her with an old friend." And he put his arm about Cassie's waist in a snug circle, never looking away from Louis's impassive face. "I guess he doesn't mind, *cara mia.*" He tugged and Cassie came away from Louis's side with a murmur of complaint to sag into Gerard's embrace. Louis never betrayed a flicker of reaction much to his friend's amusement.

"You see," he told Bianca. "Faithful Gino has no eyes for any other. Your cause is lost, my love. You cannot steal him from a ghost any more than you could take him from his bride."

And with a low chuckle, Gerard bent over Cassie to purr, "I promised you a dream, did I not?"

Vaguely aware that she and Louis were no longer alone in the carriage but not conscious of any separate entities, Cassie gazed up in search of that crooning invitation only to be snared in the glimmer of Gerard's pale gaze. Like a helpless victim frozen on light-flooded tracks as an el bore down upon them, she could no more express her disapproval than she could pull away as Gerard overwhelmed her with his cold kiss and enveloped her in the fullness of his dark cloak.

Nor did Louis have time to react as both figures were surrounded in the flat black fabric then magically were gone from the seat beside him. He looked to Bianca, holding to his stoic expression though his spirit screamed with alarm. Damn Gerard and his theatrics. If he harmed Cassie . . .

"Are you satisfied, *il nemico?*" came his icy drawl.

She gave him a small, unconvinced smile and a serene, "I wonder," then was gone.

* * *

Cassie fell back upon her bed, limp as the stems of the white rosebuds on her dressing table that had been picked too soon to ever open. The room whirled about upon senses lost to time and place. And a cold settled over her, a cold that seeped right through the cloak and garments she yet wore, through flesh and muscle and bone. A cold that was death in the form of Gerardo Pasquale.

"So it was for you that he was so willing to cast off his eternal bride."

The silky sinister tones played about her mind expecting no response. She tried to drag up her eyelids but the struggle was too much. The best she could manage were slight slits which revealed a dark shape hovering over her. Alarm quivered through her like a mild shock.

"She was extraordinary, you know, far and above the cut of you insignificant mortals. She had . . . worth. And now she is gone and Gino thinks to supplant her precious memory with one such as you. A blasphemy, that's what it is. A betrayal I would not have believed of him. One I would never have made were she mine. But she wasn't mine, never mine. I would have cherished her and held her spirit up to the heavens like a goddess. I would not have put away her memory with things past to go on to a pale comparison. You will never be what Arabella was."

Cassie heard but didn't understand. Arabella. He spoke as if he loved her, a woman three times his age. If it made sense, her dizzy thoughts couldn't grasp the obvious. But she did cling to enough presence of mind to understand the threat lacing through his tone, to fear the cool stroke of his fingertips along her cheek and down her throat.

"You do not deserve the honor he bestows upon you. You will not take her place."

And his strong fingers gathered to press down the column of her neck, his thumb pushing her chin to one side so his breath could feather like a blast of icy breeze over bare skin. She couldn't fight him. She could scarcely move her lips to whisper one word.

"Louis . . ."

"Is it because she is mine that you find you absolutely must have her?"

Gerard paused in his purpose to regard his old friend. Louis stood on the opposite side of the bed, making no move to intercede. The dark Italian chuckled. "But you have always had such exquisite taste in everything, Gino. I could do worse than to follow in your example." His gaze, his touch, caressed the woman upon the bed almost lovingly. "Like this one. She is *magnifica*. Such beauty, such spirit, such fire. How could I argue with your choice?"

"One would think after all these centuries you would have developed your own opinions, Gerard, instead of blindly feeding upon mine."

"An amusing play on words. Ah, *bell'amico*, you try to provoke me, no? I was merely stating that I admire your choice. It is your timing I object to." And then his amiable facade fell away. His pale gaze glittered with a mercurial brilliance. "You shame her memory, Gino. I had expected better from you who claimed to love her."

Her confusion deepening along with the intensity of their conversation, Cassie surrendered her struggle for consciousness knowing Louis was there to protect her, trusting him even when he could not trust himself.

Seeing her go slack upon the bed, Louis assumed an aggressive posture, casting off his ploy of disinterest. One twist of Gerard's wrist, one slash of his razor-sharp teeth and Cassie would be gone from his life, too. Suddenly, that was too great a risk to take.

"Leave her alone, Gerard. Your quarrel is with me. She was Arabella's friend, the only one she had. Harming her would be a slap to my wife's memory from one who has vowed to respect it. Would *you* so shame her with this senseless act?"

Gerard was still for a long moment, his hand yet curled about Cassie's throat, his head yet bent at a predatory angle. Then slowly he began to smile. "I never had the mental quickness to best you in a duel of wits, did I, Gino? I miss those times we had as friends. Do you ever think back to them?"

"No."

With an exaggerated sigh of regret, Gerard looked down upon Cassie's softly composed features. Almost to her rather than Louis, he said, "I have been guilty of many wrong things but this will not be one of them." And he eased his hand away, sliding backward as he did and off the bed. "One cannot hold on to the past, Gino. The curse of our kind is going ever onward and leaving all we love behind. *Arrivederci, amico mio.* Would that I could go back to make things right between us. Ah, well."

And his image began to fade, the color ebbing from it to the point of translucence. Then that shimmer dissolved into swirling motes that vanished like dust upon the wind.

Louis waited until the prickle of disturbance in the air was gone before crossing quickly to the bed. He forced himself to act without thinking, without feeling, as he knelt down to touch his fingertips to the base of Cassie's throat. There he found a faint pulse of life.

"Grazie di Dio," he breathed aloud then let the shivers of restraint work through him to the point of a weak relief. He hadn't dared admit to the feelings flowing through him, not until he was faced with the thought of Cassie's demise. Gerard forced him with a

thrust to the heart to realize how much the fragile mortal had come to mean to him. More than just a next meal. More than a simple refuge.

He wasn't staying with Cassie to fulfill a promise to Arabella. He was staying because he wanted, needed, to be with her. She was his reason for continuing on. He smiled wryly. Just as his very clever Arabella had intended.

But how long could he encroach upon Cassie's life without revealing what he was? How long before he exposed her to the danger of his past? His spirit was wounded by loss and it was so easy to seek his comfort here with her gentle and passionate soul. But what could he give her in return? A loss of self? The possible sacrifice of her very life? He'd allowed one woman he loved to make that choice already. How could he live with the pain of leading another down that same shadowed path?

He wouldn't if he loved her.

And that was the hell of it.

The barrel house was stale with smoke and unwashed bodies pressed close around the bar. Quinton Alexander hunched over his nickel slug and stared moodily into the amber liquid brimming in his shot glass. The liquor was most likely cut with prune juice and water then revitalized with a generous dash of cayenne but after five of them, what did it matter? He wanted to feel his money's worth burning all the way down to the unsettled clench of his gut.

She'd said no.

Just like that, ruining everything.

How could she? He knocked back the fiery drink and grimaced as it collided with the others.

It was that man, her neighbor, the one making intimate silhouettes upon her draperies with her. It was his fault. He was distracting Cassie from her true purpose at Quinton's side. Otherwise, smart woman that she was, she would have realized his solution was the only viable one. The two of them together, united in an infallible force.

Let his father try to manipulate things then!

But there would be no two of them, no unified front because some slick-talking trespasser had slid into his spot. He'd been dreaming as long as he could remember of that big house and the seat at the head of the *Lexicon's* table. Both empty and waiting for a man to fill them. That man was going to be him. And Cassie was soon going to realize it. Then she would appreciate all he'd done for her— for them both.

"She should, you know."

Quinton gave a startled hop as a female voice answered his hidden thoughts. He glanced to the previously vacant spot beside him to find a simply gorgeous woman standing there. With hair as bright and blonde as the midday sun. Hair like Cassie Alexander's.

He smiled.

"Were you talking to me?"

"You are the only one in this wretched place worth communing with. I could feel that all the way from the door."

"Really?" He smirked. Nice line.

"You are the man I've been looking for, the one who could partner me through eternity."

That was a new twist! Quinton peered at her more closely. She had black eyes— solid black! And completely opaque, without a hint of reflection, without the glimmer of a soul. Alarm started to worm its way up to his sodden brain. This woman was not the usual tart who hung about in the seedy district of sin. She was sin itself.

"I'm waiting for someone else," he muttered, hoping she would just fade away so the hair on the nape of his neck would resettle.

"I know what you're waiting for, Quinton."

That she knew his name astonished him. That she knew his dark heart terrified him.

"I can give it to you, all of it. The woman, the dream, the revenge. Isn't that what you were looking for in the bottom of that glass, a way to make it all happen?"

Quinton's throat was suddenly dry with fright but his cold mind was whirring on ahead, feeding on her silky words. "And how will you do that?"

"Oh, my dear, I can do anything. I am what you might call your guardian angel." She smiled and nodded, liking that turn of phrase very much. "You have what I want and I can give what you want. Can you think of a better match than that?"

"And what is it that you want?"

"Your devotion."

"Lady, I don't even know you."

"Yes, you do." She laughed softly and leaned in close, capturing him in the black pool of her gaze. "Look into your heart and I am there. Look into your soul and I am the darkness showing it the way to hell. Look into your mind and I am there, delighting in their fear, in their struggle, in their death right beside you."

Quinton stared, aghast, then looked about to see if anyone had overheard her vile insinuations. All were contentedly drinking and carrying on their conversations. Odd, how none of the men were ogling a woman of such refined beauty in their midst. It was as if he were the only one she appeared to. And that was when terror sank in deep.

She was there for him, the punishment for his crimes.

"My God!"

"Don't involve Him in this," she crooned. "We both turned our backs on Him long ago. We are damned, you and I, so why not make the best of it? I can teach you things, show you things. I can give you the gift of immortality. Think of it."

Slowly, Quinton's fear fell away as he did just that.

Immortality.

"What do I have to do?"

"Exactly as I tell you."

Fifteen

Cassie awoke with no idea of how she had gotten to bed. Or how she'd gotten home from the city.

When she tried to sit up, she found the sense of weakness had returned, and with it came the flood of fright. The terror that she was losing control of her life.

She glanced about her bedroom. The door to her cupboard was slightly ajar and inside she could see yesterday's gown neatly hung away. She was wearing her sensible combination underwear beneath her sheets. A sudden fierce tremor shook through her and she clutched the covers up under her chin until the terrible chill of panic subsided. Who had put her to bed?

Moving slowly, cautiously, Cassie eased out from under the covers and sat upon the edge of her bed. Her body felt curiously drained of energy and her head was spinning. What was happening to her? The only possible solution that came to mind filled her with a consuming terror.

She forced herself to get up and dress even though her overwhelming impulse was to crawl back under the covers for a day of hibernation. Even managing the strokes of her brush was an effort but she refused to succumb to the weakness. As long as she could continue her regular routine, she held the inevitable at bay. So continue she would.

She dressed in a dove gray breakfast jacket of cashmere with lace at the cuffs and a waterfall of it zigzagging down the front. Gathers at the neck and waist created a flattering female silhouette and she was glad for the choice when she started down the stairs and discovered Louis waiting for her at the bottom in the pooling shadows of early morning. He didn't speak but continued to watch her descend, his expression inscrutable. Until her ridiculously watery knees failed her and she stumbled, having to grab for the rail to keep from rolling down the flight of steps into a heap at his feet.

He was instantly at her side, one arm curling about her waist in support, the other curving about her shoulders to pull her gently, firmly, against the solid strength of his body. She wanted to draw away, to assert her own independence but she was so aggravatingly helpless.

"Let me take you back up to your room," he murmured softly.

Cassie's reaction was immediate and almost violent. "No! I will not go back to bed!"

"All right. I'll help you down to breakfast then. Lean on me. Trust me. I won't let you fall."

She hadn't much choice. She couldn't navigate the stairs alone. Knowing that put a point to her anxiousness and by the time he steered her into the breakfast room, she was shivering with distress and agitation.

"Don't be afraid," Louis urged gently. But his reassurance did nothing to alleviate her anguish. She was clutching at him, losing her fight against the swelling terror.

"W-what happened last night?"

"What do you mean?"

"How did I get here? I remember nothing of the trip, of the evening, of how I got into— I remember nothing at all."

He moved her gradually over to the settee where he settled them both in a close proximity. He wouldn't let her move away from him, the circle of his embrace loose but unbreakable. His lips were pressed to her temple. She could feel the warmth of his breath stir her hair when he spoke his calming words.

"You suffered a minor collapse in the carriage. Nothing to fret over. Just fatigue and worry. Stresses anyone would fail before. It was rest you needed so I saw you— comfortable."

He'd put her to bed. He'd removed her

clothing, her shoes, her stockings, the rest.
Cassie's face was burning where he held it
to his shoulder. But having Louis Radcliffe
see her in her undergarments was the least
of her concerns.

"Collapse, you say. Did I faint?"

"Something like that. Don't distress yourself. I would not let anything happen to you,
Cassie." And he held her tighter, his manner, his voice, all soothing and cossetting as
if to a child. A weak rebellion sparked
within her. She shoved away from him.

"I will not be cooed over, sir. I am not
some frail creature in need of your patronizing attention."

To her dismay, she saw he was smiling
slightly.

"Do not laugh at me!"

He sobered immediately. "I assure you, I
was not. I admire you very much for your
self-sufficiency."

She stared at him, suspicious, wondering
if he was yet mocking her, but he seemed
sincere enough. Well, she didn't feel self-suf-
ficient at the moment. She felt helpless and
scared and frustrated by her own lack of
concentration or control. And determined
not to let him see it. She smiled thinly.

"I'm afraid I am not a very good hostess
this morning."

"Don't concern yourself over it." His hand
moved against her hair, the gesture disturbing more than it quieted.

"I must not have recovered as fully as I'd hoped from my earlier illness."

"I'm sure that's all it is." He was watching her closely, his eyes warm with worry, his smile contrarily calm.

"I'm not usually so vaporish," she rambled on in growing upset. She'd said that to him before. Hadn't she? All was becoming jumbled in her head. She could find no proper order, no logical sequence of events. It seemed as though months had passed since they'd laid Arabella to rest and Louis had come to stay with her, but it had been only days. Days. And she was so disoriented, she could remember less than half that time. And her illness of the body? Not like any she'd ever known. But she'd seen the symptoms before. And a frantic desperation kept growing, a want to deny it.

"You don't have to apologize," Louis was saying, but she felt the need to make him understand this was not normal behavior for her. Something was wrong . . . very wrong.

"I don't know what could have come over me." Then her breath gave a sudden hitch and her carefully crafted composure shattered. She could no longer pretend. Sobs shuddered up through her as she turned her head away from him. "That's not true. I do know what's wrong."

Louis went completely still. "Oh? And what is the name of your malady?"

"A flaw in the family, one inherited from

my mother." Cassie took a fractured breath and told him all.

Her mother was from a very wealthy and overweaned family, blue bloods, all. She had the necessary requirements of the day; she was fragile and beautiful with a head full of wit and little else. She believed nothing could be tasteful unless it was expensive, a dreadful misconception that still cluttered their mammoth home. She could play on the piano but didn't play the piano, spoke just enough French to be fashionable, spent winters in town with her family and summers in Newport, and her one purpose in life was never to disgrace herself.

"My father came up from nothing with a taste for the aristocracy. He thought it a grand idea to combine my mother's name with his business acumen, so he married her." She spoke of this softly as she had to no one before him. "Only wealthy marriages were tolerated, you see, and it was almost a crime to marry beneath one's standards. Society would not forgive my mother for her choice in men even though she spent much of her fortune trying to bribe his way in. Of course, he didn't care a fig for prestige. He was building his dream in publishing. I was born in a boardinghouse and raised in a hotel. We had no home until this one, my father's one surrender to Mama's push for respectability. She was sure a powerful address would assure a social success. She was wrong. Realizing she would be forever the outcast was too much for her in the end."

One day Eugenia Alexander took to her bed and never left it again. Brighton would have been content to let her go quietly, properly mad up in that room. He had little patience with weakness and had no idea how to deal with her. A doctor was retained, one who pronounced her a hopeless mental invalid and sure enough, the treatment he gave her provoked an increasing mania, delusions that frightened her young daughter and kept her husband at work long into the night. Finally, when the fits grew violent, the delicate Eugenia Alexander was shut away in a fashionable upstate facility where she would disgrace no one with her ranting. And Cassie had been cut emotionally adrift. She'd loved the flighty, fluffy-headed Eugenia but her loyalty to her father kept her distanced from her mother's plight. She wasn't allowed to visit and that loyalty prevented her from begging. And when her mother died, it was a guilty relief to both husband and daughter, neither of whom had ever forgiven themselves for not knowing how to help her.

"The doctor hinted that the affliction could be a weak link in my mother's family. Her grandmother suffered from it as did her great aunt before her. Now it would seem my poor mother has left me something other than her dwindling fortune. I am becoming a slave to her dementia."

"Nonsense," Louis pronounced firmly. "You are no more mad than I am."

She lifted teary eyes, her expression wild with resignation. "It's the only explanation, don't you see?"

"For what? Falling ill? Swooning with fatigue after several very trying days?"

She looked away in distress to admit quietly, "There are other things, too. Things that cannot be explained. Voices in my head, delusions of the most bizarre nature, gaps in my memory that leave me lost and uncertain of what I've done." The strong line of her shoulders faltered. "I don't know how to stop what's happening to me. Louis, I'm so afraid. I don't want to end up like—like my mother."

He swept her up in his arms, crushing her to the hard bastion of his chest, holding her there as tremors racked her body and terror tormented her mind. What could he tell her? That madness was not the name of her circumstance? That it was not her but rather the world around her that suffered from detours from reality?

"You are not mad, Cassie."

He sounded so convinced. She wished she could believe him.

As if he'd read her doubts, he held her away by a compelling grip on her shoulders. He stared down into her distraught features, commanding the fright-brimmed eyes to yield to his penetrating gaze.

"Cassie, you are not going crazy. You are the sanest person I know. You will accept that as truth."

And slowly, like a demon exorcised, the fear began to leave her. And an equally disturbing question remained. If not mad, how did she explain the events of the past weeks?

Louis felt the increasing brightness of the hour push against the tightly closed draperies. A mounting discomfort had him struggling against his need to console Cassie. He had only minutes left, then he would have to seek the safety of the cellar. Minutes to convince her that insanity existed without, and not within her.

"I'm losing everything, Louis," she whispered brokenly. "If not my mind then my very world. Events are moving out of my control. What am I to do? How can I keep my father's dream alive when I am terrified of its only salvation?"

"And what is that, *cara*?" The endearment slipped out quite naturally in his want to comfort her.

"If I can somehow make sense of this killer's plan, if I can aid in bringing him to justice, the story could be the instrument of saving the *Lexicon*. But the closer I get to the heart of the case, the more frightened I become of its conclusion. Louis, I am afraid that it's only a matter of time before I become this maniac's next victim."

Louis seized her damp face between his

palms as if he could contain her fear within the span of his fingers. His words were gruff with intensity. "Nothing will happen to you, Cassie. This I vow. I will not allow it. I will not lose another that I— I will not lose you."

She took a fractured breath, stunned by the possible meaning of his confession. "Louis, I— "

To halt the questions because there simply wasn't time to address them with the sunlight starting to heat and burn along his veins, Louis dragged her to him, silencing those uncertainties with a fiercely possessive kiss. She made a plaintive sound then a surrendering sigh that had him damning the daylight and his own guilt-ridden conscience that forced him to pull away.

"Louis, don't stop." That soft plea was issued through lips slightly swollen from the pressure of his own, from a heart as confused by longing as his own.

"I must."

"Why? Don't you— don't you care for me?"

What could he tell her? That the woman he just laid to rest was his wife of sixty-four years, not his grandmother as she supposed? That he, himself, was an unaging demon who'd already betrayed her naive trust by feasting off her blood? That madness was the preferable explanation to the truth? That if he remained any longer, he was in danger of becoming a pile of ash?

"I must go and time does not allow for an adequate answer. We will explore it in further detail this evening when I return."

He rose and Cassie fought the urge to clutch at him. "Where do you go?"

His smile gave a twist of irony. "To see to matters beyond my control. Do not take any foolish risks in my absence."

And because she looked so forlorn, so cast adrift by emotional rifts she could not understand, he let his palm caress her hair, her cheek, her throat.

"I more than care for you."

And while she stood rooted by that rumbly admission, Louis made his escape to the cool, impenetrable darkness that would house him until the twilight hour.

Cassie woke with a start, the abrupt jerk of her body as she came upright in her desk chair creating an avalanche from the mound of papers stacked next to her flailing elbow. Blinking her eyes to clear them, she grumbled an unladylike phrase and bent to retrieve the mess.

"I'll get those."

She peered up at Walter Rampling with a blank relief, then settled back in her chair as he scooped up the errant pages. That was the dozenth time she'd found herself dozing at her desk. She was beginning to wonder why she'd bothered to come in at all if she was going to drift through the day in a stupor. Consuming a pot of harsh black coffee had all the effect of warm milk at bedtime. She simply could not keep her eyes open or the thick batting of lethargy from cushioning her mind.

"Thank you, Walter. I seem to be awfully clumsy today."

He started to smile back, then his gaze was riveted to where she was rubbing her neck. His entire expression went tense with distraction.

"Was there something you wanted, Walter?"

"I—um, no, not really."

"How's your research going?" And she couldn't keep the tone of amusement from creeping into her voice.

Rampling looked anything but amused as he replied rather stiffly, "I'm discovering some unexpected details. Now it's just a matter of knowing how to use them."

"In good journalistic taste, Walter," came her mild rebuke. Then she closed her eyes for a moment, the glare of the office lights beginning a pulse of discomfort behind them.

"You look tired, Cass. Are you getting enough sleep?"

That fatherly concern touching her heart, Cassie was about to murmur her reply when she was perplexed by the intensity of his expression. "Yes, almost too much as a matter of fact. I'm fighting off a touch of influenza. It has me worn to an absolute frazzle."

"Maybe you should go home a little early and put your feet up."

"That's the best suggestion I've heard all day," she admitted with a sigh. "I think I'll do just that. I'm not doing any good here anyway. Do you think you'll have something for me before deadline? Surprisingly, we've gotten an abundance of mail on the subject. I guess you were right about the nature of the human mind for morbid subjects of curiosity."

But Rampling didn't smile in victory or show a sense of gloating pleasure. He was all rigid concentration. "I'll have something for you. Maybe something more than any of us suspected." And with that cryptic claim, he left her office.

Too weary to muse over her reporter's odd behavior, Cassie began to gather her materials to finish the necessary proofreading at home.

"Sneaking out early? Shame on you, Cass."

She glanced up at Quinton and offered a cautious smile. "All the extra hours are getting to me, I guess. But I won't be going home empty-handed." She patted the bulky satchel of paperwork. "I'll have to get two seats on the el—one for me and one for my relentless companion."

"Don't bother with the train, Cass. I'd be glad to take you home."

She hesitated, too well recalling their last conversation to feel comfortable with his suggestion. But her cousin was in amiable spirits, clear-eyed and seemingly without a grudge. And the idea of fighting for a space on the always-crowded el was less than appealing.

"I'd appreciate it if it won't put you out."

"Are you serious? Any excuse to escape this place." He helped her on with her wrap, his hands lingering just a second longer than necessary upon her shoulders before he picked up her papers and offered a gallant arm. "Shall we make our getaway?"

As their progress uptown was slowed by a snarl of conveyances, Cassie was aware of a growing restlessness of mood between them. Quinton was watching her with quick furtive cants of the eyes. It was hard for her to get a fix upon his attitude. He wasn't sulky, nor did he appear to be under the effects of any mind-altering influences. In fact, rarely had she seen him so lucid and sharp of wit. She just couldn't decide if it was a change for the better. This was a Quinton she didn't know— secretive, cunning, introspective.

As if he could read her concerns upon her face, he reached out to drape a companionable arm about her shoulders. It took all her resolve not to flinch away. He smiled at her and it wasn't a seductive gesture nor one of genuine good will. It was a smooth pull of facial muscles that implied no emotional involvement. And she was looking forward to the end of their ride together.

"I hope I didn't upset you yesterday with my blundering proposal." The meaningless smile widened. "It was ill-timed and, I see now, ill-conceived."

"You needn't apologize to me, Quinton. Let's just put it behind us, shall we?"

"If that's what you want, Cass, then by all means, let's forget the whole incident. I was unaware that your romantic interest was pegged elsewhere or I would not have put my case before you."

She stared at him blankly. "My romantic interest— ?"

"I assumed as much since the gentleman is residing with you," he drawled out dryly. "It's the talk of the entire office staff. Really, Cass, if I were you and struggling to maintain my control of the magazine, I would not put forth my private life into controversy."

Aghast, she sat open-mouthed at his suggestion. Everyone knew Louis was living under her roof. And all assumed she was carrying on with him in an improper fashion. Would that she was! Still, the stigma of their censure was not lost upon her. Unstable and immoral, that's what her uncle would be claiming. And that cry would not go unheard if he did go through with his threat to challenge her father's will.

There were only two ways she knew to escape the scandal to come— publish an exclusive on the killer's identity to send the *Lexicon*'s sale skyrocketing . . . or marry Louis Radcliffe to quiet gossip and preserve her control of the magazine through him. Of the two, she wasn't sure which would prove more difficult but she had no doubts as to which she would prefer.

Quinton was studying her and she could only hope her expression was suitably impassive.

"Thank you for your advice, cousin. You can be sure I will do whatever I can to hang on to what is mine."

And that seemed to satisfy him, for he was smiling to himself for the rest of their journey.

"What are you up to, *cara*? You have that look about you, that cat picking its teeth with canary bones satisfaction."

"Why Gerard, you always think the worst of me. Why is that?"

"Because it is usually the truth, is it not?"

Bianca smiled and said nothing as she brushed by him. She'd spent the past evening away and that was not like her. They were both careful never to let the dawn find them far from the protection of their lair. That was the reason they had lived so long. That and the fact that they trusted each other about as much as they trusted the world around them. Gerard was immediately suspicious of his lethal companion's good humor.

"This is about Gino, isn't it?"

"Gino! Everything does not revolve about Gino."

"Since when, my love?" And he continued to study her with a speculative eye. "Don't you think it's time you let go of that obsession? Carrying a cold torch for four centuries in hopes of finding a spark is a wasted effort, wouldn't you agree?"

For an instant, her glare gleamed black and malevolent then she came to put her arms about his neck and cooed, "How unkind of you to paint my failings in such pitiful colors. But do not fear, my interest is not in Gino."

"Oh?" He was so surprised, he let her press a cool kiss upon his lips without reacting to it. "Who then?"

"Jealous, pretty one? Perhaps you should be." She sauntered away with an enticing swing to her hips.

Gerard wasn't jealous. He was worried. "I will not let you interfere with Gino's hopes for happiness. You've done enough there already."

"Threats? From you, Gerardo? Since when have you had the nobility to carry through on your convictions? That would require character and you, my love, have none. Do not think to dictate to me. You overestimate your importance."

With that chill warning, she turned away, dismissing his words with a contemptuous tip of her head. And left him to a slowly mounting anxiety.

Sixteen

It was a habit ingrained over the decades, one that came without thought but rather straight from the heart. As Louis swung out of the box that housed him during the daylight hours, his first action was to look to Takeo and ask, "Bella, how is she this evening?"

The stricken look on his loyal servant's face didn't register for a moment. Then remembrance came swamping back and it was like confronting the pain all over again.

Master? Takeo placed his hand on Louis's arm in concern when he reeled away overcome by renewed despair.

It took a few minutes for him to find the composure to fix a tight smile of reassurance and say, "It's all right, Takeo. It just takes some getting used to, is all." And he climbed the stairs of his borrowed house, to get on with his pseudo-life, suddenly so dissatisfied with it all, his mood could not be safely contained within the cluttered rooms.

"Where is Miss Alexander?"

She called upon the telephone to say she didn't require the carriage. She had found another to bring her home.

"Who?" That crackled with tension, and Louis's agitation mounted because he was aggravated and jealous and lonely, and had no right to the first two and too much of the last.

Her cousin, I believe she said.

Cousin? Louis scowled darkly, recalling the parting glimpse he'd gotten of Quinton Alexander the time he'd come to visit Cassie when she'd been abed. He remembered a pale, handsome figure with the expression of a poet and an aura as dark as his own. Thinking of Cassie in his company troubled Louis more than was acceptable to his struggling conscience. Because he was wondering if this was the man who had offered for her hand.

Surely she was not still considering wedding another?

"I am going out, Takeo. I need to— get away for a time."

And Miss Alexander? What shall I tell her?

"Tell her nothing. You aren't supposed to be able to speak. Remember?"

The Oriental bobbed a quick bow but Louis caught a glimpse of his wry smile. *And if the gentleman comes in with her, do you wish me to be conspicuous?*

"She does not need a chaperon, Takeo. She may see whomever she wishes."

But his curt tone told his servant an entirely different tale.

He skimmed the edges of the night, one of the park's more dangerous shadows. It was one of Louis's favorite hunting grounds because no one traveled its paths after dark except victim and predator. And he preyed upon the latter.

He moved fast, stalking the footpaths with the speed of his kind, just a shimmer and a gust of wind to those he passed; the lucky ones he left unaware, allowing himself to revel in the power. It wasn't often that he gloried in the superior nature of what he was, but on this night he sought the speed, the flush of hunger, the simple instincts that would overrule the torment of his mind. That was his hope, however futile. The anxious energy just kept building, steaming like an overheated engine, roiling like water left on to boil too long, and there seemed to be no outlet for the restless churn of emotion knotting up his soul. Even the night with its cool breezes and infinite peace could not control the foment of his darker passions. The pressure continued to grow, straining for release.

"You cannot outrun it, *bell'amico*."

He felt Gerard fall into that preternatural pace beside him but refused to acknowledge his presence.

"Let go, Gino, before it consumes you. Hunt the winds with me tonight, my friend. Feed from these glades at my side."

"Leave me alone!"

Louis streaked away from him, down the elm-bordered mall like a cannonball on a path of destruction with Gerard behind him, a spark racing along an explosive trail of gunpowder. They reached the imposing double set of stairs leading down from the terrace to the brightly tiled esplanade, both rocketing outward instead of down. Unconfined by the laws of mortal time and space, they traversed the currents of air as easily as the ground below, soaring like dark birds of prey upon the night above the winged bronze statue in the Bethesda Fountain, round the lake's rim. The adventurous couples embracing within the rustic bench-equipped shelters paused to look up in alarm, wondering what sort of selective wind tore past them.

Growing bored with the chase, Gerard caught Louis about the knees and they plummeted like flaring meteorites to skid upon the grass, tumbling free of one another. Louis was up at once, running, leading the way into the esplanade's large, cool hall where colorful Milton tiles set in gilded ironwork covered the ceiling above. There, he turned abruptly to become the aggressor.

Gerard stumbled back, hand pressed to the side of his face where Louis's unexpected blow had taken him. Slowly he began to smile. "Come on then, *amico mio*." Chuckling with delight, he began to circle the seething Louis, drawn to this deadly play by age-old animosities. "You've never been able to best me in a fight, Gino. Well, just once, and that loss all but killed me." He grinned with dark humor and sent his fist out to collide lightning-fast with Louis's jaw. "Take me if you can. What shall we fight for? Your pretty little *inamorata*? Come. There can't be a contest without a prize."

He gave a grunt of surprise as Louis's heel took him in the chest with rib-splintering force, knocking him back across the huge hall. He laughed and chided, "You'll have to do better if you mean to make good on your plan to destroy me. Come on, Gino. Here's your chance. Come on."

And with a savage snarl, Louis came at him. They went down in a tangle of unnatural limbs, struggling with powers far beyond human limits, two lethal and immortal combatants, feeding off the fuel of an ancient feud.

"You killed my wife!" Louis growled as they grappled upon the floor.

"I loved you, Gino, and you betrayed me. You took the woman I loved. You sent my soul to hell!" A viciously driven elbow to Louis's throat punctuated that claim.

"She was hell and you went of your own accord, blindly, foolishly, dragging me with you, damn you!" And he forced his fury home with several punishing blows to the mid-body. "Damn your greed and your stupidity. Your hell is of your own making. Burn in it." And he found the leverage to toss Gerard over his head, sending him airborne at least thirty paces. Gerard rolled to his feet to meet his fighting stance. All traces of civility and amusement were gone.

"How loud you wail of this injustice. What have you lost, Gino? The chance to warm your skin in the sun? What is that compared to eternity? You should thank me. You are the fool. You never used the gift you were given."

"Gift? You mean curse! Prowling the night, feeding off the innocent? Is that a blessing?"

"I speak of the power. You never knew what to do with it, not when you were alive, not now when you could rule a nation. Gino, if I had your mind, your talent, I could be a king, a god."

"King, god, neither would satisfy you for long. Nothing is enough for you." He took to the air in a flying spin-kick, twisting his entire body into a weapon of lethal force the way Takeo had taught him. His foot caught Gerard in the face, sending him spinning away in an arc of blood to tumble to the ground. And he stood over his friend as he wobbled on hands and knees, venting his frustrations in a furious roar. "I gave you everything I had, everything I was, and it was never enough!"

"You let me have scraps from your table of plenty," Gerard panted fiercely, swiping at the split in his mouth and chin with the back of one hand before weaving to his feet. "I was never good enough to sit with you at my own place."

"You were!"

"No! The times would not allow it. Your family would not allow it. I was a child of the middle class, a nothing, a nobody. You let me sip from the wines of privilege but the cup was never mine to hold."

"The barrier was in your mind!"

"No! You were so blind. You could not see how much your family hated me. You never heard the sneers, the insults hurled upon me by your rich and scholarly friends. Damn you, you never defended me to them."

"They were nothing to me. You were my friend!" Louis settled back into a defensive pose, fists and feet ready, uncertain of his friend's mood. "My family thought all you cared for was my title and my wealth. They didn't want to see me hurt. I told them they were wrong, I told them money didn't matter between brothers. But I was the one who was wrong, wasn't I? Because it always mattered to you. Didn't it?" His pulse was racing with the rush of combat, hammering with the potent sense of despair, a loss of all he'd cared for. He didn't want to fight anymore. There was no answer in the bruising of flesh. The venting of souls caused the deeper cut.

"I wanted to be your equal. I loved you, Gino. And I hated you." His fury blown out with that admission, Gerard dropped his offensive pose, his hands falling lax at his sides. His cry of anguish echoed back centuries. "All those things you gave me, what could I give you in return? You don't know how that tormented me."

"You don't know, do you? Even after all this time, you've learned nothing," Louis murmured sadly. "Your friendship was more valuable to me than any of the things I possessed."

"My friendship destroyed you. What happened to us, Gino?"

"A woman, a demon."

Gerard gave a soft laugh. "And I won her in the end, didn't I? Four centuries of heartless misery. Would that I had your sixty-odd years of devotion from a woman who loved me."

And all at once, Louis's anger drained away, replaced by the unhappy plight of his friend. "Gerardo, leave her. Find peace with yourself."

His smile was mocking. "I am not like you, Gino. I have no . . . character. You live an endless search for betterment. I just— live."

It was then their poignant conversation was disrupted by the outside world.

There was no noticeable cry for help, just rapid breathing inaudible to human ears. The pattern was a familiar one: one labored and frantic, one heavy and determined—prey and predator. Frowning, Louis moved to the opening of the hall, Gerardo blending in behind him. A desperate female stumbled past the sandstone balustrades, her grasping hands pulling her along the lovely carvings of birds and fruits. She was followed more slowly by the pursuing figure of a man. He held her torn coat and discarded bag and was obviously after greater treasures.

"It would seem we are not the only ones terrorizing the night."

Gerard's nonchalant observation sparked an angry want for justice in Louis. When he stepped forward, meaning to go to the woman's assistance, Gerard retained him with a reasoning grasp.

"Do not concern yourself. Why meddle in their petty problems?"

Louis gave him an impatient glance and a gruff, "You have lost all trace of compassion over the centuries, haven't you?"

Gerard let him go, smiling with amusement. "Go ahead, *amico mio*. But whom do you think she'll fear more?"

The woman had reached the edge of the fountain and was clinging to it to support her flagging strength. She gave a plaintive moan of fright as her assailant closed in. He was so assured of his victory, he was smiling even as a vengeful Louis swept down upon him, spinning him about and away from the horrified woman. That smile altered to a contortion of fear when he saw what had him. With fangs exposed and gleaming, his eyes ablaze with lurid appetite, Louis Radman was a terrible sight to behold.

For it wasn't the frightened woman who goaded him into a fury. Upon that woman's face, within that woman's plight, Louis saw Cassie, helpless and abused, and the rage came bubbling up like a volcano.

The man had opened his mouth to scream in terror when Louis's hand closed about his throat, strangling off the sound. His eyes continued to widen until they bulged almost comically. Feeling the fear pulsing from the terrified mortal sparked a psychic surge and Louis drank it up, reveling in the richness, the taste, until his brain burned with it. It was a rush of pure energy, this draining of the soul, as powerful as the lure of live blood he'd soon drain from the man's body. It was the ecstasy of the kill and Louis let the dark glory of it overtake him as he sank his teeth to tap the hot well of life. He pulled away only when he felt Gerard's nearness.

Gerard reached out to wipe Louis's chin, collecting a dark film of blood on his fingertips. He stared at it for a long moment, then up at Louis. The blue of his eyes burned with a white-hot brilliance but his expression held an almost dreamy sense of wonder.

"I've never seen you kill before. You do it as you do all else, with an infinite beauty. I am awed, *bell'amico.*" And slowly, with a decidedly sensual pleasure, Gerard cleaned the stains from his fingers. Once that was done, he cast his glittering gaze to the huddled figure of the woman. She whimpered at his attention. "Shall we ask her which she prefers, her human assailant or her monstrous rescuer?" He walked to the petrified female and extended his hand. She quivered like a frightened rabbit.

"Gerard, let her alone. Hasn't she suffered enough?"

"Suffer?" He gave Louis a sly smile. "What I have planned for her she will not consider suffering. Come, *cara bella,* and let me take the memory of this ugly business away from you."

She started to reach up tentatively for Gerard's smooth hand.

"No!" Louis cried, breaking her trance. "Go, run! Save yourself!"

With a moan of confusion, she staggered to her feet, backing away from the two unnatural beings. Louis tossed her the stolen bag and she stared at it upon the ground as if she feared to touch it. Then, with a bleat of sheer terror, she snatched it up and ran, stumbling up the steps and across the wide terrace.

Gerard was chuckling. "Gino, you have just chased off my dinner. Why?" And his expression grew mystified. "Why do you care what happens to them?"

"They are all that's perfect in this world. We are the aberrations."

"With an attitude like that, you could well starve to death. I do not plan to go hungry, not on this night or any other. I bid you a good evening, *amico mio*. And I leave you with a warning that I hope will not spoil your appetite. Bianca has not forgotten you. Be careful, my friend. I would hate to lose you."

And Louis was motionless for a long while, considering the terror upon the woman's face, a reflection was what he was. No amount of outward sophistication, no fine address, no huge bank account, would ever change their reaction to what he was. An unnatural being. A demon. A ghoul. They saw no humanity in him. Arabella was the only one who'd known it was there.

And if Cassie were to discover what lurked within the darkness of his heart, would she believe there was more to him than monster?

After disguising what he'd done to bring about his victim's demise— no sense in giving the papers new fuel for their fires— Louis found himself wandering with an unconscious purpose until he ended up at the gates of the Woodlawn Cemetery. And there he realized he had to take an old friend's advice. He had to let go.

His hands stroked over the cool marble, so pale and pure and yet unravaged by time. He closed his eyes and leaned his cheek upon the smooth stone.

"I miss you, little one. I long for the wisdom of your counsel and the tenderness of your care. You were so much more to me than the term wife could ever imply. You were lover, friend, and confidante. I wish you could tell me what to do." But of course, she couldn't. That voice was forever stilled.

"You were right about her, Bella. She is a fine woman. I can see why you thought we would suit. She has many of your strong qualities . . . and your prideful stubbornness, too. I am glad you were friends. I know it was your wish that she and I be together but— but I wish I were certain that you knew how much I loved you, how much I will always love you. I wish I could make you understand that in saying goodbye to you here tonight, I am not walking away from the memory of our life together."

It was faint at first, then there was no mistaking the light floral scent of Arabella's perfume. Louis lifted his head, half expecting to see her there beside him, and it was an agony to be met with only moonlight and the silent tributes to the dead. Then he felt the stir of a soft breeze upon his face, stroking along his cheekbones and ruffling through his hair. Like a loving caress.

And very slowly, he smiled, content with his answer.

"Buona sera."

The softly purred greeting brought Cassie about with a gasp. She clutched her night robe up about her throat as the elegant figure emerged from the shadows of her bedroom. "You." Recognition didn't bring a lessening of fear.

"Forgive me. We have never been properly introduced. I am Gerardo Pasquale. I am a friend of . . . Louis's."

"What are you doing here? What do you want?" Her nervous gaze darted to the unmade bed and back. He smiled.

"Oh, I assure you, nothing so sordid as that."

"I think I would be more inclined to believe you were I not standing here in my night clothes with an uninvited man in my room."

He chuckled at her tart speech. "You have fire. I like that."

"How did you get in? I don't normally allow strangers free access to my home."

"You mustn't think of me as a stranger, *cara*. Think of me as— family." And his smile widened, growing warm with seductive charm. It was a fight not to succumb to it, but something was disturbing about Louis's foreign friend. Something in the way he moved, the way he appeared without a sound and left the same way. Something disquieting in the residue of fear she felt when in his presence. He was like the rest of Louis's family— attractive, mannerly, and totally unnatural.

"Why are you here?" she asked again, this time with a bit of authority in her tone. That seemed to amuse him all the more.

"One reason only. I came to warn you of a danger to your Louis. It is a subtle threat, one you may not see or even believe, but you must be on your guard. Dark forces are at work here and the danger deepens with the night. He scoffs at my cautionings. Perhaps you will be wiser."

"What is this threat and from whom?"

"He may choose to tell you. It is not my place to interfere. Just coming here to impart this knowledge is rather out of . . . character for me. Do with it what you will. And now, I must go before Gino— Louis returns. He may not be thrilled to find me here." He rubbed the side of his face as if his jaw pained him. "We have had enough discussion between us for one night."

"I thought you said you were friends."

Gerard grinned. "Friends, yes. Allies . . . not always. We have a lot of history between us."

She might not have understood the innuendo but Cassie could read between the lines. She squared up to present a formidable female barrier. "I will not allow you to harm him."

"Really?" He laughed, delighted by her futile threat. "Oh, *cara,* perhaps I underestimated you. I had not thought there could be two mortal females who would dare confront me with an ultimatum." He bowed to her and the gesture was only slightly mocking. "I stand corrected."

Mortal. What an odd way to refer to her. Cassie's discomfort increased. "I believe you were leaving."

"And now I find I don't wish to go. Another time."

"I will see you to the door."

A smile. "That is not necessary."

"I insist."

"Then by all means, escort me." And he crooked his arm and made a great show of tucking her hand there. Up close, Cassie found him even more intimidating, but oddly she was not afraid anymore. She was remembering the way he'd mourned over Arabella's passing and the way Louis's sister had embraced him. Like family. Just another piece to an increasingly discordant puzzle.

At the front door, Gerard paused, letting her open it to offer the way out. He was still smiling over some inner joke as he lifted her hand between the press of his.

"*E stato un piacere conoscerla. Adesso devo an-*

darmeme a casa." At her blank look, he translated loosely. "I am glad we had this opportunity to meet but I must return home. You are very lovely, Cassie Alexander. As always, Gino's taste is exquisite." He brought her hand up to his lips and the touch of them was as strangely cool as his manner was intimate. *"Grazie della serata."*

"Good evening, Mr. Pasquale."

"Gerard," he corrected with another chill caress across her knuckles. "Family, remember?"

When she didn't argue he chuckled with pleasure and stepped back so she could shut the door between them.

"Ah, Gino, where do you find such jewels?" he sighed before turning to start down the walk. He stopped abruptly, senses quivering. A quick glance about revealed the figure of a man standing off to the side of the house, wreathed in the shadows. A human, no threat to him. But perhaps a fortuitous meeting considering he'd not yet dined.

"Who is there? Come forward."

Gerard waited as the man approached. He was handsome in a weak and pretty way, a bit pale, his eyes a little too piercing. But Gerard was looking past those slight flaws, concentrating upon the sound of his heartbeats, on the luring scent of his blood. Hunger stirred. Gerard smiled in a seemingly harmless greeting.

"Are you Louis Radcliffe?" There was an edge to that question.

"If I am, what is your business with me?"

He was closer now, close enough for Gerard to be distracted by the rhythm of his pulse, by his human warmth. And because he was consumed by appetite and blinded by a superior ego, he never saw the danger.

There was a swift glitter of steel. Gerard had no chance to express his alarm as the blade opened his throat from ear to ear. He dropped down on his knees, eyes wide with shock, breath gurgling awfully as he pitched over onto his side.

Quinton Alexander observed his work dispassionately. "That wasn't so hard. She said it would be difficult to convince you to come with me. You weren't planning to put up a fight, were you?" He nudged the now still form with his toe and smirked. "I thought not."

Seventeen

Louis slipped in through the back of Cassie's home. He never used the front door, partly to protect her reputation, partly to conceal his presence. As he moved easily through the unlit lower rooms, his well-honed senses began to fix upon a familiar odor, one that tantalized with dark fascination. Blood. Freshly spilled and too near for comfort.

"Cassie? Takeo?" He advanced into the front foyer, dread quickening with each step, for there the scent intensified until he was almost dizzy with it.

Master?

Louis whirled to face his loyal servant. "Takeo? Is everything all right?"

A nod and a questioning look.

"Miss Alexander?"

I believe she has retired for the evening. She had a visitor, the Italian, Pasquale.

Louis was already racing up the stairs, his thoughts numb with panic. Gerard had deceived him with his nostalgic talk and pretended concerns. It had been a ruse to double back and strip him of his second chance to know some happiness. Cursing his faithless friend, he flung open the door to Cassie's room, steeling himself for whatever he might find.

"Cassie?" He knelt down upon the edge of the bed and gripped her shoulder to turn her over onto her back. She came awake with a cry of alarm and even her fierce curse of recognition sounded like music to him. Because it meant she was unharmed.

"What are you doing in here? Last time I looked this was still my bedchamber and not the second floor of some house of ill repute where men feel free to come and go as they please."

He was smiling foolishly in the face of her fury, too relieved to do otherwise. "And have you been entertaining other men up here?"

She sat up, dragging the covers up to her chin. "Only that wickedly flirtatious friend of yours who insists I think of him like family."

Louis was suddenly serious. "What did Gerard want?"

"He asked me to watch out for you. He said you were in some kind of danger, only he wouldn't say the nature of it. Who is he, Louis? There is something . . . odd about him."

"Odd is an understatement," Louis muttered. Then his focus sharpened. "He did not try to harm you?"

"No . . . actually, he was quite charming.

Though I can't say I approve of his penchant for appearing in my bedroom." She saw the question form furrows in Louis's brow so she hurried on. "What did he mean by danger?"

"Nothing you need concern yourself with." The cool reserve was back as he settled in a seated position a neutral distance from her.

Cassie watched him silently for a moment, trying to screw up her courage to put her desperate plan into effect. But how to go about convincing him that he needed a bride? Not just any bride, but her. It was hard to concentrate with him so near. Her heartbeats were scurrying with an unbidden urgency and the starch of her will was already beginning to wilt with the strength of her longing for him. The need to reach out and touch just his sleeve was so intense it was nearly erotic. Emotions woke within her, becoming as powerful as images. Thoughts pushed her toward action with a restlessness that would not be stilled.

I love you, Louis. I must have you. Anything for you. Anything!

Cassie shook her head to scatter the seducing whispers. They frightened her because they were not coming from her heart or mind but from some unnamed source deep in her soul, a source Louis Radcliffe seemed to command regardless of her will.

"Since you are here, we must talk." The words sounded stiff and stilted upon her lips

with all those hungry, needy pleadings echoing behind them. *I need you, Louis. Take me,
Louis.* She sucked in a deep breath, hoping
to dismiss those despairing inner cries.

"What did you wish to discuss?" He was
staring at her steadily, his expression inscrutable. She would have sooner died than have
him guess at her internal struggle. Thank
goodness he couldn't read her mind as the
thoughts continued to come with increasing
frequency and in embarrassingly explicit detail.

"Things cannot continue as they stand,"
she began firmly, as her gaze traitorously following the shape of his mouth. *Kiss me,
Louis. It would be heaven for you to kiss me.*

"And how do they stand?" he asked with
an unencouraging nonchalance.

Cassie tried to speak but her mouth was
so dry. She moistened her lips with the tip
of her tongue, imagining how it would feel
to exchange wet, soulful kisses with Louis
Radcliffe. Growing uncomfortably aroused
with her own thoughts, she lowered her eyes
until her gaze rested upon the graceful
hands he had tented upon one knee. She
cleared her throat, studying those long,
beautifully shaped fingers, wondering what
delights they could awake upon her bared
skin.

"You staying here with me in the same
house, the two of us alone," she all but
stammered.

"Have I made you afraid to be with me?"

"No." An odd question. He was deliberately misunderstanding her. She shifted beneath the covers, her body unbearably sensitive to the chafe of her nightdress, to the heat of the sheets. "Because of my position at the magazine, I must consider how it looks to others."

"And how does it look?" he drawled out silkily.

"Like we are involved in . . . in something improper."

"But you and I know that is not true."

"But it looks— "

"I thought you did not care what other people thought. You have always been outspoken to that effect. Were those bold, independent words not worth the expense of breath to say them?"

"Of course, I meant them," she mumbled irritably. Her knees were rubbing together beneath the covers. Oh, to have the lean hard strength of him clenched between them, his weight upon her, his power within her. Claiming, possessing, conquering the weakness of her female form. Cassie grabbed an unsteady breath. Heaven above, where were these shameful ideas coming from? She brushed the back of her hand across her brow, wiping away the dampness beading along her hairline as she struggled to retain her calm long enough to explain her plight. "Louis, I cannot afford the speculation. Not now. My feelings on the matter do not apply. My uncle is trying to take the *Lexicon* from me. If he brings the common knowledge of me living, unwed, with a man not in my immediate family, before any court, I will not have a case. My innocence will be irrelevant. The circumstance will damn me. I cannot afford the loss of respectability in the public eye. Louis, you must understand—"

"Is it him, your pale cousin?"

"Quinton?" She was confused by his sudden shift of topic.

"Have you decided to have him for a husband?" Again, that slightly gritty undertone that made her think . . . that made her hope he objected to the idea.

"Would it bother you if I did?"

He didn't react to her silky baiting as she'd wished. There was no notable change in his expression, but his eyes, when he lifted them to fix upon her, held a sudden flare of intensity. "Are you in love with him?" was his quiet question.

Under the penetrating heat of his gaze, Cassie found she could not continue her charade. "No."

"Yet you would marry him?"

"He asked. I said no."

Louis never so much as blinked but, all the same, she could sense his relief when he said, "So that leaves us."

"Us?" The enchantment of the word seduced her. Us. *Oh, yes.*

"You would like me to leave."

"No!" That denying cry exploded before she could catch it. Then it was too late to make any other argument. "No," she concluded softly. "I don't want you to go. I promised Arabella I would care for you."

He smiled slightly. "And do you?"

"What?"

"Care for me?"

Her gaze danced away shyly, then returned to boldly claim his. "Yes." She glanced down, shocked by her own behavior. "But the talk—"

"Let them talk. I cannot leave."

"But surely you can afford to move into one of the new grand hotels. It would be ever so much more comfortable for you than here in these stuffy old rooms."

"I like it here. I enjoy the— company."

"Oh." Coherent thought fled.

"And I, too, made a promise to Arabella. I vowed I would see you safe. There is a maniac out there who means to do you harm."

Predictably, Cassie gave a huff of indignation. "I am perfectly capable of taking care of myself."

And Louis suffered an uncomfortably clear recall of her staggering along the iron fence row, of the woman's dead eyes staring upward in that grimy flat, of the frightened creature in the park this very night. Victims all. One a permanent statistic. Cassie wouldn't become one if he could help it.

"I will not leave you."

"Well, I don't want you to stay," she countered with surprising vehemence. "Not out of some death-bed obligation. Not against your will."

Then she gave a tiny gasp as his hand eased up over her thigh, moving there against the soft curve of flesh with a deliberate, seducing skill. "It's more than obligation. And it was never against my will."

Cassie held herself perfectly still as he leaned toward her. His kiss was like none of his others. This one was soft and slow and succulent with a sliding luxury. She squeezed her eyes shut and let the sensations sweep her away. His hands had come up to cradle her face in the vee they made between them, gently imprisoning her as his tongue easily breached the barrier of her lips to press deeply into the wanting cavern of her mouth until she thought for sure she'd swoon.

After what seemed like minutes but was probably closer to several long seconds, he withdrew just far enough to whisper, "Was that the heaven you sought?"

Her eyes flickered open. "What?" And she stared at him, wondering how he'd known—but then he couldn't have, could he? Then it didn't matter how he knew, just that he knew and he was kissing her again, just as deeply, just as wetly, until she thought she'd go mad with the pleasure of it.

His hands were on the ribbon bows of her nightdress. She could hear rippling sighs as the satin ties gave way, then her own sigh as he pushed the barrier of fabric from her shoulders. His hands rode up along the rapid rhythm of her rising and falling rib-cage until possessed of the ripe underswell of her breasts. Those he molded to fit the cups of his palms as he woke their tender tips to an agony of yearning with the brush of his thumbs. Just as she'd imagined he would, she thought in a sensual daze. And if he followed that pattern of longing, he would be turning his attention to—

Cassie caught her breath as he lowered his head to feed an aching nipple into his mouth. Her body shuddered in response. She'd never dreamed . . . She knew of such things from sneaking peeks at the naughty books her father thought hidden from her view. There on those pages such activities between men and women were described in graphic detail. But picturing the acts themselves had in no way prepared her for the way they would make her . . . *feel*. Reading those tantalizing passages had stimulated a guilty sense of shock and curiosity that touched nowhere near the searing darts of delight Louis created with a gentle suction and the teasing tug of his lips. Those exquisite feelings quivered clear to the soul. From those pages she hadn't experienced the shattering awareness of her female self, the awakening of her body that was like a flush of fever in the blood. She was trembling with it, every inch of her sensitized and desperate for his touch.

Arms that had hung lax at her sides for lack of direction came up to curl about him, not to clutch at him or pull him tighter but simply to contain the wondrous strength of him. Her hands moved restlessly over the rough material of his coat and she wished it to be the smooth heat of his skin instead. She was at first dismayed then wildly expectant as he leaned away from her so he could rid himself of his own garments. All the while, he held her gaze captive with his own, his intense with passion, picking up the reflections of light so that one moment his eyes were brilliant with the glitter of emeralds and the next were hot and smoky like dark jade.

When he was bared to the waist, he gave her scarce time to admire him but one glimpse was enough to tell of his perfection. Though not impressive in height, his body was heavy with muscle. The well-defined swells slid beneath her palms as he drew her in close, and learning the terrain with timid strokes revealed an awesome power. His arms and shoulders were thick and hard, ridges of steel overlaid with the most supple satin. She found him amazingly beautiful and had lifted her head to tell him as much when he caught her mouth with the commanding heat of his own, making her lose all threads of cohesive thought.

While he controlled her will with his exquisite kisses, Cassie arched against him to indulge in the heady luxury of hot skin on hot skin. His hand stroked down the curve of her spine, sweeping the tangle of her night clothes lower as she lifted to meet him more fully. Somewhere in the back of her modest mind, she was scandalized by the way it pooled about her knees, allowing him the freedom to follow the soft flare of her hips and the plump shape of her buttocks with that exploring hand.

She stiffened slightly as his fingers raked gently through the down concealing her virginity, but he rubbed the tension from her even as his kiss grew distractingly and explicitly deeper. When he reached the slick wetness of her, Cassie started to moan wild objections, then she forget them as his sliding fingertips began to mimic the plunge of his tongue within her mouth— swift, relentless seeking, penetrating beyond the limits of imagination to the secret pleasures of her feminine self. She started to moan again but this time in wonder and anticipation.

Then his intimate touch ceased and his intoxicating kisses slowed and finally stopped as well. Louis eased back just far enough to observe her flushed face and passion-dark expression.

He was not unmoved by the sight. He'd come to a decisive crossroads, the past behind him, the future stretching out ahead. If he continued down the sweet road of Cassie's sensual education he would be putting behind the vows he'd never expected to break. Vows that swore fidelity and undying love. He hesitated, unsure of what to do, of whether to deny the urgency of the flesh for the sanctity of remembered bliss. He had loved Arabella with the special intensity reserved for a first and forever passion. She'd awakened him to human desire after nearly five lifetimes of dormancy. He'd never believed another could stir him to that same level of need but Cassie had, and had done so with Arabella's blessing. It was the strength of Arabella's love encouraging him to go on, her generosity of spirit that refused to deny him what she could no longer provide. She had picked this woman to succeed her as his lover and companion, a gift as rare as it was unselfish. How could he turn from her last wishes and the chance for happiness that would see her truly at peace?

"Louis?"

Cassie's husky plea for his attention helped pull him from the past. Her fingers splayed wide upon the hard wall of his chest, endearing in their timidity, undeniably enticing with their innocent caress. He lifted one of her small, mortal hands and pressed the back of it to his lips. He could feel the surging flow of life traversing beneath the skin and the allure was unmistakably there but muted now that his vile appetite was sated. Even stronger was the fragile scent of human warmth and the delicate bouquet of her perfume. Those stirred a response more male than monster.

"Louis, if you don't make love to me, I shall surely perish."

He chuckled at her dramatic claim. "That I could not stand upon my conscience," he murmured, and hooking one arm about her, he jerked her up close and fell with her upon the tangle of covers.

Cassie was in paradise. The most exciting man in the world was here within her arms, showing her down the enticing road to womanhood. He filled up her senses with awareness of him, of his power as he settled over her, of his masculinity as hard contours rode boldly over feminine softness. She couldn't stop touching him, charmed by the surprising smoothness of his skin, by the sleekness of his hair and amazed by the rippling strength of muscle moving beneath her hands. His lingering kisses spoke of heavenly bliss, his thorough caress of hellish delights. And she responded to him without a maidenly fear, without a reluctance to experience the unknown. She wanted to learn all there was to know about love and she wanted this man to teach her. Because there was more than desire between them. A sense of trust, a bond of belonging prohibited even the slightest doubt as he lifted her knees slightly to wiggle the bunch of her nightdress free. She felt no shame as his gaze took in all she had to offer.

And because she was a journalist, the need to know all forbade modesty. Her hands smoothed down the tapering breadth of his torso to the concealing barrier of his trousers, determination supplanting timidity as she worked them open and coaxed them down. Her hands returned to chart the newly bared terrain, skimming up the firm curve of his thighs to caress the taut contour of his seat. Louis was far from shocked by her aggressive interest. Her curiosity, her obvious appreciation, fanned the flames of passion higher. He shifted onto his side, rolling her up against him and holding her head tucked beneath his chin. His eyes closed tightly as she continued her investigation with inquiring strokes that had his breath rattling noisily in a matter of minutes. He put an end to her fact gathering by rolling up over her again. She looked up at him through eyes all dark and rich with desire.

"It was my intention to teach you about pleasure," he chided gently.

"Sometimes the greatest pleasure comes from discovering for yourself," she replied

with a smile so smugly sultry his will gave
way without a whimper.

"I like you, Cassie Alexander."

"Well, that's nice to hear . . . considering."

He smiled and rubbed his thumbs up the
stubborn line of her jaw. Then his mood sobered and his voice softened. "I don't want
you to regret this."

"I won't," she swore with enough conviction to conquer his anxious heart. "No matter what happens later, this is what I want
now. No regrets. Not ever."

And he sealed her vow with a searing kiss,
and from there things moved quickly, with
escalating intensity toward the desired end.

He made her imaginings come to life.
There was no awkwardness because she
never spoke her needs aloud. She thought
them and he fulfilled them with a dizzying
degree of sensuality. He primed her body to
a point of restless desperation, preparing the
way with the gentle insertion of his fingers,
using them to ease the stiffness of surprise,
to encourage a welcoming flood of wetness
that would insure a minimal amount of pain.
He taught her the motion, the rhythm of
love and, a quick study, she was soon straining beneath him, moaning for more, panting
his name with a wild yearning.

He saw that she was too aroused to feel
much discomfort at his first possessing
thrust, or if she did, it was soon lost before

the indescribable feel of oneness. She clutched at his shoulders, shivering beneath him not with pain or fear but with anticipation.

He took his time cultivating her passions, building sensation to the edge of ecstasy and beyond, if her soft keening cries were any indication. He'd forgotten the compelling power of human love but it returned to him with an exquisite sharpness of detail, the flooding prickles of heat, the pulling grasp of paradise, slowly, surely wringing pleasure from the remaining mortality of his soul. The feelings were hot and urgent and beautiful as was the woman yielding up the tender heart of her femininity to him. The rush of galvanizing satisfaction was like none other, except the erotic thrill of swallowing down the very essence of life.

And when Cassie snapped rigid beneath him with an almost tortured cry of his name, he crushed her close, devouring the hard pants of her breath until her tension released in violent quakes of completion. As she sank into a lethargy of relief, he shuddered with the strength of his own conclusion and gradually relaxed above her.

Louis was aware of her steady stare, perplexed by its intensity. He came up on his elbows to study her just as intently and to ask with a reverent hush, "Was it everything you wished for, *cara*?"

Her smile was small but infinitely pleased.

"How could I wish for something beyond all I could imagine?" Her gaze darkened. "I love you, Louis."

She watched the shadows fill his eyes and as he was about to speak, Cassie touched her fingertips to his lips to silence his words of apology.

"No. Don't say anything. It's all right. No regrets, remember?" And her caress eased up along the dramatically sculptured angles of his face to soothe the lines of anxiousness away. "Allow me to love you. That's all I ask."

He caught her hand and pressed an expressive kiss against its palm. "That, alone, could prove to be more than you ever bargained for."

Cassie was remembering Arabella's warning. A sacrifice was demanded as the price of his devotion. Well, whatever it was, she would make it. Nothing could be so monumental as to overshadow what he'd just given her.

As if he could read her thoughts, Louis smiled somewhat sadly, resigned to her decision as if sure she would soon regret it.

She would prove him wrong. No regrets. No turning back. She'd made that promise, just as she'd promised Arabella that she would love him.

She slept curled up beside the heat of his side, safe in the strong band of his embrace. She slumbered deeply, without dreams until

the early hours of morning, when she awakened to the feel of his hand stroking
through her hair. She lifted her head to accept his possessing kiss and the dregs of weariness were quickly chased away as he
covered her once more and showed her the
way to a soul-shattering heaven.

Louis cradled her slumbering form while
troubled thoughts plagued him. It was a
vague uneasiness, something external that refused to go away. Something he was forgetting in his daze of sensual satiation. His
brow furrowed in the darkness. What was it?

The blood. The overpowering presence of
it when he'd stepped into the foyer below.
He'd dismissed it when his fears for Cassie
were absolved.

But if not hers, then whose?

The answer shot through him like a piercing bolt from a bow. His mind was momentarily stunned by the force of the psychic call
impressed upon it, clouding his thoughts
with an intense shock of panic.

Gino, help me! Don't let me die!

He came up with a gasp.

Gerard.

Eighteen

Bianca du Maurier was in her gloating glory. Finally, after centuries of frustration, the fate of the man she loved was in her hands. Hands that could bring limitless delight as well as an infinity of pain. An equal attraction often confused within the darkness of her heart and mind.

Luigino Rodmini was her one great obsession. She'd become desperately infatuated with the pious green-eyed Florentine. His chaste nature and intellectual innocence had inspired her to heights of erotic depravity. She'd had to have him, even if it meant destroying all that he was. And she had. In her greed to possess him, she'd lost her chance to seduce him slowly into her control. It wasn't often that she underestimated the human male. They were easily led by their physical lusts and not very clever once their libidos were provoked into an animal rut. She'd found two exceptions. One was the damned Parisian, Marchand LaValois, who was wed to Louis and Arabella Radman's daughter Nicole, both legally and vampirically. He was the one creature on the face of the earth that she truly feared. He, with his fierce code of justice and nobility had almost cooked her in his fires of retribution, and would have had Gerard not been there to extinguish the flames that still marked her perfect features. For him, she was planning a special vengeance when the time was right.

The only other to scorn her advances was her handsome Gino, her eternal love and lasting enemy. He'd managed to escape the charms that snared his friend, Gerardo, and he had gone over to the life of the damned without her intervention. He'd been schooled not in darkness but with a philosophical light under the tutelage of the only vampire older and more clever than her, another thorn in her side, Eduard D'arcy. Under Eduard's counsel, her gentle, scholarly Gino had become a force to be reckoned with. And an undeniable source of frustrated craving.

His marriage and subsequent happiness with that meddling mortal creature never failed to chafe Bianca's vanity, knowing that a mere human could tame and enjoy that which she in all her power had not been able to hold. Even her faithful and lethal lover, Gerard, had been smitten with the wretched human. But now Arabella was gone and Bianca had no patience to wait while her Gino toyed with another mortal female. She would have him now as her rightful slave or she would destroy him and rid herself of the constant irritation of knowing him content with another.

The plan was perfect in its evil. The place was exquisite in every detail. It was in the rear of the Radmans'— no, she must remember they had called themselves the Radcliffes in this decade— burned-out home. She'd noticed it by accident when she'd paid her respects: a slightly sunken room with a slanting wall of glass, constructed to catch the morning sun to cultivate the exotic greenery Arabella had been so fond of. Most of the glass had been broken out of the frames by the fierceness of the fire but an idea had taken root, one of appalling consequence for those of their kind.

She completed her project with the aid of her new fledgling. Quinton Alexander had proven to be remarkably suited for evil deeds. She was quite impressed with his amoral viciousness and his readiness to do her bidding. He was very creative in his initiative. He'd thought of the silver shackles and promised to deliver her black heart's desire.

And as she entered the shadowy greenhouse still redolent with charred wood and pungent smoke, her anticipation spiked deliciously.

"Did he put up a struggle, Quinton?"

"Not really. He was surprisingly easy to subdue. He never knew it was coming."

Bianca smiled at his sinister boasting and advanced into the hazy darkness. She could see the figure of a man hanging from silver cuffs nailed into the wall. And she could smell blood.

"What have you done to him, fool? I did not say you could hurt him!"

"Well, how did you think I was going to get him here? By asking nicely? He's all right. He recovered almost before I had a chance to secure him but those manacles seem to hold him."

"As well they should," Bianca mused. Silver ate through unnatural flesh like a ravaging infection. The more he fought against the bonds, the weaker he would become. Genius, really, but quite painful for him if he sought to struggle.

Bianca could see him stir as she approached. He knew she was there even though he didn't lift his head. His shirt front was black with an alarming stain. What had the enthusiastic Quinton done to him? Slit his throat? She grimaced at the idea more than at the thought of his distress.

"So, Gino," she purred with a venomous amusement, "this is what our four-century struggle comes down to. I told you it was only a matter of time before you were mine once again. May I tell you what I have in store for you if you should decline? Curious about your position? I understand when the sun comes up, it warms this whole area with its radiant glow. Of course, all you'll feel is that first burst of flames before you incinerate. Even your tolerance of diffused light shouldn't stand that kind of test for long.

"Consider my offer again, since you have, oh, I'd say about ten, maybe fifteen minutes before the fires of hell consume you. I offer you my undying devotion. All you must do is remain by my side. Is that such an awful fate? Worse than the flames? It is your choice."

There was a moment of silence then the sound of low, raspy laughter as her prisoner slowly lifted his head. Bianca froze, recognizing the mocking tones but not understanding until she found herself confronting not eyes of verdant green, but those of silver blue.

"Were I Gino, I would take the fire, *cara mia.*"

"You!"

"I am so sorry. You always seem to be forced to settle for second best. Perhaps that would not happen if you found yourself less moronic assistance."

Fury overcame Bianca as she whirled on a confused Quinton. "How could you be so stupid?" she screeched at him. "You brought me the wrong man!"

Quinton blinked and stammered in his defense. "B-but he told me he was Radcliffe! How was I to know? I have never seen him. Who is this then, and why would he lie to me?"

"I am your worst nightmare when I get free," Gerard drawled pleasantly, his voice still rough from the rapidly repairing damage to his vocal cords. "I did not say I was Louis Radcliffe. I merely asked why you wanted him. That was all I could manage before you nearly took off my head. *Cara,* have him release me. I have endured quite enough for one evening's folly."

But Bianca was pacing angrily, seething at the failure of her plan and just as determinedly readjusting her plot. "What's one mistake? No one saw you, did they, Quinton? Good. Then we can go ahead as planned tomorrow night. Only this time I will point him out so there will be no mistakes. Then nothing can get in our way." Then she paused in her restless travels and looked thoughtfully at Gerard. "You would not warn him, would you, my love?"

Gerard stared back through expressionless eyes. "Why would I do that?"

"Why, indeed?" was Bianca's pensive reply. "Why were you at Gino's tonight? Talking over . . . old times?"

"I was there for the woman."

"I could almost believe you, Gerardo. Almost." She came close and let the backs of her fingers trail down his cheek. "But if you had, you would not be so cool to the touch."

"Of course I'm cold. I'm freezing. Look what that *idiota* did to me! Free me so I can recover myself. I will even fight the temptation to make a meal of your buffoon."

Bianca smiled softly. "Quinton serves me well and without question. As you once did. He will learn." Her fingertips ran up the length of one arm, stopping short of the silver cuff. Beneath it, his flesh was raw as if eaten away by some harsh corrosive. "This looks terrible. Are you in much pain?"

"Release me, Bianca! Now!"

Her narrowed eyes returned to his and he could see his mistake at once. "Orders, Gerard? And so impolitely given."

"Forgive me, *cara*, you are right, I am in much distress and not myself. Please, let me go. I do not find this funny anymore." His gaze flickered nervously to the wall of windows, gauging the time before the first rays would crest over the sill. He could scent the dawn and he didn't need to try the shackles again to know he couldn't escape them. Not on his own.

Bianca ran her hands up his chest and over his shoulders as she leaned against him, her lips touching lightly to the savage wound in his neck, kissing her way along it. Gerard shut his eyes and rested against the brick wall behind him, relieved to see her carnal nature overcome her.

"You are so beautiful," she mouthed as she slid her way up to feast upon his lips. And when she eased back, he was smiling, sure of his dark charm. Until she sighed and said, "A pity I can no longer trust you not to betray me. I shall miss you, Gerard."

He took a quick breath and attempted another smile. "Bianca? Do not tease me. Release me, my love. I do not like this game."

But she pressed her fingertips to her lips, then to his. "*Arrivederci, caro mio.* I will think of you fondly from time to time and may even regret this. But I will have Quinton to coax me out of my melancholy." And she turned away from him to loop her arm through her new companion's.

Gerard gave a soft laugh, still not totally believing. "Bianca, you punish me most unkindly. The woman, she is nothing compared to you. Release me and it can be as it once was— you and me and Gino."

But she didn't look back.

Gerard swallowed hastily and pulled against his bonds, gritting his teeth against the bolts of agony that shot down the length of his arms. "Bianca? Have you forgotten that you owe me a life?"

That brought her around with a vicious hiss. "Yes! I remember! I remember how you waited before stepping in to smother the flames. You left me in hell then gloated about it. Do you have any idea how much suffering one endures with each second in the fire? You will, *caro*. You will!" And she swept out into the spreading pastels of dawn, never to glance back.

"Bianca? Bianca! Don't leave me like this!" With a wail, he jerked against the cuffs until too weakened by the pain to do more than hang in their damning embrace. "Don't let me die like this," he moaned. *"Dio del cielo,* show me mercy."

But he knew there would be no mercy for him, not after the dark existence he'd enjoyed. Panting frantically, he tried to think of a way out.

"Nicole!" But as soon as he uttered that call, he pulled it back. There was no time. If he called, she would come. She might save him, but she would not have the chance to return to safety and save herself. There were few things he placed above himself in a heart so old and scarred by self-indulgent pain. Nicole LaValois was one of them.

There was one chance, one faint hope. He fought against the effects of the silver streaking through him like a raging fever, trying to summon the last of his strength for one plea, one last avenue. He didn't know if he could do it. The pain, the weakness, was already clouding his mind, and he would need full faculties to attempt a mind link with one so loosely joined to him as Louis was. They'd shared the dark kiss only once, when Louis had come to him with the offer of salvation and he, in his incredible arrogance, had laughed and stripped his friend of the fleeting humanity granted him by Arabella's father.

Maybe he wouldn't come at all, even if he heard.

Gino, help me! Don't let me die!

That was all he could manage as fingers of daylight etched a faint line at the top of the wall above him.

"Madre del Dio!" His panic-stricken gaze was riveted to that downward-seeping brightness even though it burned his eyes. "Gino, hurry or there'll be nothing but ash for you to rescue."

"What have you gotten yourself into, *amico mio?*"

Gerard laughed hoarsely and supplied a wide smile for his friend. "You know me, always the poor judge of character, never listening to good advice. This is not the kind of price I wish to pay for my foolishness."

Louis stepped closer to examine the situation. It was grim, indeed. His friend was in desperate shape despite the smile that etched a poignant contrast to his sunken and strained features. There was a fatal amount of blood on the front of his clothing and Gerard was shivering fitfully for the loss of it. The fine bones of his face stood out against colorless flesh, skull-like with shock and suffering. The ghastly wound at his neck was healing but those on his wrists where the silver bound tight were fresh and terrible.

"Gino, I don't mean to rush you but I am growing quite uncomfortable."

Louis could feel it, too, that heating of the blood that came with the sunrise. If his was streaking along his veins like liquid fire, Gerard's, in his pure vampiric state, must have been boiling. Louis gripped him by the forearms— there was no way he could touch the silver himself without being burned by it— and pulled. Gerard's screams were so horrible, he could not continue.

"I'm sorry. I'm sorry, *amico mio*. But there is no other way."

Gerard was shuddering with shock and fear as his wild gaze fixed upon that horizon of light banding the bricks a scant inch above his fingertips. "Gino, don't let me burn! Take off my hands if you must but don't let me burn." His unnatural flesh above the silver cuff had already begun to smoke and smolder. "Gino, please! Do something!"

Steeling himself, Louis murmured, "Steady, my friend," then he took a firm grip beneath the cuffs and jerked with all his strength. With an awful cry, Gerard came away from the wall, slumping against him, carrying him to the floor with his unresponsive weight.

And at that moment, sunlight flooded down through the wall of fractured glass. Louis had no time to consider his act as he threw himself over Gerard, shielding him from the direct rays with his own body. Heat seared through him in tongues of quicksilver agony, but he bundled Gerard beneath him determinedly, his own breath beginning to labor with the pain.

"Gino, save yourself. Don't do this for me."

Louis didn't answer. He was using all his strength to block the debilitating effects of the light as he pushed both of them along the glass-littered floor to the cooler safety of the shadows. It was a temporary solution and each knew it.

"Thank you for trying, my friend," Gerard panted faintly. He was already blistering from the indirect exposure and in too much distress to care much about his own death; in fact, it seemed like a welcome alternative. But he was concerned about Louis's. "Go while you can. You cannot save me now any more than you could centuries ago. My foolishness has sealed my fate."

"I will not let you die."

Gerard laughed weakly. "So stubborn." His eyes squeezed shut in torment and the rest of his words were gritty with strain. "I love you, Gino, my *bell'amico*. Forgive me and let me go."

But Louis wasn't listening to him. He was concentrating, sending a frantic summons.

* * *

With a gasp, Cassie sat upright in bed. "Louis?"

One quick glance told her she was alone, but she'd heard his call so plainly. Without hesitation, she threw off the covers, not taking time to blush over her own nakedness, and dressed hurriedly in answer to a subconscious command. Not knowing why, she gripped the coverlet on her bed and ripped it free before fleeing the room and racing down the stairs.

I will take that.

Cassie gave a start to find Takeo beside her. Wordlessly, she handed him the comforter and together they left the house, running barefooted across the dew-dampened grass to the rear of the gutted Radcliffe mansion.

"Louis?"

"Here! Quickly!"

She entered the greenhouse, mindless of the glass that crunched beneath her vulnerable feet, and rushed to the back of the room where Louis was crouched over another figure in the fast-evaporating shadows. She got one good glimpse before Takeo tossed the concealing covers over the both of them and the sight that would haunt her dreams for nights to come.

Help me.

It was Takeo's voice she heard. There could be no doubting it and no time to wonder how, as the two of them arranged the bedcovers into a suitable cocoon and held the ends closed as Louis stood, the limp body of his friend held close in his arms. It was an awkward trip back to her home and, once there, they did not go into one of the comfortable front rooms but rather to the basement steps. Again, there was no time for her to ask the questions bursting to be spoken. Tossing off the covers, Louis went down the stairs into the damp void of darkness. Reluctant, frightened, yet helplessly drawn by curiosity, Cassie followed behind Takeo.

Is he alive, Master?

I don't know.

What can I do?

Get me some torch light. Hurry.

Cassie approached the spot where Louis knelt on the dirt floor. Fear and alarm warred with a deeper sense of concern. It had been Gerard Pasquale she'd seen, she was sure of it even though he'd been barely recognizable. She sank down on the cold earth, aware of the ragged rush of Louis's breathing, of how it caught and spilled out anxiously.

"Don't you die, Gerardo," he urged in a husky tone. "Don't you die and leave me."

Just then a muted artificial brightness filled the dank chamber and Cassie could not contain her cry of horror.

"Oh, my God! Louis, what's happened to him? Was he burned?"

"Yes but that's not what worries me now."
He lifted one limp arm. "Takeo, get these
off. It's the silver that's killing him."

It sounded like an incredible claim but
one look at Gerard's wrist convinced Cassie. She'd never seen wounds so raw and
running with what she could not imagine.
In moments, Takeo knelt down with some
sort of gardening shears meant to clip
through wire. Lacing his fingers through
those of his friend, Louis held Gerard still
while Takeo cut through the clasps of the
cuff. Gerard gave a soft groan of relief as
the silver fell away. Quickly, the other side
was similarly freed and Gerard returned to
a frail lucidity.

"Gino, it is too late. My hold on life is
fast fading. I will not see the next moon
rise."

"No! No, I won't let you do this. You will
recover. Fight it. Without you, who will be
there to bedevil me through eternity?"

A weak smile spread across the blistered
face. "Gino, don't make me laugh. I hurt too
badly. Forgive me for Arabella. It was an act
of love from me to the both of you."

"I know. Save your strength."

"Why? I have no noble qualities worth re-
deeming. You were never able to teach them
to me."

"Then live and learn. It's not too late.
Please . . . Gerardo? I did not sacrifice my

soul for you so that you could desert me now!"

"I'm sorry, Gino. I am doomed to disappoint you."

"No . . ." He dragged his friend up into a tight embrace. Gerard's eyes were open now and Cassie could see through their glittering veil of blue to the swells of red and to the soulless darkness beyond. And she knew right then that he wasn't human—as she had suspected but had never quite dared believe. What then—?

And as she sat frozen at Louis's side, the truth overtook her with a chilling clarity. All the laughable details of Walter Rampling's article fit like a well-cast mold over the two beside her.

Somehow, impossibly, these two friends were vampires.

Her hand touched the base of her throat where the evidence of two tiny wounds remained. The mark of Louis's kiss. The reason for her weakness and disorientation. He'd taken her blood to survive and go on. Was that, then, the answer for Gerard's life as well?

Looking at him, she could scarcely picture the wickedly handsome charmer who'd stood at her bedside with Arabella's last request, and had mourned at her funeral as one of the family would. That he was more to Louis than an old friend was readily apparent by the tracks of wetness upon her lover's cheeks. She could not endure the thought of his renewed pain at losing another that he loved.

"Will blood revive him?"

Louis stared at her as if she'd sprouted another head upon her shoulders. "What?"

"I'm not well versed in these—matters. If he has fresh blood, will he recover?"

"I-I don't know. Cassie, what are you saying? Do you have any idea—"

"I'm beginning to. I hate wearing black, Louis. The color does not become me. What do I do?"

He gazed at her with an expression akin to awe, then gently took up her hand in his. Quickly, he raked his thumbnail across the veins of her wrist and pressed the bright fount of blood to Gerard's mouth.

For a moment, nothing happened and Cassie blinked against the throbbing ache. Then she felt the briefest movement against the tender flesh of her wrist, just a whisper of breath. Suddenly, Gerard's hands flew up to clamp down upon her arm, affixing the wound to his lips. A piercing pain made Cassie cry out, then the powerful pull threaded through her in streaks of fire and ice, bringing faintness and a great dizzying surge. She sank in a partial swoon upon his gory shirt front and Louis cradled them both in his embrace.

Cassie lost track of time. Hours seemed to float by in a numbing haze of near bliss.

She was aware of Gerard's coldness, of the very heat from her body leaving her to infuse through him. She could hear the beat of his heart growing stronger as her own began to fail and falter. And then there was just his, invading her, becoming hers, joining them together. She experienced a fleeting mingling of minds, could actually read his thoughts within her head, could see his memories, could feel the enormity of his pain. There were tears upon her face as she heard Louis's distant call.

"Gently, my friend. Easy. This was a gift, not a sacrifice. Do not make it one."

And slowly the connection broke from between her and Gerard, and yet a part of it remained. She could still feel the texture of his mind imprinted upon hers. Just as she could feel Louis's there. Gerard released her, his mouth moving up slightly so he could press a bloody kiss into the well of her palm.

I am in your debt, signorina. You may call upon me at your convenience. I will be there.

She sat back, woozy and unsure of her balance.

"Takeo, take her," Louis was saying. "We must retire. Come, my friend, you can share my resting place."

"Mille grazie. Mi sento stanco. I am very weary," came Gerard's weak reply.

From Takeo's supporting arms, Cassie watched Louis rise up with his friend easily borne. He carried Gerard across the room to where the shadows lengthened into blackness. There she could just make out the shape of a large box laid out horizontally. It looked like . . . a coffin.

She must have lost touch with the bizarre reality for a moment because her next awareness was of Takeo lifting her to her feet.

Come, mistress, you must rest, too. There is nothing more for us to do here.

She struggled against that logic and pulled free, needing to see, needing to know for certain.

She approached the closed box in a drunken reel. Her knees wobbled with weakness, with fright. Pain began to pulse from the lacerations on her feet and as her hands settled on the cool wood, her courage almost failed her. Then she rallied and determinedly lifted the lid.

They were stretched out upon a slippery bed of white silk, Louis upon his back, his eyes softly closed as if in slumber, Gerard on his side wedged in next to him. Already the terrible blisters were beginning to fade from his face. But Cassie could see from where his hand rested in a graceful curl atop Louis's chest that the open sores were still inflamed and just as awful.

They both looked so peaceful, so unaware of her as she stared down in mounting horror.

One thought came to Cassie as she slid toward a thankful unconsciousness.

The man she loved— the man she'd allowed to make love to her— was no man at all.

Nineteen

Cassie watched the evening approach with the sweep of the clock's hands. She would never feel the same way about this particular time of day again, the slow seeping darkness that meant the awakening of her love.

"You look deep in thought. You must have many questions."

She wasn't quite brave enough to face him yet, even though the soft drawl of his voice shot a shiver of longing through her. Was that real or what he'd done to her?

"Cassie?"

"Yes," she answered at last. "We have much to discuss."

"You are still here, so that says much." But she could tell from the uncertainty in his tone that it didn't tell him enough. "I am still here and that speaks volumes as well."

"Had you thought I would try to destroy you while you slept?"

"I don't know. Did you?"

She'd had time to think about many things after she'd woken from a deep sleep of exhaustion. Takeo had greeted her with a hearty breakfast and after it had somewhat fortified her, she'd made a call into the *Lexicon* to make an excuse for her absence—a recurrence of her stubborn illness, she'd said, not exactly a lie—then had spent the afternoon hours piecing together the implausible but apparently possible truth.

Cassie looked up at Louis then. He lingered in the doorway, hesitation skirting the impassive lines of his exquisite face. She was surprised that he looked no different to her now that the scales of innocence had been shed. He still looked—gorgeous. And there was no denying that the sight of him made her pulse race. He was sedately dressed in a conservative suit of clothes, appearance dapper and correct, much like the men who frequented the downtown business district. How easily he concealed the unholiness of the creature within him.

"You are a vampire."

"Yes."

"Thank God."

He blinked at her odd reply. It was not what he'd expected. "You are not upset. I don't understand."

"It's an easier truth to accept than the fact that I was going mad. You cannot know how relieved I am that there is some—logical explanation for the mysteries my mind could not answer."

"Knowing what I am has done that?" He was still puzzled and cautious with his relief.

Cassie gave a nervous laugh. "I had thought such things were fiction. No wonder you were so discomposed by Walter's article." Her gaze skewered him directly. "Was it true?"

"The facts or his supposition?"

"Both. Either."

"He did his research well on my kind."

"Did you kill those women?"

He flinched slightly at the coldness of her accusation. "No."

"And I should believe you?"

"That's up to you, Cassandra."

She preferred to change the subject for the moment. "A vampire," she mused. "As in the undead, sleeping during the day, drinking blood to survive?"

"Yes."

"You drank mine, didn't you?"

"Yes."

"More than once."

"Yes."

She let his answers assimilate with what she'd already guessed. Because she'd had the better part of the day to prepare for this meeting, she was handling it well. Better, she supposed, than most would. After the initial shock, her reporter's mind had taken over, supplying an endless parade of questions. They helped keep the basic fear at bay. He made it easy for her to think. He didn't come closer nor did he try to influence her thinking. She had to wonder why he was being so truthful now. Was it just to lull her into a false sense of security?

"No," he said, as if in answer. "If I had wanted to harm you, I could have done it long ago when you suspected nothing. It's time you knew the truth."

She gave a small start of surprise. "You can read my thoughts."

"You do not guard them very well, *cara.*"

And she flushed deeply, thinking of what had been in her mind just before they'd made love. No wonder he'd known exactly how to please her. He was fulfilling her every fantasy by pulling them directly from her dreams.

They'd made love. She'd let him . . . touch her, join with her. A sudden shudder overtook her.

"I've not in any way contaminated you, if that's what is worrying you," he drawled out in an inflectionless tone. She couldn't tell if he was insulted or hurt or angry . . . or indeed, if he really felt any of those things at all. "In fact," he continued rather crisply, "sexual relations with me are probably safer than with the majority of Manhattan's prowling male populace. Unless it's the idea itself that you find so repugnant."

Repugnant? The word confused her. No, it had not been repulsive then and wasn't now. "I'm sorry if I have offended you by the implication that I found our union less than— enjoyable. It's just the idea that you were privy to my most private thoughts."

A small smile shaped his mouth. "You did not seem to mind so much last night."

She blushed hotter, and the embarrassment of it made her reply curt. "That's before I discovered your performance was less than— spontaneous."

"Forgive me, Miss Alexander, for trying to be sensitive to your wishes. I should have been like any other man and considered only my own."

She had no doubts then. He was insulted and hurt and angry. And before she could do anything to soothe those ruffled emotions, there was a gruff throat clearing from the hall.

"I am interrupting something, no? A lovers' tiff, perhaps?"

"No," Louis growled as he turned to face his pale and yet wobbly friend. "You should not be up."

"You know me, Gino, so easily bored with my own company. Thank you for the loan of your shirt. My own was rather— unpresentable."

"You look like hell."

"What a thing to say to a creature of my vanity," Gerard exclaimed with feigned affront. "But better to look like hell than wake up there. And for that, I have you to thank. *Mille grazie, bell'amico.* I was not sure you would care to answer my call. After all, we do have our share of—" He smirked and continued. "—bad blood, shall we say, between us. I am grateful that you are more compassionate than I would have been."

Louis smiled. "You would have done the same thing."

"Please." Gerard made a dramatic clutch at his chest. "You flatter me with your estimation of my good will, misguided though it may be. I am a singularly selfish being with no thoughts for anyone but myself. You would do well to remember that."

But Louis's smile didn't ease as Gerard put a fond hand to his shoulder then advanced into the room.

"And you, *signorina,*" he purred, coming to perch beside Cassie on the sofa, "you have my undying— and I do mean undying— gratitude." He scooped up her hand, kissing her knuckles, the back of her wrist, turning it to taste the well of her palm, the fresh wound at its base. His lips lingered there until she felt a sizzle of sensation course down the length of her arm. He grinned up at her, his pale eyes all mischievous dazzle. "There are many ways I could choose to show my thanks. Would you like me to show them to you now? I could take you away with me and shower you with delights."

She said nothing because suddenly she was overwhelmed with the lascivious desire to beg him to do just that. He chuckled softly, recognizing her weakness of will and the strength it took to deny it, and him.

"She is not interested in your thin charade, Gerard."

"No?" His devilish gaze slid to his friend then back to a yet entranced Cassie. He leaned closer to her, letting the brilliance of his stare bewitch her. "Are you uninterested?"

Louis growled impatiently. "You said you were leaving. When?"

"Tired of my company so soon, Gino? You wound me." He turned to Cassie with a sultry smile and a whisper of, "He is jealous. Shall I give him reason?" His lips brushed hers but the gesture was so passionless, it shook Cassie from her spell of fascination. She cupped his cheek and levered him back a safe degree.

"You tease your friend most unkindly, sir. You know it is you who has no interest in me," she chided.

Gerard laughed at her astuteness. "You see through me too easily. Gino expects me to behave badly. To do less would have him worrying that I was not as well recovered as I appear. He is like a smothering mama when he is concerned. That is because he loves me, though I do not deserve it. Poor Gino, you have always had too much heart and I, too little."

Louis's features sobered. "Are you all right?"

Gerard leaned close to Cassie to whisper conspiratorially, "See, I told you. Just like a mama." And there was no way to miss how pleased he was with that. He sighed contentedly. "But I must go. It would be bad manners to remain when you two so obviously wish to be alone."

Louis crossed to them, still frowning and apparently not convinced by his friend's claim of good health. He lifted up one neatly bound hand and, despite Gerard's pull of protest, unwound the wrapping Takeo had applied that morning. He uttered an expressive curse at the sight of the horrible injury.

"Madre del Dio! You are far from fine." He caught Gerard by the chin, tipping it up so he could not avoid Louis's gaze. "Let me see how you really are."

For a flickering instant, Gerard let down his guard of pretense and Louis winced away.

"Amico mio, the fever still consumes you. It is madness for you to think of leaving."

"And it is too dangerous to think of staying," Gerard amended with a sudden sobriety. "For me and for you."

"Who tried to destroy you?"

Gerard supplied a wry smile. "You might say Bianca and I had a parting of ways. She is not very sympathetic to those she casts away."

"Bianca did this?"

"She has a dim view of disloyalty in any form."

Louis made the connection all at once. "You tried to warn me last night and I wouldn't listen. You came here to warn Cassie."

"And see what that moment of insanity cost me—a fate I would not have wished upon you . . . even though that was her plan. She is quite mad when it comes to you, you know. I don't envy you her affection. As far as she knows, I am ash and I would prefer she continue to believe that, at least for now. Attack from a point of strength, never from weakness. One invaluable piece of advice I learned from her. I will reveal myself to her when the time is right—for me."

Louis sank down on the arm of the couch beside him, stunned by the grim revelation. "You are wise to leave, my friend. Only go, stay with Nicole until you are stronger and less vulnerable. She will take you in."

"I'm not sure I trust that husband of hers any more than I trust Bianca. He is not fond of me, you know. No, Gino, it is better if I spent some time in my own company. And maybe develop some opinions of my own, eh? I think I'll go south, some place where the nights are long and warm and the menu selections are varied." He grinned irreverently, then allowed his gaze to shimmer with true feeling. "I will see you again. When one has an eternity, what's a decade or two?"

"That's what Bella said."

Gerard heaved another long sigh. "Ah, Gino, you did always have exquisite taste in all things." He rubbed Cassie's cheek with his thumb then stood, wavering slightly. Louis rose to support him with a hand beneath his elbow. "Be careful, *amico mio. Il nemico,* she is not alone. The one she has picked to replace me makes me seem a papal candidate in comparison. She will try again tonight. Do not let her succeed. I would miss your pretty face too much." He gripped Louis by either side of the head and kissed him grandly on either cheek. "I have a sudden taste for Creole. *Arrivederci,* my friends. Call if ever you should need the favor returned."

And Cassie blinked in amazement as abruptly she and Louis were the only ones in the room. "How quickly you come and go," she murmured.

"Gerard and his flare for the dramatic."

Then the awkwardness of their earlier conversation began to settle back between them. Slowly, Louis assumed the spot his friend had vacated on the sofa, but he made no move to close the distance. His expression was atypically unguarded, and for once Cassie could read all upon it: his worry, his sadness, the wistfulness of parting with one so obviously tied to his heart.

"You are very close, the two of you."

Louis smiled. "We were boys together in Florence."

"And when was that?"

His smile took a wry bend, sure his candor would shock her. "In the early fifteen hundreds."

"That's a long time to remain friends," was her only comment.

"We have grown much since those simple days, regrettably apart. He is all I have left to remind me of what I was."

"And what were you, Louis?"

"Naive, young, human. I had the bad luck to meddle in my foolish friend's love affair with a mysterious woman. The woman proved a demon from hell and her kiss of death damned us both to this eternal life of darkness."

"She's the woman Gerard warned you about?" At his nod, Cassie rallied possessively. "What are we going to do to stop her?"

Her attitude nonplussed him. "You will do nothing but be careful and stay close so I can protect you."

"And who protects you? I do not want you to end up like Gerard."

"Does it matter to you that much, *cara*? Enough to risk your life for someone who is not what he pretended to be?"

She didn't answer, and for Louis that was answer enough. He rose up and strode to the windows. She could read tension in every elegant line yet was unprepared to ease it. Not yet. Not when her emotions were separated from thoughts by the shock of her discovery. He spoke to her quietly while looking outward toward the night.

"I asked you before if you wanted me to leave. You said no. Is it still your wish to have me here?"

"If I said it was, where would that answer come from? My own desires or from those you instilled in me?"

"I do not know."

"You don't know?" Her tone had taken on a crust of agitation. "How much of what I feel, of what I think, is truly my own?"

"Most," he replied without turning to face her mounting indignation.

"Most. But not all."

"No. What we— shared placed within you an instinct to see to my safety and my needs."

"Shared? You mean what you took from me?"

"Yes."

"You've been using me, Louis. You've taken advantage of my isolation, of my loneliness, of my friendship for Arabella and my— my interest in you— or rather in what I thought you were. How could you do that, then claim to care for me?"

"It's part of what I am, Cassie. The desire to survive, to protect, it's deeply ingrained in all of us or we would not continue beyond our own lifespans. We become masters at disguising the ugliness of our existence."

"You're a parasite. You live off those who would love you like a tick upon a dog. You suck up their affection and prey upon their weakness the same way you devour their blood. Don't you?"

"An unflattering but quite accurate summation."

"And you kill."

"Yes. Sometimes."

"Like those two men who attacked me."

"You, yourself, said they deserved what befell them. I could not let them hurt you."

"And those women. What danger did they present to you?"

"I told you, that was not me."

"But you said you must kill to survive."

"No. I must drink to survive. I do not kill those who sustain me. They give me the gift of life. I do not repay them with their own death."

"How very . . . noble."

He fought not to writhe beneath the sting of her sarcasm. He expected her condemnation. He could not argue the vile circumstances under which he lived. Nor could he in good conscience try to explain away what he was or what he did in a manner that would be more palatable to this woman he'd come to love. He was remembering the mortal he'd saved in the park, her horror, stark and unrelieved by the fact that he had rescued her. Which had she feared more, Gerard had taunted. Indeed, he believed she preferred the known and recognizable peril of the man who'd assaulted her. Would Cassie turn from him now that she knew the truth? She would have to make those decisions and it was becoming quite apparent that she had no sympathy for his plight. Nor could he beg for it.

"So," she concluded with a raw edge of injury, "let me see if I have a complete picture. You needed a place to hide during your daylight rest. You needed an available source of sustenance. And you didn't have to look far. I all but threw myself at you. You came into my home at my invitation. You abused my generosity, took advantage of my hospitality, preyed upon my emotions and clouded my mind so you would be safe. You drank my blood, you stole my individuality, well knowing it was the one thing I cherished most. You let me believe I was going mad. And then you seduced me and took my body the way you had already violated my soul. Have I gotten all the facts straight?"

"The facts, perhaps, madam newswoman, but not the motives behind them."

"So tell me your pure-at-heart motives. Convince me that I am more to you than a passing convenience." And the tears standing in her dark eyes begged him to make it into a good argument.

"There was nothing pure about the state of my heart. It belonged to another and yet I could not stop myself from coming to care for you. I did not make this situation. It was forced upon me. But I did not fight against it as I should have. I wanted you, Cassie. I wanted you in ways that defiled my vows to another. I could not permit myself to love you but I could not defend against my need to have you. I can offer you no excuses. But do not accuse me of using you without conscience. My feelings for you run too deep to express, so close to the loss of another love. For that, I do apologize. I have unfairly enjoyed your giving heart while mine was not free to give in return."

"I don't understand, Louis. Are you talking about your grandmother?"

"No. My wife. Arabella was my wife of sixty-four years."

Cassie stared at him, too stunned to make a sound. If she'd not been sitting down, she would have dropped like a stone.

"We met when I was going to her father, a renowned London doctor making brilliant headway in studies of the blood. I had hoped he could cure my affliction. Bella and I fell in love and we wed when I thought his treatments had succeeded. They did not, but Bella refused to leave me even knowing the manner of beast she'd married. We had a daughter between us, Nicole, and she was doomed to inherit my curse and pass it on to the man she loved. Frederica is their child, my granddaughter."

It was too much to absorb all at once. "They are all vampires."

"We do not age beyond the time of maturity. We will stay as we are through centuries of darkness. Bella would not come over as one of us. She loved life too dearly and it was her stubborn humanity that I adored. She was my hope that I would someday know salvation. She had hoped that you— " He broke off suddenly, looking disturbed, then just as quickly all emotion seemed to leave him. "She had hoped that you would provide me with a reason for continued optimism."

Cassie thought back upon her conversations with the elderly woman, refocusing them to fit Arabella's shift in status from grandmother to wife. And she was aghast when she thought of the things she'd said to the older woman, expressing her longings and desires for the man who was her husband.

"I've been such a fool," she murmured wretchedly.

"No," Louis argued gently. "How could you have guessed? It was a well-conceived deception, one necessary to explain our relationship as she aged and I did not."

"And it was so easy to deceive me. How it must have amused the both of you." She surged up off the sofa, refusing to acknowledge her weakness in favor of her distress.

"What else have you hidden from me, Louis? What other secrets have you concealed under the guise of my supposed illness and mental confusion?"

"Nothing of any great importance." But she could see the remoteness settle in his gaze and knew he wasn't speaking the entire truth. And that mild rebuff was enough to send her into a rage of wounded fury.

"Tell me, Louis! What bits and pieces have you stolen from my memory? I want them back! How dare you decide what is inconsequential! You have managed to invade my life but I will not allow you to tamper with my mind. Give me back those images."

"Not all are good."

"I don't care. Restore them to me now if you wish to remain safely in my home."

"Very well," he stated and, just as quickly, details came flooding back into her head. She reeled beneath the magnitude and the intensity. Louis emerging from the fog, his eyes unholy, his fangs distended. The cruel way he'd dismissed her as she'd come crawling to him down the stairs desperate to serve him. The details of Arabella's death. The carriage ride with Gerard and some frighteningly beautiful blonde woman who had laughed when Louis claimed how little the foolish mortal female meant to him. All of it returned from the veil he'd cast to protect himself from her knowledge of what he was and how little she mattered to him.

Just then there was a knock at her door, putting a halt to any further discussion. Without a word, Cassie went to answer it, wiping at her eyes as she crossed the huge foyer.

"Walter. This is a surprise."

"Might I come in for a moment, Cass? There are some things I must discuss with you that are best not left for the office." Even as he spoke the mysterious words, he was glancing about nervously.

Concerned about what might have the flamboyant editor so obviously discomposed, she held the door wide. "Please come in. I happen to have an excellent brandy in my father's study. You look as though you could use a glass. Or two. I think I will join you in at least one."

"Are you alone?" he asked, looking anxiously about. From their commanding position in the front hall, they could see clearly into all the adjacent rooms. All of them were empty, even the parlor she'd just come from.

"Yes," she told him, leading the way to the brandy, needing one as badly as her employee. She poured while he fidgeted about the room, stopping before a mammoth portrait of Brighton Alexander.

"I quite admired your father."

"I know you did, Walter. You and he got into a number of scrapes together in your earlier years. Father spoke of them fondly."

"A tragedy, his death. So sad. So unexpected. So wasteful."

"Yes," Cassie agreed, washing down the ache of loneliness with a toss of amber liquor. It burnt through the pain of reminiscing. "But that wasn't what you came to see me about, was it?"

"No." If possible, he looked even more agitated. "Cass, this is going to sound crazy."

"Try me, Walter. You'll find I'm amazingly open-minded this evening."

"I think you are in danger, Cass. And I don't think your father's death was any accident."

"What?"

"Dark forces are at work. I know you are not going to believe this. I didn't at first. I started this investigation on a lark. I never expected to believe in the subject of my research."

Cassie's features stiffened. "Walter, if you are trying to tell me my father was killed by a vampire, you are wasting your time. He was killed investigating a story. You know the details. You wrote his obituary yourself. He was stabbed in an alley."

"But why was he there? What story was he on? Did he ever tell you?"

"No. No, he didn't. He was very closed-lipped about the whole thing." She closed her eyes, distressed by the memory of their last conversation. "All he'd say was that it was something he had a hard time believing."

"Something like vampirism?"

"No," she scoffed, almost angry that he would suggest such a ridiculous— But it wasn't ridiculous, was it? "Walter, you're allowing the strain of this investigation to color your judgment."

"Where did you get those marks on your neck?"

His sudden question startled her. Reflexively, she covered the bite with one hand while an unconscious cunning provided an excuse. "I gouged myself with a hat pin. What are you suggesting? That I am the victim of some beast out of superstition? Walt, please."

"I'm worried about you, Cassie. Your change in behavior, your absences from work, these killings that seemed somehow linked to you and the *Lexicon*. And to your father."

Glib assurances abruptly failed her.

"I've been tracing the paths of those women who were slain. They seem to have some mysterious gentleman in common, one who is generous with his wealth, who visited only at night and was careful not to be seen. Cassie, forgive the personal nature of this question, but are you involved with anyone, anyone who would have a motive for murdering women who resemble you?"

"No, Walter. I am not."

It took some doing to convince Walter Rampling that his fears were groundless and to send him home. But in his absence, Cassie could not dismiss the seeds of doubt he had planted.

Had the Radcliffes begun their careful plotting earlier than she suspected?

Had Louis killed Brighton Alexander?

Anxious because he'd made no impression, Walter Rampling started down the front walk only to be distracted by a movement in the shadows. His initial reaction gave way to the relief of recognition.

"What are you doing here so late at night, sneaking about in Cassie's bushes?"

A flash of metal was his reply.

Gurgling for his last breath, Walter Rampling collapsed and died with the bulk of his suspicions yet unspoken.

Twenty

Bianca du Maurier felt a faint stir of air behind her and whirled with a gasp.

"Expecting someone else?"

She forced a smile to shape her narrowed lips. "Gino. What a— pleasant surprise."

"Is it? Why do I get the impression that you expected our next meeting to be under vastly different circumstances?"

"I-I don't understand. But what does that matter now that you are here?" She sidled up to him, slipping sleek bare arms in a sinewy circlet about his neck. "Oh, Gino, dare I hope this means you've missed me?"

He smiled blandly in the face of her skilled seduction, not nearly as affected by it as she had hoped. In fact, he was almost wearied. He glanced about her opulent rooms with a bored air. "Where is Gerardo? I would say hello to him as well."

Her smile never faltered. "You know Gerard. One can never be sure of him."

"Apparently you weren't, were you?"

"I don't know what you mean, Gino."

"The only reason I didn't hunt you down and destroy you centuries ago is because of the misguided feelings my friend had for you, and my reluctance to face him down once again over such a worthless cause. Perhaps I should thank you for freeing me to seek vengeance at last."

She had gone very still, her eyes reflectionless, soulless pits of hell. They widened as he drew a pouch from his coat and upended it on her Persian carpet. Candlelight glittered off the silver cuffs she'd used to bind Gerard, cuffs Louis had torn from the wall.

"Unlike you and even my late friend, Gerardo, I am not a vengeful creature. But I am protective of my right to live this sham of a life you left me as I see fit. I will not tolerate your interference again. If I see you near me or anyone I care for again, I will have these fashioned into the nails for your eternal coffin."

Bianca took a step back, rage building, billowing about her like a hurricane wind. "You dare threaten me? Me?" she roared, and her syllables were like cracks of lightning and volleys of thunder. "I made you. I brought you back from death to exist as you are now in a hybrid state between their world and mine. You have not the power to intimidate me. Gerard was the only one who came close to matching my strengths, and in the end it was his own vanity that played him false. That and his foolishly sentimental fondness for you. Without him to intercede for you, you are in no position to make idle promises."

"Perhaps he isn't, but I am."

Bianca retreated as an involuntary cry escaped her. Marchand LaValois stepped from the shadows, his dark features etched with menace.

"This does not concern you, Frenchman," she spat.

"My wife takes her father's health and happiness very seriously. So must I. Forgive me for being tardy, Louis. It took some doing to convince your stubborn daughter to stay behind. I finally made her see that we could handle this witch on our own—with pleasure." Then he smiled thinly at the momentarily subdued vampiress. "Your burns have healed nicely. One would hardly guess how close you came to resembling fireplace soot."

Bianca reared back like a viper readying a strike, but Marchand showed no trace of fear. In fact, his smile broadened insolently.

"Give me an excuse to come for you. I place family above all things in my life. I have not forgotten my brother whose soul you forced me to lay to rest. Give me a reason to seek you out and send you permanently to hell where you will probably rule—until I get there. You will never best me again. Never. Remember that. I hope it makes your slumber an uneasy one for the remainder of your cursed life. No man stands alone when he has family behind him. I would watch where I fling my own threats were I you, madame." He looked to Louis. "Was there anything I missed or any personal converse you wished to have with her? I promised Nicole I would return in time to take in some eclectic gallery opening with her. She fancies herself quite the expert on paintings these days."

"I think we've made the desired impression on Madame du Maurier. I trust she will not be bothering any of us again. Will you, Bianca?"

"We will meet again, be assured. And then the pleasure will be mine." She turned abruptly, causing the voluminous cape she wore to swirl around her until she was enveloped in its folds. They seemed to collapse in upon her like a closing fan, becoming thin, thinner, then nothing but air.

Marchand gave his father-in-law a lift of one black brow. "She certainly knows how to make an exit."

"As long as she stays gone," Louis concluded.

The two of them went out into the night, moving as equals. Louis had the experience of centuries but Marchand's was the superior power. Combined, they made an awesome whole, one Bianca was wise to fear.

"I'd forgotten how sweet the mountain air

tastes," Marchand reflected then he sighed. "How is your treacherous friend, Pasquale? Has he recovered? It would quite break Nicole's heart if something bad were to befall him. I don't know why, but she has some great attachment to his black soul." He sounded annoyed by it. Louis tried not to smile.

"Gerard is fine. I know him. He is hiding somewhere, nursing his wounded pride. He will be back."

"I cannot wait," Marchand drawled out dryly. "And you, how are you? Nicole has driven me close to crazy with her pleas to visit. I thought you would like to have time to make your own adjustments before being swamped by family."

"I am— better."

"And the woman, are you still with her?" He phrased it so casually that if Louis hadn't known Marchand as well as he did, he would have missed the sharp interest he had in the answer.

"Tell my daughter I will inform her of the details of my private life when I feel she has the right to know them."

Marchand grinned suddenly. "She won't welcome that news. But I will tell her. *Au revoir.* My regards to the lady."

The lady was very much on Louis's mind when he returned to her home toward the hours of dawn. He stood at the edge of her bed watching her sleep, at points with his intentions regarding her but oddly at peace with Arabella. There was no less love for the woman who'd shared so many of his years but he'd come to terms with the meaning behind her sacrifice. He was to go on for her through Cassie.

Not an easy task, considering Cassie was contemplating driving a stake through his heart rather than risking her own on him.

As if she could feel the disturbing texture of his thoughts, Cassie came awake with a jerk and a defensive, "What are you doing in my room?" An odd question, considering how they'd spent their hours the last time they were in it together.

"I mean you no harm," he told her softly. "I only came to assure myself of your safety."

"The only danger I'm in is from believing the illusions you placed in my mind. Please go." She'd drawn the covers up to her chin as if they offered some security, and her gaze was fierce in its denial of her own heart.

He sketched a brief bow of acquiescence then murmured, "If you need me, call out and I will be there."

"Unless, of course, I happen to need you during the daylight hours."

He managed not to flinch at that but instead, replied even more quietly, "Then Takeo will answer. You may trust him . . . probably more than me. Forgive me for disturbing you." And he stepped back to be consumed by the shadows.

Cassie sat for several heartbeats wondering if he was truly gone. She was disturbed, deeply. By the questions that plagued her heart and mind and the uncertainties that twisted about her soul. By the agony of longing that would not go away. She finally lay back, managing a few more hours of fitful sleep, and by the time she prepared to go in to work, her nerves were as frazzled as her attempt at a smooth, upswept hairstyle. She provided Takeo with a stiff smile as she ate the breakfast that was much better than any her scowling former housekeeper had ever prepared. The woman hadn't said anything about her as yet, at least that she knew of, but Cassie knew she'd been scandalized by the turn of affairs. Just like those at her own office. A tortured laugh escaped her as she buttered her biscuit. All this fuss over her living with a man. What would they say if they knew he was no man at all?

Her knife paused in mid-stroke. What would they say? What an incredible sensation it would cause if the public got wind of a real vampire.

The story of the century.

Her hands were shaking as she finished her meal. She didn't dare look Takeo in the eye as he escorted her out to the carriage. Could he read her mind? She didn't know.

There was no privacy, not even within her own head and heart.

And there was no one she could trust.

She slipped in the front door of the *Lexicon,* pausing to lose herself in the sense of normalcy. This was her life, the one thing that mattered to her. The one thing that had never betrayed the efforts she applied. The lover she understood. She'd been foolish to think any other could satisfy.

"Good morning, Miss Alexander. I trust you're feeling better."

"Yes, thank you, Sanford."

"Miss Alexander, do you have a minute to look over this ad layout?"

"In my office in about a half hour. All right?"

"Fine. Thank you. Glad to have you back."

Glad to be home, her soul sighed.

"Cassie, Mr. Alexander's been waiting for you. He said you should go right into his office."

So much for a moment's peace, she thought wryly. "Tell Mr. Alexander that I am otherwise occupied this morning and that I will try to fit him in later today. Has Walter come in yet this morning?"

"Haven't seen him." That was echoed by several shrugs and negative head shakes.

"Have him come to my office at once when he does." Then she shut herself behind her door and fell limply back into her desk chair.

As she sat watching the bustle in the room outside her window, her hands stroked along the old desk that had been her father's when he'd started out. He'd passed it down to her with pride. His eyes had actually filled with moisture when he'd seated her in the chair and showed her where he'd kept the personal stationery all done over with her own name on top. She'd vowed that day never to disappoint him. But she had. Gravely. With her continued fears. With her weakness of resolve. She had at her disposal the means to save the *Lexicon*. All it would take was the betrayal of a man— of a *being* who had already played her affections false. Why was she hesitating?

Her father had been right about Louis. Had he begun an investigation on his own, not speaking of it because of her bias on the subject? Had he uncovered the facts of Louis's dual life, that he was both man and murderer? Had he then become a victim? Her vision blurred as she considered the possibility. Had it all been carefully staged: her father's death, the killings, the frightening gifts and threatening notes, all aimed at weakening her to the idea of taking Louis in as her protector? She was the perfect foil: alone, vulnerable to his sophisticated charm, distanced from family and friends who could offer cautioning counsel. Louis and Arabella Radcliffe had found the perfect fool for continuing his deception.

Suddenly she became aware of an odd stillness settling in about her. Unnerved by it, Cassie glanced up to see a strange hush had fallen over those in the outer work area. Police sergeant Dan Hooper stood right in the middle of the lull of activity. One by one they were looking back in her direction with faces etched in shock and sorrow.

No! her mind cried out in objection. No more! She couldn't take any more bad news on top of all else. She sat frozen in her chair as Danny came slowly across the room. Her thoughts went numb, refusing to guess at the terrible tidings his expression foretold. He tapped once on the door and came in, closing it behind him.

"I don't suppose it would do any good to beg for this to be a social call." Her attempt at a smile bent like a crooked bit of wire.

"I'm sorry, Cassie."

"Just tell me straight out, Danny."

"Walter Rampling— "

"No!" The cry choked from her before she could stifle it behind quickly raised hands. She squeezed her eyes shut, wishing the rest of his words away. But they couldn't be denied.

"Walter Rampling's body was found early this morning under one of the el stations in mid-town. His throat had been cut. His money and his watch were still on him so robbery wasn't the motive. What the hell's

going on here, Cass? What are you involved
in?"

"Oh, Danny, I wish to God I knew."

For the next hour, she listened to the
grisly details and gave her own abbreviated
statement. For some reason she didn't even
understand herself, she didn't mention Walter's last visit to her home. For that same
reason, she didn't mention her growing certainty that her preternatural houseguest had
been his killer.

Proof. She needed proof.

The moment Danny left to interview the
others in the office, Cassie went straight to
Walter's cubbyhole office space with a promise to turn over anything she might find of
any bearing on the case. In her heart, she
knew she was searching for any evidence that
might convict Louis of the crime. What she'd
do with that link, she didn't know. She
wanted to believe she'd do the right thing.
But if it was that simple, why were her hands
cold and her pulse-beats going like crazy?

With a stack of Rampling's papers clutched
to her breast, Cassie slipped through the somber newsroom to the isolation of her office.
Dumping the disorganized lot upon her desktop, she sat with the determined purpose of
sifting out any damning references. Unfortunately, she couldn't seem to focus her gaze
long enough to see to the task. Just as her
shoulders began to shake with shock and

grief, they were spanned by a supportive embrace, one she turned into gratefully.

"We're all devastated by the news, Cass. No one expects you to hold up like a martyr."

"Oh, Quinton, I can't stop thinking that this is all my fault."

"What do you mean? How could it be your fault?"

"I provoked him into doing that story. He came to my house last night with the most disturbing news. Things he'd found out about my father's death, about the murders that are still happening. I refused to take him seriously. And now—and now he's dead."

"What news did he have, Cass?"

"Nothing solid, just some story leads he'd been following. I was trying to find something in this mess he keeps upon his desk."

Quinton's hand was stroking gently through her hair, but his glittering eyes were upon her desktop. "Did you tell your police officer friend?"

"No. Not yet. I wanted to do some investigating on my own first."

"First and foremost a newswoman, eh, Cassie? Do you need some help going through all this? I'm not sure I'd know exactly what to look for but if you tell me—"

"I don't know, myself. Thank you, Quinn, but I'd rather do it alone. I need something to occupy my mind or I fear I'll go mad."

He pressed a brief kiss to her temple, a

strictly brotherly gesture. "I understand. If you need me, call. Promise?"

Cassie nodded and gave a heavy sigh. "Oh, Quinn, I am so overwhelmed by all this. When is it going to end?"

"Soon, Cass. I promise. Soon."

"You what?"

Fitzhugh Alexander strode to the door and slammed it closed before turning to confront his son. Quinton was seated on the edge of his desk, negligently swinging one leg while he toyed with a piece of colorful millefiori glass his father was particularly fond of.

"Put that down and repeat yourself."

"I said, Walter was getting too close to several truths so I killed him."

It wasn't the news but the delivery of it that had Fitzhugh so shaken. His son was blandly indifferent while a small smile played about his refined lips, almost as if he was secretly amused by what he'd done.

"Walter was my friend."

Quinton shrugged. "How long would that friendship have served when he found out that you plotted your own brother's death?"

"That was business. That was to save the *Lexicon.*"

Quinton's laugh was low and gritty. "That was to save your miserable job. You know Uncle Brighton was about to cut you loose.

So let's not make it sound any more noble than what it is."

Fitzhugh stared at his son, trying to fathom the change. Quinton was— harder somehow, harder and even more ruthless than his own ambitions could imagine. There was a glaze to his eyes not put there by drink or drug. It was an opaque sheen that was oddly lifeless. And for the first time, Fitzhugh experienced a chill of alarm at what he had created from the sensitive clay of his son's soul.

"Brighton is dead and now Walter is too," he said at last. "There's nothing we can do to change those things. Now, we must be very careful to protect our own interests."

"Cass is going through Walter's papers," Quinton remarked idly.

Fitzhugh's attention narrowed into the furrow of a frown. "Will she find anything?"

An elegant shrug. "Who knows? Nothing, perhaps everything."

"She must be stopped. She must be— "

"Eliminated?"

Fitzhugh hadn't dared speak it, but now the solution was obvious. "Yes."

"I could take care of it for you, Father. For a partnership in the *Lexicon.*"

Fitzhugh bit back his harsh laughter and studied his son through new eyes. "All right."

"And a column where I can publish my own work."

He ground down on that a bit harder, unable to believe his own son, his weak-willed son was attempting this kind of blackmail. Perhaps the boy wasn't worthless after all. Wasn't a column or two of sentimental pap worth the right to rule the *Lexicon* as he chose? With no interference?

"All right, Quinton, you take care of it. And son, today you've made me proud of the man you've become."

Quinton took a ragged breath, his heart filling up with the torturous bliss of a lifetime dream fulfilled. And that was worth one more life.

Twenty-one

Cassie was searching through pages, through scraps of paper, through squares torn off hotel menus with Walter's illegible scribbles on them until her eyes were watery and unfocused with fatigue. She had two stacks on her desk, one a collection of useless details that chronicled Walter's six years at the *Lexicon*, and the other, possible leads worth following. In all her weary scrutiny, she'd yet to find a single link to Louis. It seemed much of Walter's investigation shadowed his so-called vampire killer. He had pages of names but no hard facts.

And then, just as she was about to scoop the whole lot into her satchel, she came across a lone piece of paper that made the blood stand cold in her veins. It wasn't so much the cryptic message stating, *Schiavone's, nine o'clock*, it was the handwriting that leapt right off the page. That bold script she would never mistake. The same hand that penned the messages accompanying the murdered women's clothing.

Schiavone's. The name was familiar. Nine o'clock. What was the significance?

Then it came to her all at once in a sickening swell. That was the name of the small ethnic eatery behind which they'd found her father's body. Nine o'clock. The estimated time of his death.

There was a link, just as Walter suggested. But what and who? And why?

Too exhausted to continue, she swept the pertinent papers into her case and looked up, surprised to see how quiet the outer offices had become. It was late, far past quitting time for her staff. Anxiously, she gathered up her things and hurried to see if she could catch a ride with one of the others traveling uptown. She wasn't ready to confront Louis. Not with her heart and mind so unsettled. She hadn't found anything to condemn him. Nor to exonerate him, either.

How could she love a man who might have the blood of Walter Rampling as well as her father upon his hands?

The outer office was alarmingly empty. She had waited too long to find a suitable escort. And then she caught a glimpse of Sanford Raines, one of their copy editors. She found him to be whining and cloyingly ingratiating, but these were desperate times.

"Sanford, would it be possible for me to beg a ride with you?"

"Why, Miss Alexander, it would be an honor." And he was all simpering smiles as he helped her on with her wrap. "I'm meeting my fiancée at the corner, but I'm sure she won't mind."

Cassie hesitated, ashamed of the imposition but needy enough to overlook it. "Are you certain, Sanford?"

"Oh, yes. My Mim is a pip of a girl." He reached for Cassie's satchel with a gallant, "Let me carry that for you," but Cassie pulled it back.

"Thank you, I can manage." She placed her hand on the proffered arm and allowed him to lead her down to the street. Once there, she clung to his arm and refused to look toward the sleek brougham waiting to carry her home.

It was drizzling and the street and walk were awash with a dampness that reflected the city lights in vivid smears of color. Dry beneath her bonnet and cloak, Cassie nonetheless felt a shiver overtake her.

Cassie?

The soft call sounded from behind her. She stiffened her resolve and hugged closer to Sanford's side. The prissy young man looked at first surprised then smugly pleased.

"Beastly evening, what? Just a bit farther. See? There's her carriage."

Cassie.

She couldn't resist a quick glimpse over her shoulder. Louis stood a block behind, coatless, hatless in the chilling rain, yet oblivious to it. He looked sleek and dark and dangerous and he had eyes only for her. The burn of his golden gaze streaked through her like lightning. She pulled her attention away and continued on with Sanford, rushing his mincing, puddle-hopping steps with a gruff, "Come on. A little water won't hurt you."

Sanford's Mim was far from a good sport. Her pale gaze cut through Cassie with a rapier-swift thrust of dislike.

"Mim, my darling, I hope you don't mind but I've offered to take Miss Alexander home." His tone was almost pleading as he handed Cassie up opposite the rigid female.

"Sanford, my dear, you know we have theater tickets. We are late already. Surely Miss Alexander would understand—"

"Mim, you are not being your usual charitable self. I promised Miss Alexander we could—"

"You needn't take me all the way to my residence," Cassie put in with a sweet smile. "A few blocks walk would be invigorating. I don't wish to put you out."

"See there, Sanford, Miss Alexander understands."

Yes, Cassie understood perfectly. The pretty peacock didn't want to share her beau's attention any longer than necessary. Charity had nothing to do with it. It was sheer female possessiveness.

"In fact, you can let me off at Schiavone's. Do you know it?"

Sanford made a face. "That little Italian place? Isn't that a little— ethnic?"

Now Cassie could add snobbery to his already impressive list of faults. "I'm meeting someone there. I guess it would be to everyone's benefit if I forewent to trip home to change."

"I say, you look positively topnotch to me, Cass."

Then Sanford grunted from the force of his sweet Mim's elbow tunneling into his ribs.

"Schiavone's, it is," he muttered.

In the light of day, the small Italian restaurant boasted a bustling clientele seated at round tables on the walk beneath a cheerfully striped awning. At night, it looked particularly uninviting, the patio furniture stacked up for the evening and only a tiny glow from within to beckon patrons. Sanford glanced out at the desolate facade and grimaced.

"Cass, are you sure? It doesn't look as though anyone is waiting."

"For heaven's sake, Sanford," the icy Mim snapped at him, "If she says someone is waiting, someone is waiting. We've only minutes until curtain."

Sighing in henpecked resignation, Sanford stepped down and handed Cassie out, looking every inch reluctant but not man enough to protest.

"I'll see you at work tomorrow?" He

sounded anxiously hopeful as he glanced at the surroundings.

"Yes, of course. Thank you, Sanford, and again, I appreciate your inconvenience."

He nodded sheepishly and climbed back into the carriage. Almost as soon as the door closed, it was rocking into motion and she was left glaring alone on the rainswept walk with no choice but to go inside.

The restaurant was dark and for the most part empty except for a few furtive-looking men crouched over wine at one of the back tables. A young man approached her, his expression both anxious and wary.

"*Signorina,* may I help you? We are about to close but if you wish a glass of wine, that we could manage."

"Thank you, but what I'm really interested in is some information. Concerning the murder that happened here several months ago."

His swarthy features had gone suddenly blank as if understanding of the English language was lost to him. "*Non capisco,*" came the surly growl of his reply.

"*Come sta?*" The soft drawl sounded from over Cassie's shoulder. She didn't turn but stiffened beneath the light press of Louis's hand upon her arm. "*Un tavolo per due, per favore. Qual e il piatto del giorno?*"

"*Trance di pesce alla griglia.*" Then he switched to English for Cassie's benefit. "But as I explained to the lady, our kitchen has closed."

"Some wine then, unless your bottles are also sealed for the night. *Che cosa mi consiglia lei?*"

"*Il vino della casa.*"

"*E vino secco?*"

"*Si.*"

"That would be fine. Is dry all right with you, *cara?*"

"Considering the weather, I think it would be most appropriate."

Louis smiled. "But not as dry as your tone, I hope."

An elderly man had come from out of the back and approached with a quizzical smile on his face. He looked as though he might be the owner.

"*Buona sera.* Forgive me but I have not heard my language spoken so beautifully since I left Pescara in my youth. *Lei di dov'e?*"

"Firenze, but it has been many years since I have seen my home. Please. Would you care to join us?"

"*Grazie.*" He motioned them toward one of the tables and gestured for the young man to hurry with the house wine. "*Mi chiamo Paulo Schiavone. Lei, scusi, come si chiama?*"

"Luigino Rodmini. *Posso presentarle il mia ragazza,* Cassandra Alexander."

"Ah!" The little man beamed at Cassie and grandly kissed her hand. She smiled and shot Louis a venomous glance, wondering how he had introduced her. As his lover, most likely, from the way the elder man sighed.

"So, what brings you to Schiavone's, *amanti appassionati?*"

Louis's gaze touched upon Cassie's, his simmering with enough suggestion to make her blush. Then to their host, he exclaimed, "Nothing so pleasant as that, I'm afraid. We are here to ask about a man's death some months ago. He was my sweetheart's father."

He made a regretful noise and patted Cassie's hand. "Terrible business. We told the police everything."

"Everything?" Louis lifted a questioning brow.

The older man flushed uncomfortably and confessed, "My nephew, he got in a bit of trouble with the police so we no want them here asking too many questions. We tell them we see nothing so they go away quick."

"But you did see something." Cassie leaned forward expectantly.

"*Si.* There was a man in here that night, one known about the neighborhood as no good. He asked for a table where he could watch the door and was interested in knowing about the exit to the alley in back. When the *americano* come in, this man, he followed him into the back. That was all we saw until one of my waiters found the body when he was taking out the garbage."

"And you told none of this to the police?"

"Please, *signorina,* understand. We did not

want this bad man or his friends coming back. It is our way to keep our eyes down and our mouths shut."

"But you would recognize this man if you saw him again?" Louis asked quietly.

"Oh, *si*. He comes in for dinner every Friday night. He will be here tomorrow."

"Would you point him out to me? Discreetly, of course."

"Discreetly, perhaps. We want no trouble, but we all feel bad about the lady's father."

"But not bad enough to help catch his killer."

"Cassie," Louis warned gently.

"Is all right," Schiavone sighed. "She has right to be angry with us. You come tomorrow. I show you this man. Now, here is your wine. Please drink, enjoy. It is on Schiavone."

Cassie said nothing as the wine was poured. Her gaze was riveted to the table but Louis could tell from the fractured way she was breathing that the silence would not last long.

"Schiavone? One more thing."

"Yes?"

"Have you ever seen me before?"

"You? No."

"You're sure."

"Yes, *signore*."

When they were alone with the two glasses of untouched wine, Louis said very softly, "Cassie, I had nothing to do with your father's death. Please believe me."

She didn't look up as she spoke. "Am I to believe you had nothing to do with Walter Rampling, either?"

"Who?"

Her gaze shot up to confront his, hers fierce and tear-filled, his perplexed. *"Who?* The man who came to my home last night. The one who was ready to expose this vampire killer in his next column in the *Lexicon*. The one you must have overheard from across the hall. The one who was slain probably right on my doorstep and was found this morning with his throat cut. That Walter Rampling." She shoved back her chair and surged up, her voice rising accordingly. "So excuse me if I don't care to have a glass of wine with you or whatever other vintage you would prefer." And she stalked from the restaurant, her vision skewed and her upset roiling.

She started up the block, making for the nearest el station, her breath coming in quick sobs of anger and distress. The street was empty of traffic as she began to cross, but as soon as she neared the middle a carriage appeared, seemingly from out of the midnight mists, and came bearing rapidly down upon her.

She had time for one cry. It was Louis's name that escaped her as she glanced to either side of the road where safety seemed miles away. She started to run only to have her shoes skid and slide on the wet street, dropping her painfully to hands and knees.

Right in the path of a racing carriage.

Then darkness swirled before her terror-stricken gaze in the guise of Louis's pantlegs as he stepped between her and oncoming death. She had him about the knees, clinging tight, eyes closed and mouth working in a soundless prayer, certain they were both going to die.

But a vampire couldn't be killed by a runaway team of horses, could he?

Curiosity made her open her eyes.

Louis stood firm and unflinching. At the last moment, when Cassie could swear she could feel the breath of the beasts upon her face, Louis threw up one hand in a silent command. Both animals reared back in the traces, bugling wildly, then stood, shivering, pawing at the street while Louis bundled Cassie up in his arms and bore her safely to the walk. She couldn't let him go any more than she could stop shaking. So he held her, saying nothing as the unmarked closed carriage hurtled away into the night.

Finally, Louis loosened one hand to wave up his own carriage, then lifted an uncomplaining Cassie up into its interior. There she remained within the snug circle of his embrace, not wanting to think about what had nearly happened, but needing to feel the surrounding security of his arms.

"Louis— "

"Shhh."

"I'm so sorry I doubted— "

"Shhh. *Cara,* we can talk of this later."
And she felt the pressure of his lips against
her hair and all was suddenly right within
her tumbling world. Because Louis Radcliffe . . . or Luigino Rodmini, whomever
he really was, was at the center of it.

Louis was no monster, not like that human
creature out there preying upon innocents in
the dark. Not like the man who'd stolen her
father's light, if they were, in fact, two separate
men. She'd seen the way this centuries-old
Italian had cared for his aged wife, had witnessed his grieving over the fate of his friend,
was grateful for the way he seemed always to
be on hand to risk his life to preserve hers.
Few mortal men would have displayed that
kind of nobility and that was the attraction
Louis held for her. It wasn't the bond of
blood between them, though that intensified
what had already grown within her heart. He
was a . . . *being* of impeccable character, capable of self-sacrifice and tremendous inner
strength. The kind of integrity she admired
so much and tried to uphold with her own
decisions. Just the kind of man she'd always
longed for. But he was not just any man. He
was not a man at all.

She was still too shaken by the time she
reached her home to act on her own. Without pausing, Louis swept her up in his arms
and carried her, not into the parlor, but di-

rectly up the stairs and into her bedroom. There, without saying a word, he divested her of her wet and torn outer garments, casting them off into a sodden pile at the foot of her bed. She began to tremble, not from the chill of the night or the vestiges of her fear.

Gently, he took up her scraped palms, bathing them one at a time in water he brought from the bathroom spigots, then, more gently still, pressed his lips to the abraded flesh. Her fears dissolved in a tremulous shudder. With her gaze locked in his, Cassie encouraged her cold, stiffened fingers to hurry down the front of her gown, repeating the process on corset cover and on the rigid undergarment itself, letting all three fall at her feet until he lifted her, wearing only her thin one-piece combination drawers, up onto the bed, laying her down upon the coverlet she'd used to shield he and Gerard from the scorching rays of the sun.

She lay upon her back, the breath panting from her, as he bent her knees up and carefully washed the torn skin. Then those wounds he kissed as well, letting the cool slide of his tongue bathe the raw areas like a sensual balm. When he glanced up at her over the tent of her knees, his eyes blazed like molten gold. Her own eyes closed and her fists closed, twisting the coverlet within them as his kisses eased down the sensitive sleekness of inner thigh to the delicate cross-roads of her undergarment. She could feel the heat of his breath, the heat of his kiss against scarcely covered flesh that was hotter still.

She moaned his name in husky need as he came up over her, settling fully clothed between the wanton sprawl of her legs, upon the soft cushion of her breasts, onto the willing part of her mouth. And never once, as she was kissing him wildly, did she think of him as anything but as the man she loved and wanted to the very depth and breadth of her being.

"Louis," she whispered against the pursuing heat of his kisses. "Love me. Make love to me following your own desires, not just my dreams."

"Cara, don't you know those two things are one in the same?"

And the thought that he would want her with the same reckless abandon made her sigh rapturously and commend herself into his hands.

And when they were gloriously naked and entwined in search of mutual accord, Cassie gripped the back of his head, guiding him instinctively to the offered arch of her throat. Just the whisper of his lips upon that vulnerable curve had the hairs raising in an erotic prickle all over her body. A shiver that was more than just sexual rattled through her and she moaned her impatience.

"Louis, please."

He teased his mouth over to the corner of hers, away from that pulse of temptation, to murmur, "You don't know what you ask for, my sweet innocent."

"Yes. Yes, I do. I want to be yours."

"You are mine, Cassie. Now and forever. And what is mine, I care for. To take from you so soon would be an unnecessary risk for you."

"I don't care," she groaned, arching beneath him. "I want to please you."

"And what makes you think that this does not please me?" he crooned while sucking at her lower lip, at the impudent tip of her tongue.

"Because it's the blood you want from me. It's what you need to continue on." Suddenly, her mood was too somber to endure. He kissed her hard, then rolled so she was astride him. His hands were at her hips, moving them in a rocking, luscious rhythm upon the staff of his desire.

"What I want from you is you. All of you. I want you to love me. I want you to make love with me. And mostly, I want you to trust me. Do you, Cassie? Do you trust me?"

She was breathing hard into the surge of rising bliss, her eyes sealed shut, her pale breasts rising like lush twin moons. "Yes! Oh, yes!" she cried, lost in the maelstrom of her satisfaction.

And when he'd found his own and she

rested quietly along the hard line of his body, he asked again. "Do you trust me, *cara?*"

"I love you, Louis."

But that sighing answer was not the same thing.

"Do you still wonder if I took the life of your father and your friend?"

"No," she replied more sedately. "I don't believe that anymore."

"And you are no longer considering what a marvelous headline I would make to sell your magazines?"

She lifted up, her expression contrite, her eyes dark pools of anguish. "Forgive me. I would never betray you."

"Is that why you brought all those papers home instead of turning them over to the police?"

"I wanted to make sure nothing in them implicated you."

"And was there?"

"No," came her hushed whisper. "I'm sorry." She snuggled back upon his chest to sigh in contentment. "Besides, I have another story now that will save the *Lexicon.* Or at least I will once I discover the identity of my father's killer tomorrow night."

He pushed her back and scowled at her darkly. "You will go nowhere near that place. I will go and find out what there is to know."

She studied his fierce frown and concern-puckered brow and smiled demurely. "Yes, Louis," and was burrowing back upon that luscious stretch of skin that cradled her so exquisitely, not realizing how horrified she once would have been to make that submissive claim. Dependence was proving not quite the ogre she made it out to be.

"How do you wish to handle what we have between us?"

"Frequently," came her scandalous reply.

Louis chuckled and squeezed her slightly. "I meant our living here together."

"That's easy. Marry me, Louis. You can protect my interests at the magazine and I can protect your secret."

He was ominously silent. Aware of how flippant she sounded in the face of his recent loss, Cassie rose up, pleading, "I'm sorry. I forgot what I was saying and to whom. It's too soon for you to even think of such things again." She swallowed hard. "Maybe sometime in the not so distant future."

"Maybe," he replied softly. "Maybe sooner than either of us thinks."

She smiled weakly and her vulnerability went straight to his heart, making him hug her up once more. A thought came to her as she was grazing his smooth chest with her fingertips.

"Arabella had talked of having your family here for the holidays. I think she'd like it if you still did that. If you don't think they mind too much about me, that is."

"They won't." And he was smiling slightly, thinking of his family, thinking of Cassie among them.

"Only what on earth would I serve them for dinner? I mean, that I could acceptably purchase at the corner market."

He laughed aloud, delighted at her musings. "I think it's safe to say they would prefer to dine out." Then he kissed her brow with a sudden intensity, aware of her fragility, of her fleeting humanity. "Cassie, being with me is not without its risks."

"I know. Arabella was speaking to me about the sacrifices I would have to make. Of course, I didn't understand then like I do now."

"She was preparing you for me. For the truth. She told me I could trust you."

"Louis, she loved you so much. I feel so honored that she would trust me to assume her role, but not her place."

He was silent for so long that she worried her words had kindled a renewed pain within his heart. She couldn't expect him to just forget the relationship he had shared for better than a lifetime. And suddenly, she felt Arabella between them rather than behind them, pushing them together. Awkwardness rose as she wondered how to escape his arms when there was no place else in the world she would rather be.

She'd forgotten that Louis could read her thoughts, that her concern was as plain upon them as one of her magazine's banner headlines. And he loved her all the more for her worry. He tilted up her head, seeking her lips with a revived passion, loving her long and lavishly through the hours of the night, to convince her that she'd established a place of her own within his heart, then holding her until a time when the pale fingers of dawn would soon force his retreat.

He had never meant to, but love her he did. And as he held her crushed to his chest for as long as he dared, he vowed to keep her safe from all nature of ills—those of earth and beyond.

But in doing so, he realized the greatest danger was from Cassie, herself.

How was he going to keep his impetuous one from plunging headlong into the arms of a waiting madman?

Twenty-two

"So, you've finally made time for me."

Cassie glanced up from the papers on the conference room table to regard her uncle through a cool inscrutable gaze. "Come in and close the door behind you."

Fitzhugh paused and lifted a questioning brow, then did as she instructed. "What is this about?"

"I think you know. I think it's time we had an understanding between us in regards to who runs this magazine."

Fitzhugh supplied a thin smile. "Are you sure you want to discuss this now, so soon after Walter's death? I'm sure that must have upset you—"

"About as much as it upset all his friends. No more, no less. And not so much that I can't take care of business. Sit down, Fitzhugh."

Her curt tone had him bristling. The fact that she called him by his given name without any other form of respectful address didn't escape him either. He came in and he sat, aware that she had assumed his brother's chair at the head of the table. And appeared to feel very at home in it.

"I thought I would let you know before announcing it to the others— a matter of courtesy only."

"Let me know what?"

"That as owner and editor of the *Lexicon,* I've decided to take on an investment partner who is willing to sink in enough money to firmly establish this magazine where it belongs."

"You *what?*"

"Do not roar at me. I'm sitting an arm's length away. There is no need to raise your voice. I am not a child to be intimidated by a show of temper."

Fitzhugh took several gulping breaths, then glared at his well-composed niece. "Who is this investor?"

"Louis Radcliffe."

"Your lover?"

Her eyes narrowed ever so slightly. "A well-known and vastly admired member of the New York business community recognized for his shrewd dealings and upward profit statements."

He gave a harsh laugh. "You mean someone you can lead around by the— "

"Enough! I've told you the way it's going to be at the *Lexicon.* Now I'm going to tell you the way it's going to be between you and me. You either recognize my authority and my place in my father's chair or you find yourself another position on another magazine."

"You wouldn't dare!"

"Later this afternoon, I'm meeting with my attorneys, who will draw up the partnership agreement. I will present it at a staff meeting Monday morning. At that time, I want to hear that you've stopped your ridiculous legal proceedings or I want your resignation. All the paperwork will be signed tomorrow evening, followed by a small celebratory dinner at my home. You and Quinton are invited, of course, providing we have something to celebrate together. I hope we do, Uncle. You have always been an asset to this magazine. I would hate to replace you. But I will if you force me to it. There's only room for one person in this chair and that person is me. I think it's high time we both got used to it."

Without comment, Fitzhugh rose up and stormed out of the room, slamming the door with a glass-shivering force. Cassie sighed and slumped back in her chair.

"I'm sorry, Father. I did the best I could to keep him with us. Now I guess it's up to him."

She sat for a while, silent and pensive, until aware of how comfortable her father's chair felt enveloping her. It was like sitting on his lap with the brace of his arms about her. And she knew he was pleased. Perhaps not about Louis, but about her stand at the helm of the *Lexicon*. He would just have to understand that she could not have done one without the other. Brighton Alexander had always found his strength within himself and her mother had always gotten hers from others. Neither had understood the concept of shared strength, and that's why they'd led such personally unfulfilled lives. Power came from a broad base, from the control of a firm foundation and that was found at home, in the heart. Contentment there branched out into all other aspects of life. If hers was an unconventional arrangement, she would not apologize, for it served her well. If Louis could tolerate her demand for professional freedom, she could succumb to his command for control over her private desires. The perfect solution with the perfect— man. Now if it could only lead to marriage . . .

She was smiling, thinking along that line, when young Tim appeared in the doorway, his face very pale.

"Miss Alexander, a package for you." His voice was little more than a whisper.

Cassie stared at the brown paper-wrapped parcel and her heart catapulted into her throat. With an equal degree of quiet, she said, "Bring it over here, Tim." When he did, setting it down gingerly on the table before her, she told him, "Wait outside for just a minute."

"Are you sure?" He sounded as frightened

as she felt and that was what pulled her together. That and the feel of her father's chair surrounding her with confidence.

"Yes, I'm sure." And she smiled at him, nodding toward the door. That bravado held until she was alone with this latest killer's gift. Her determination set, her hands slightly less sure, she began to open the paper.

Fitzhugh Alexander sat in the dimness of his office making the final editorial marks on the next issue of the *Lexicon*. Though his actions were concise from long years of practice, his mind was far from engaged in the duties he performed.

How dare she? How dare she sit in the chair that should be his? Not only was she sitting in it, she was dictating from it, to him! *Him!* He'd been compiling facts and trimming copy when she was teething at her crazy mama's knee. It was time for the charade to end. Time for the publishing world to discover who was the real strength behind the *Lexicon*. And by morning, there would be no question in anyone's mind that it was Fitzhugh Alexander who would bravely recover from the deaths of both brother and niece to continue their dream. Alone. Or rather, with Quinton, but that was another matter to be dealt with at another time.

He wasn't sure quite yet what to do about the son whose instability was both blessing

and liability. Perhaps he would have to go
the way of Brighton's dear wife. A little too
much pleasure in the arms of his narcotic
mistress, and he would be in a dream forever, then safely locked away where no one
would believe his rantings.

He thumbed through the dreary poetry
Quinton was expecting him to print.
Wretched stuff. He grimaced and pushed it
aside. Perhaps Quinton would have to go as
soon as he finished with his dear cousin.

"Working late, Father?" The soft, almost
sinister drawl sounded from the doorway.

"Finishing up the dummy for our next issue."

"A convenient alibi should we both need
one. I, of course, will be here working dili-
gently at your side. That's what you'll tell
them, anyway."

Fitzhugh frowned. He didn't really want to
discuss the matter any further. He just
wanted it done. Perhaps he should have
hired a stranger to see to the task rather
than put up with his son's increasingly erratic behavior. But he'd done well in arranging things for Brighton.

"What's that you have there?"

"This?" Quinton pulled a piece of clothing and a slip of paper out from behind his
back. "Just setting the stage for tonight."
And he smiled a chilling smile. "I think I
shall miss the intrigue and all the cat and
mouse games once she is gone. Ah, well.

Once her mysterious stalker is discovered and convicted, we can't very well have him surfacing again, can we?"

Fitzhugh stared at his son, slowly assimilating the grim words he was hearing. But still, he couldn't believe it. "Quinton, what nonsense are you spouting?"

"Nonsense? Why, Father, I'll have you know I've been baffling Manhattan's finest for the better part of two months now. If it wasn't for the need to tie up loose ends and get on with a respectable living at your side, I would still be enjoying the game. It was just a pastime, after all. Just something to do until you recognized my worth." Another perfectly frigid smile. "And you have at last, haven't you, Father?"

"You?" Fitzhugh gushed. "You killed those women!"

"Thought I was weak, didn't you? Thought I was a spineless fool, there for everyone to take advantage of. So did they. Right up until their final minutes, when I had the last laugh. Well, now you know the truth, don't you? You know what kind of man I really am. The kind you can admire."

"Yes," Fitzhugh breathed in a daze of shock. "Now I see what you really are."

Quinton smiled pleasantly and deposited the items he held onto his father's desk. "I won't be long. Then maybe we can go out somewhere and share a drink together. To our new partnership. Wouldn't that be nice?"

"Yes. We'll do that."

"Good night, Father. I love you. For you."

"What?"

"What I've done, I've done for you."

An hour later, he sat still frozen behind his desk, hearing his son's last words. *For you.*

What had he done? What kind of monster had he raised in his own image?

And how was he going to get rid of him?

"I saw your light. I hope you don't mind the company."

Fitzhugh gave a nervous leap, but he'd never seen the elegant stranger standing in his doorway. "I'm very busy right now," he growled, struggling for a normal tone. "If you wish an appointment, come by tomorrow."

"What I have to discuss is business best left to after hours." The stranger with the smooth, foreign-tinged voice gave a bland smile but there was no shift in his eyes. They were remote, unblinking, disturbingly direct.

"I have no idea what you are talking about. Now if you'll excuse me—"

"No. There is no excuse for you. What kind of man kills his brother?"

Fitzhugh was careful not to betray the way his heart began suddenly jerking at a mad pace. "I beg your pardon?"

"It's not my pardon you need to beg. It's Cassie's."

"Just who the hell are you?" He'd had all the spooky visits he cared to for one night, and this one made his skin tighten and crawl in eerie ripples.

"Louis Radcliffe." There was something dangerously hypnotic in the way he stood there, completely still, a glow beginning to build deep within those penetrating eyes.

"Radcliffe? Cassie's— investor. Ah, yes. What is this nonsense about my brother? What has she told you?"

"I didn't hear it from her. I heard it from Cesare Orsini. Does that name mean anything to you?"

"No. Why should it?"

"Because he was the man you paid to take your brother's life after you lured him to Schiavone's."

"Ridiculous. Who made up these lies?"

"Lies? I think not. Signore Orsini was quite convincing before he died."

"Orsini's dead?" The crafty wheels were turning in his head. No Orsini, no damning testimony.

"Of course, I didn't let him die before he'd made a complete written confession and had it duly witnessed— by a priest."

Fitzhugh didn't think. He simply acted. The stack of loose pages on his desk he flung into Louis's face, momentarily distracting him so Fitzhugh could push past him and race out the door. Louis straightened and smiled in the darkness of the hallway.

And then he began to follow.

It was cold upon the rooftop. Fitzhugh was surprised to see it was snowing. A fine white powdered the pavilion that disguised the building's water tank and blanketed the tar paper beneath his feet. From his sixth-floor view, familiar context disappeared. The city was no longer a crowded canyon of busy streets but rather a fairy tale land of fantasy structures; towers, temples, elaborate spires, carved cornices and grinning gargoyles all frosted in white like a nightmare wedding cake. Behind him, he heard the door of the stairwell closing and he spun, seeing nothing. Nothing but his single set of footprints.

But no, that wasn't right. Radcliffe was there before him, standing in that fluffy swirl of snow without a single flake upon him, without a single dent in the powdery surface leading up to his glossy shoes. Shoes that seemed to be planted lightly on the one-inch layer without making an indentation.

Fitzhugh gave a soft cry. "What are you?"

"So surprised? Did you think such creatures as I did not exist? You should have let Rampling finish the rest of his article before you killed him, as well."

"I had nothing to do with Walter. That was— that was Quinton. It was his doing, all of it." He was backing up, his terror-glazed eyes never lifting from Radcliffe's feet, his gaze bugging as Radcliffe came forward in a gliding step . . . leaving no footprints.

"I'm sorry I cannot believe you." And suddenly he moved, rushing forward in a blur, fangs out and eyes like flame. Screaming, Fitzhugh lunged backwards and found nothing but air as he cartwheeled over the low stone retaining wall that edged the roof. And disappeared. Silence settled over the twilight world once more.

Louis was in no hurry as he came to look over the precipice. No emotion showed in eyes now calm and green.

Manhattan had a vast pigeon population that did little but fly and eat off the streets and in the park and perch on high buildings, corroding them with their acidic droppings. To discourage them from loitering, spikes lined the upper ledges, and it was on those spikes that Fitzhugh Alexander breathed his last breath as a light filtering of snow covered his fear-contorted features.

Satisfied, Louis went back inside the building, returning to Fitzhugh's office where he would leave Orsini's confession in lieu of Alexander's supposed suicide note. It was then he noticed a length of shimmering silk—a lady's stocking. All his senses were suddenly aquiver as he lifted it, identifying Cassie's scent upon it. And there, in the same brown wrapping was a single note written in the same bold hand that scrawled line after line of flowery poetry only inches away.

"Winter Drive. Eight o'clock. It's your turn."

"Oh, Cassie, no," he moaned, glancing at the desktop clock that stated half past the hour of eight.

Conifers lined the western carriage road, a mile and a half of seasonless green to relieve the barren months to come. Scores of evergreens were drooping beneath the sudden weight of snow, lacing the air with the crisp pungent scent of pine and winter, two of Cassie's favorite things. But on this evening, she didn't notice.

She walked along the deserted road huddled in her cloak, but it was anxiousness, not the chill, that had her shivering. She'd gone about a half mile and her unsuitable shoes were caked with newly laid slush. There'd been no time to prepare for this drastic change in weather. She'd been too busy readying for this sudden turn of events. And she was beginning to think the wintery trail would lead nowhere when she was distracted by a fluttery banner tied to the iron rail of a bridge spanning the road. It was part of a narrow walking path that wound off through the richly forested trees. She approached cautiously, not having to touch it to recognize the mate to her stocking pair.

It was knotted off center to the left so that was the direction she took down the all but indecernible trail.

It took all her concentration not to glance around continually for Danny Hooper and his men. The sergeant had promised that she would not see them, nor would her assailant as he stepped into their trap. She clung to that confidence as the overhead sky darkened and a huge round moon arose to gleam across the snowy patches of a seemingly uninhabited world. Uninhabited by all but herself and the man who stalked her.

The narrow footpath led off into terrain that grew increasingly rugged with bold contours of rock. Ahead, Cassie could see another of the park's uniquely individual bridges, this one a graceful arch of fieldstone brightened by a softly glowing lamppost on either side. In the center stood a dark-garbed figure. Cassie paused, feeling for the added comfort of the small revolver in her handbag, then she started forward, her curiosity almost as great as her fear. As she stepped onto the graded curve of the bridge, he turned toward her, his features sharpening in the revealing aura of artificial light. Cassie stopped, not understanding.

"Quinton! What on earth are you doing out here?"

"Why, Cass, I came to see you."

Then the cold reality hit like a fist of ice. "Oh, my God." She clung to the wide stone lip of the bridge's arch as her knees gave with shock, but an aloof, analytical part of her was wondering why she hadn't guessed the truth before. All she could think to say was one word. "Why?"

He shrugged. "Why not? Why not take advantage of those who loathe me? You were the only one I thought was different. I wanted to believe you were different."

"Quinton, I'm your friend. Why— why didn't you come to me first?"

"I did. Don't you see? I gave you every chance. The notes, the gifts. I wanted you to use those things to save the *Lexicon*, to save our future. You see, my father wanted to destroy you, but I couldn't let that happen. I used the others to try to make him happy, to try to make you happy."

"Quinton, don't you understand there's no pleasing men like your father?"

"Oh, you're wrong! He's come around, Cass. He appreciates me now. He and I are going to share the *Lexicon*."

"What are you talking about?" She started to back down off the bridge, wondering rather frantically when Danny was going to make his move. Of course, he would wait until he'd heard something incriminating and it was up to her to get her cousin to condemn himself. "You killed those girls and now you mean to kill me, too?"

"That wasn't the way I planned it, Cass. I wanted it to be you and me together. But no, you had other plans, another man." He laughed with a gust of madness. "Well, I've made other plans now, too. Unfortunately, your part in them is going to be rather short-lived."

"You won't get away with this." Her hand closed over the hard metal in her bag even as she prayed for a quick intervention.

"Of course I will. It's perfect in every detail. Walter investigating the murdered girls, citing a vampire killer. He, himself, gets too close and becomes a victim. You following clues to your own regrettable death. The *Lexicon* under my father's and my control, breaking the tragic story of your lover's mad obsession. Of course, the truth would make more interesting reading, the fact of what Louis Radcliffe really is, but who would believe that? Classing him as a madman will do just fine. A very satisfying end for all involved. Except, of course, for you and Radcliffe, but that can't be helped. You don't know how truly sorry I am."

"You're the madman, Quinton."

"Why, Cass, what an unkind thing to say. Who would recognize a madman amid a world gone mad?" He laughed again, this time a cold, emotionless chuckle that had Cassie trembling all the more.

Enough, she thought frantically. Surely Danny had all the evidence he needed to close in for the arrest. Why didn't he? What was he waiting for?

"I'm sorry, Cass. I truly am. I did like you, but you are the price for my reward in my father's eyes. It's all I've ever wanted, you know, for him to approve of me."

"Not this way, Quinn. Come with me. Let me get you the help you need."

"Help? The kind your mother got? No, thank you. But you can help. You can help me greatly." From out of his coat, he withdrew a thin-bladed knife.

Cassie retreated another step and looked about wildly. But the silent snow and indifferent backdrop of evergreens were all that met her desperate gaze.

"Looking for something?" came Quinton's humorless drawl. "Or should I say for several someones?"

He held out his hand, opening it slowly so the metal of the four police badges he held caught the light with impotent flashes.

"No help is coming, Cass. It's just you and me."

His smile never faltered when confronted by her small bore pocket pistol.

"Always the resourceful one, aren't you, cousin? Did I ever tell you how much I admired that about you?"

Suddenly, he lunged. The report from her gun was tiny, well muffled by Quinton's body. He grabbed her so fiercely, for a moment she feared she'd missed. But how could she have when he was engulfing the muzzle?

She hadn't. Even as she pushed frantically

away, he was going down upon one knee, badges scattering on the new snow as he clutched his hand over an ever-widening stain at his midsection. Cassie staggered free of his grip, panting wildly, waiting for him to fall as she continued to confront him with the wavering pistol.

Then he looked up at her, his expression one of surprise before dissolving into one of unholy delight.

"My God, you shot me!" His laughter put the chill of death into her veins as he slowly tottered up to his feet.

Bracing her hands and her nerve, Cassie fired again, but this time the only sound was a hollow click.

"Sweetheart, don't you know anything? That's a single shot and, unfortunately, you didn't make the first one count."

Twenty-three

Cassie threw the useless pistol with all her might, striking Quinton just above the right eye and distracting him long enough for her to dart around him. She heard him curse and the sound of heavy movement, assuring her of pursuit. Grabbing up her weighty skirt, she ran as fast as her slick-soled shoes could carry her along the treacherous walk, slipping several heart-stopping times but managing to catch her balance and race on. To where, she didn't know. No help was coming from Danny and his men and she had no time to consider what Quinton had done to them. She was too absorbed in trying to think of how to save herself.

She headed for the carriage road, hoping luck would provide her with some passersby. But even as she ran, she knew the unlikelihood of that plan. Few would head into the darkened park on such a discouraging evening. They would be home building up a cosy blaze upon the hearth or sharing cheerful companionship in some society watering hole or restaurant. Where she should have been, instead of stalking the night in search of a criminal.

And now she very likely was going to be his next victim.

Suddenly, she was aware that she'd been running uphill and risked stopping to look about. Somehow, she had managed to confuse her bearings and had headed off into the wrong direction, away from the main road rather than toward it. The path she'd taken was carrying her farther and farther into the dense, craggy wilderness area of the park. Where no one would see her. Where no one would hear her screams.

She thought briefly of leaving the path, of trying to hide herself, but cast off that idea. She was encumbered by her female garments and in the midst of harsh, unfamiliar ground. Her best chance was to out-distance the wounded madman.

Then Quinton came reeling into view. Moonlight glinted wickedly off the blade in his hand as he stumbled toward her at a surprisingly strong pace. So she ran on through the nearly blinding haze of snow, placing all her faith in the hope that his strength would expire before her own.

The stinging slash of flakes obscured her vision. Cassie saw the vague outline of a structure up ahead. She increased her pace, thinking it was another bridge, only to discover too late that it was not. It was a pretty wooden pergola perched on the very edge of a twenty-foot plunge. Gasping for breath, she clung to the railings, peering in momentary fascination at the white oblivion below. Then she turned, readying to flee along the sharply veed trail, only to find her wheezing cousin there to block the way.

Cassie backed against the rail, panting frantically, blinking the dampness from her gaze as it filtered down through the open roof slats. Her only escape was to get past Quinton and he seemed determined not to let that happen.

"How perfect," he rasped, clutching his wounded middle. "It will take them days to discover your body once I push it over. Imagine the amount of public sympathy we can arouse in that time as we launch a desperate search for our magazine's missing owner. Missing and presumed dead. Only we'll know better, won't we? Perhaps I'll even become a hero, having been wounded in a struggle with your determined murderer. What a wonderful witness I'll make; the distraught cousin who'd risk his very life for you. But to no avail." Then he smiled. He started toward her in an awkward shuffle, knife brandished before him.

Cassie refused to just stand there and let him slay her. She wouldn't make it that easy for him. Flinging her curse as hard as she swung her bag, she struck him in the head with the beaded confection and attempted to slip past him. To no avail. She shrieked with all her remaining breath as his fingers bit into the flesh of her upper arm. Her futile twisting and turning seemed only to enrage him more. He pinwheeled her around hard, causing her head to strike one of the pergola's supporting beams. Blackness surged up in a tide of death. At least, she thought numbly, she would not suffer. As she sank down upon her knees in the cold, trampled snow, one last thought swirled within her mind.

I love you, Louis.

"Let her go."

The soft-spoken command brought Quinton staggering about, dragging Cassie with him. "Well," he sneered, "if it isn't the mysterious lover. Sorry I missed you the first time, Radcliffe. I won't make the same mistake twice."

"No, I'll see that you don't."

"Louis," Cassie sobbed as she scrabbled in the slush to get her feet under her. Suddenly, it was as if he was with her, the warmth and comforting support of his mind embracing hers.

Don't be afraid, my love.

His love. It was almost worth dying to hear him use those words.

Has he harmed you?

"No." *No.*

Assured of that, Louis began to approach, moving in the mesmerizingly minimal way of a drifting shadow. Quinton was nowhere near as distressed by the sight as his father had been. He'd seen a vampire before. He hauled Cassie up before him and laid the razor-shape blade at her throat.

"Come no closer," he snarled, yanking Cassie's head back at an impossible angle and bringing a line of blood to bead along his blade.

Louis stopped, an uncanny stillness coming over him. His eyes took on a deep, pulsing brilliance, a magnetic pull meant to smother a weaker mind. Quinton wavered briefly, then shook his head to scatter the dreamy coercion Louis was trying to force upon him.

"Your magic won't work on me, vampire. I am already under the protection of another."

"Bianca," he whispered in a soft expulsion of breath.

"Yes, and she's quite eager for me to finish here."

"You're wrong, Alexander. You won't benefit from these actions. There is no one left to applaud your fit of violence. Your father is dead."

Quinton gasped. "No. You lie!"

"It will seem as if by his own hand, but we will know better. It is by yours."

"What? Why do you say that? You are trying to trick me, demon."

"No trick. He could not live with the monster you'd become or with the guilt of his own brother's death and that of his friend upon his hands. You killed him. There is no future for you there."

"No!" He wailed in a frenzy of grief. Then he seemed to compose himself. His breath seethed past Cassie's tear-glazed cheek, a hot scorch of fury. "If not at my father's side, then at Bianca's."

"She is gone. I've driven her away. If you do not believe me, try to reach out for her and see if she replies. No, you can feel only emptiness as an answer."

He gave a choking cry as he realized that was true. His unfocused, fledgling mind could make no contact.

"Cassie is the only one who has ever really cared for you. Why harm her? Let her go." Louis's voice held a low, seducing cadence. Once again, he started to reach out his hand.

"If she cares so much for me, then we can both go, together!"

But Louis was no longer standing there before him. His image had paled, thinning, separating to become like the tiny drifting dots of snow. Quinton was transfixed by the flickering particles as they disappeared against a field of blackest night. Then, before he had a chance to recover from his stupefaction, a grip like steel had a hold of his wrist, wrenching it down, away from Cassie's throat, twisting to shove the blade to a new home deep within Quinton's chest. But even as Quinton began to fall, dying, his last act of strength was to thrust the woman he still held prisoner back and over the rail with a flutter of skirts, her thin scream rapidly falling away into the darkness below. The hand was instantly gone from Quinton's wrist for there was no way to retain him and save Cassie from certain death.

Snow and wind flew by her, stealing away the rest of her cry as Cassie plummeted downward. Then abruptly Louis's arms were wrapped about her and the out of control plunge became a gentle drift to the ground in the embrace of the man she loved.

"Are you all right?"

His question had her laughing, crying almost hysterically until she was silenced by his kiss. Of course, she was all right, her fervid response decreed. Now that he was here. With her arms in a tight knot about his neck and her chilled face pressed against the shelter of his throat, Cassie was content to linger in the enchanted circle of his love, reluctant to let reality intrude until she heard the sound of her name being called from far above. She lifted her head to listen against the moan of the night wind.

"That sounds like Danny. Quinton— where is he?"

"I had to let him go, my love, but he won't get far with the nature of his wounds." Louis was kissing her face, warming the wind-chapped, rosy skin with repetitious strokes of his fingertips. "Do not concern yourself with him. He cannot harm you anymore."

"Oh, Louis, I can't believe he did those awful things. And my uncle . . . is he truly dead?"

"There seems to be justice abroad this night. And the time has come to take you home."

He rose up with her still clutched tight in his arms, lifting effortlessly while his gaze locked into hers, radiating a message of love. When they'd reached the level of the ground, he stepped to it and helped her back onto the snow-covered path where a very bewildered Daniel Hooper was floundering about, his red hair streaked even darker from a ghastly wound at his temple.

"Where did the two of you come from?" he muttered in confusion. "And Alexander, where is he?"

Louis gestured to a path of gore leading off into the dense foliage. "My guess is that you'll find him at the end of that trail."

"Are you all right?" Danny and Cassie both asked one another at the same moment. Then he smiled weakly and went first. "I don't know what hit us. He took out all three of my men without me hearing a thing, and he must have left me for dead after bashing my head into a boulder. I'm sorry, Cass. I let you down. I was supposed to have been there for you."

"That's all right, Danny. I'm just so grateful you survived, that we both did."

"I guess we have you to thank for that," the sergeant muttered, holding out his hand to Louis. It was taken and firmly shaken.

"It was just luck that I happened upon them," Louis volunteered, as if the reluctant hero. "I found some references to Cassie's father's death in the papers she brought home and went to question her uncle about them. I believe you'll find the same thing I did—that the strain of living with his guilt and the knowledge of his son's deeds were too much for him. He threw himself off of the roof."

Danny grimaced in appropriate horror. "I'll get a man over there and some officers here to follow this trail. I don't want you to worry, Cass. We'll have this madman in hand by morning. I promise."

"Until then, could I take her home? She's been through quite enough for one night."

Danny nodded absently at Louis's suggestion, but he was already distracted along that generous trail of blood, at the end of which he fully expected to find Quinton Alexander dead from exposure and the complications of his wounds.

Quinton floundered through the trees, stumbling frequently but dragging himself onward until too weak and cold to move another inch. He fell face first into the chill cushion of snow and waited there for peace and death to overtake him. He was unprepared for the tender touch of female hands, rolling him over, wiping the wetness from his face. He blinked up vaguely into a field of hazy brilliance. An angel. His groggy mind was dazzled by her pale ethereal beauty. Then she smiled and he saw the points of her teeth gleaming. He made a small outcry of terror as she bent to his throat, drinking deep of the rest of his life's blood.

Then, just as he hovered upon the brink of final damnation, she brought him back with the promise of hell on earth, the taste of her own warm blood upon his lips as he obediently swallowed, fashioning on that cold, dark night a new companion from his black soul. One she could lead, one whose own ruthlessness was unending.

And as he awoke, changed, a new and more deadly being, Bianca kissed his lips and whispered upon them that together, there was nothing they could not have.

In the gleaming twilight, her seductive vow sparkled with lethal clarity.

"Come, my love, I have much to teach you."

And smiling with malicious anticipation, he reached up for her hand.

Cassie murmured her thanks as she took another glass of brandy from Louis and sank back on the sofa as she waited for him to see the police detectives out.

It had been an exhausting evening piecing together the puzzle of Fitzhugh Alexander's deadly greed and his son's lethal madness. She was still troubled that the official search had turned up no sign of Quinton or his body. The bloody trail they'd been following had seemed to come to an abrupt end. However, the detectives assured her that he would turn up, most likely as an unidentified corpse in the morgue, but they had all the hospitals staked out as well. The confession, note, and stocking found in Fitzhugh's office, as well as the scraps of evidence Walter Rampling had put together, were enough to implicate both father and son, and Danny's eyewitness account of Quinton's murderous attack collaborated her own. Cassie was weary and grateful that it was over. But a sudden restlessness overcame her, a sense of unfinished business.

Louis paused at the door of the study, bemused by the sight of his bruised and beautiful Cassie making copious notes upon the margins of the pages littering her desktop.

"Haven't you had enough intrigue for one night, my love?"

She didn't look up at first, jotting down one more thought before glancing up with an apologetic smile. "I have a special edition to ready for press tomorrow. If someone is going to print this story, I would as soon it be us.

Perhaps knowing them, I can shed some insight into why they would feel forced into such dreadful acts. I would prefer the world to see them as victims pressured by the world around them rather than monsters."

"They were monsters, Cassie," Louis corrected, unwilling to feel charitably toward the ones who had almost stolen her away from him.

"Read this and tell me it is the work of a monster."

He took the sheet of paper with a guarded frown and found himself transported by the poignant verse printed upon it. He frowned, not liking the way his anger was being complicated. "He was a good poet."

"He could have been a good man, Louis. And I'm angry that he was not allowed the chance."

"He made his choices. We all make them. We cannot go through our lives blaming others for our failings. All we can do is look ahead with hope."

And Cassie smiled gently, intuiting that he was speaking of himself. She laid her pen aside and reached out a hand to him. He took it and came down on one knee beside her chair.

"I love you," he told her simply, emotionally. "You are the good that my future holds."

She continued to smile somewhat wryly. "I am not a conventional choice, Louis."

"That is probably why Arabella chose you for me."

"Here. I think you should read this."

Looking pained, he took the paper she produced from her desk drawer. "What's this? Another poem?"

"Something like that." And she watched his face as he read Arabella's last words, the ones Gerard had delivered on the night she died. Wordlessly, he folded the paper and smoothed it with his fingertips before returning it to her.

"Do you mean to honor your vow?" he asked at last, in an almost inaudible hush.

"I never break my promises, Louis. This one will be a pleasure to keep." She leaned forward to taste of his lips, fighting against the desire to put all aside to savor more. But sighing with an age-old discipline, she sat back. "I have much to teach you if you plan to enter the publishing business."

"And I have much to teach you about the nature of my love."

Her frown was rueful. "I have a morning deadline."

"So do I. But beyond that I have an eternity."

Cassie hesitated, glancing between the papers on her desk, words needing to be written, and the smolder of his eyes, the promise of a relationship needing a strong beginning. Her eyes lifted to the portrait of her father and her answer was there in all his failings.

Smiling, she switched off her desk lamp and took Louis's hand in hers with a philosophical, "The work will still be there in the morning. The night belongs to us."

"And as many nights beyond as you could ever wish for," came his sultry vow.

Her lips were moving impatiently upon his, then paused only to suggest, "Let's start with this one."

Author's Note

This book was for all those who took the time to write me, sharing their love of the supernatural and generous words of praise; I didn't know there were so many of you out there! What is it about the dark side that invites our imaginations to run wild? I've had great fun developing this series and hope to extend it to three more titles, bringing Louis and his ghoulish friends up into the twentieth century. But I think the greatest pleasure was in reading letters from those who've said, "I swore I'd never read a romance but . . ." Glad I had a chance to convert you!

If you'd like to receive my newsletter with updates on my future projects and past titles along with any signed promotional material I have on hand, send a legal-sized SASE to: P.O. Box 526, Kalamazoo, MI 49004. Or just drop me a note to share your opinions . . . I'd love to hear from you!